THE MAN
WHO MADE
NO MISTAKES

AND TEN OTHER TALES

THE MAN WHO MADE NO MISTAKES

AND TEN OTHER TALES

Scott William Carter

FLYING RAVEN

PRESS

THE MAN WHO MADE NO MISTAKES

"The Man Who Made No Mistakes" originally appeared in *Realms of Fantasy,* October 2011. "The Bear Who Sang Opera" originally appeared in *Analog,* July 2009. "The Time of His Life" originally appeared in *Realms of Fantasy,* February 2011. "The Problem with Polly" originally appeared in Cat Tales II, April 2010. "The Android Who Became a Human Who Became an Android" originally appeared in *Analog,* November 2011. "Stone Creek Station" originally appeared in Beneath the Surface, February 2008. "Deep Down in the Diggyback" originally appeared in *Full Unit Hookup,* August 2008. "A Witness to All That Was" originally appeared in *Analog,* July 2011.

For more about Flying Raven Press, please visit our web site at
http://www.flyingravenpress.com

ISBN-10 0615642969
ISBN-13 978-0615642963

Printed in the United States of America
Flying Raven Press paperback edition, June 2012

Contents

The Man Who Made No Mistakes

It may have been the steady drone of the rain on the church roof, or it may have been the second bourbon he'd had with dinner, but Father Holder found himself dozing in the confessional. His whole body was slumping against the heavy oak panels when the young man spoke.

"This won't be your usual confession," he said.

The voice jolted Father Holder awake—heart pounding, breath catching in his throat. For a moment, looking through the thick gray mesh, he thought he'd dreamed the voice, that it was a fabrication concocted from a stomach full of beef stroganoff—but then the young man opened his eyes and Father Holder saw the bright whites, luminescent almost, surrounding a pair of penetrating dark pupils. That's when he realized the reason he was having trouble seeing the young man was because the young man had skin nearly as black as the darkness.

"Oh my," Father Holder said with a nervous laugh. His heart was still thundering in his ears. He also had an embarrassing line of slobber on his cheek, and he wiped it away with his sleeve. "You do know how to make an entrance, son."

"Sorry," the young man said. "I didn't know you were sleeping."

He had just a tinge of a Southern accent, but of a particular variety—Cajun, maybe? It was barely there, like a radio playing faintly in another room. Whoever he was, he certainly wasn't from around here. Of course, that was true of just about everyone in Las Vegas.

"I wasn't asleep," Father Holder said, even as he blinked away the bleariness in his eyes. "Just resting my eyes a little. I was— what time is it anyway?"

"Late," the young man said. "Very late. Midnight almost."

"Ah," Father Holder sighed, and he was going to say that he should have closed the church an hour ago, but then he would have to admit he'd been nodding off. Instead he said: "Well. I do need to be getting home here soon. You didn't start by asking for my blessing, son. Did you really come to make a confession?" He felt vaguely guilty for the accusatory tone, but he knew it was because he was feeling defensive.

"Yes. Of a kind."

"Of a kind?"

"Well … I didn't ask for your blessing, Father, because I don't think I sinned. I did something awful, I guess, but I can't see how it's a sin. I don't know. Maybe you can tell me. All I know is it wasn't a mistake. I don't make mistakes."

Father Holder chuckled. The young man didn't.

"I'm sorry," Father Holder said. "I assumed you were joking."

"No. I wouldn't joke about this."

"Hmm."

"I just don't make mistakes. Even now, after everything, I can say it. But maybe a mistake and a sin aren't the same thing. I guess that's why I'm here. That and to tell you my story—I want you to hear it."

Father Holder rubbed his eyes. He didn't want to deal with this foolishness right now—he wanted to be home, tucked into warm sheets, the rain lulling him back to sleep. "Son," he said, "I have to say, that's not a very Catholic idea. Scripture tell us—"

"Honestly, I'm not even Catholic."

"Ah. Well. Then I'm not sure I'm the person you—"

"I'm not saying I don't believe in God," the young man said. "I haven't until now … But lately, yeah, I've been thinking there's somebody up there. Some*thing* up there at least. My mama—mother, she certainly did. Always Jesus this, Jesus that." His Cajun accent was creeping into his voice, but it was obvious now to Father Holder that the young man had worked hard to suppress it.

"I see," Father Holder said. "Well, I know you want to talk, son, but a confessional is not intended to be a cheap replacement for a psychiatrist's couch. I could give you some phone numbers—"

"Let me ask you this, Father. Has God ever given you a sign that what you're doing is right?"

Now *that* was a question Father Holder hadn't expected the young man to ask, and there was something about the *way* it had been asked that put him on the defensive. When he'd entered seminary—what, two decades ago now?—he done so with such fervor and passion, such certainty that this was the path He had chosen for Joshua Holder. But over the years, where had that certainty gone? How many times, lately, had he prayed for some sign, however small, that He truly wanted him to stay on this path? And had he been blessed with any response? Had there been *anything* but a deepening of the silence?

"No," he said to the young man.

It surprised him. He could have said yes. It wouldn't have been a lie, at least not to the young man all those years ago who'd felt the call, the young man who'd traded in his camo and his guns and all the dreadful memories of those years in the jungle, the young man who would have insisted that with conviction that he saw signs with great regularity. *That* Joshua would have been able to say yes and believe it.

But not *this* Joshua. He looked at those early years and saw only naiveté and foolish idealism. He looked at his dilapidated old church and his measly congregation and wondered how much longer he could even keep his doors open. If only he had a few generous donors, he might be able to do some good, build a treatment center for gambling addicts, like he'd long wished, but he'd stopped hoping for that long ago. The Bishop said they'd support him if he could raise the money, but he didn't see it just falling out of the sky.

And building that treatment center was the one thing that had kept him going. Without it, what kind of purpose did he have? A man without purpose was a man without hope.

"No," he said again. "No, I've never gotten a sign."

"Has that been enough?"

"Why are you asking me this? Why does it matter?"

Father Holder was embarrassed at the bitterness in his own voice. He wanted to add, *My faith was more than enough,* as a way of making things right, but he couldn't. He didn't want to say it, and he saw himself indulging in his own pity. It took the young man on the other side of the confessional a while to respond, but when he did his tone had changed. He sounded relieved.

"Well, I have," he said. "I've seen a sign that what I'm doing is right. In fact, I've seen it again and again. And I want to tell you about it—if you'll listen. Will you listen to me, Father? It's important. It may be the most important story you'll ever hear."

It was unorthodox, of course, but Father Holder didn't feel right just turning the boy out into the rain. And course he was intrigued now. Anyone who believed he'd never made any mistakes was either a megalomaniac or delusional—and maybe both. In which case Father Holder doubted he could do much good.

But so far, he didn't detect either malady. The young man sounded reasonably sane and polite. It was a mystery, and getting to the bottom of a mystery was much more appealing than going back to a cold and empty bedroom, no matter how tired he was.

"I'll listen," he said.

"Good," the young man said. "You also have to promise me you'll never tell anyone. Not a soul. You priests have to do that, don't you?"

"Yes."

"I'm taking a chance on you, Father, so I need your promise. You have to promise that no matter what I tell you, you'll take it with you to your grave. It's very important."

Father Holder sighed. "Son, the confidentiality of all statements made in here is absolute. I have no choice in the matter."

"Oh, we always have a choice, Father. Take it from me, we always do. But I'll take that as your word." The young man shifted, his kneeling pad creaking. "I don't know how much time I have, so I'll try to make it quick. The first thing I guess I should tell you …"

… IS MY NAME. It's Michael Palmer. That's not the one my mother gave me, of course, but it's my legal name. When you're born poor and black in Baton Rouge, you don't need a name that's going to keep you there, and that's what would have happened if I would have stuck with the one Mama scrawled on my birth certificate. You ever noticed that, Father? As soon as you hear someone's name, you decide certain things about them. Certain doors open, other doors close. I wanted a name that would keep all the doors open. Once I found out what I could do, that was important.

Especially when you got skin so dark that lots of white folks instinctively reach for their wallets or purses. Even without my special talent, I probably would have changed my name. No offense to our current President, but how far a black man gets in life is directly related to how dark his skin is, not how much he jazzes up white folks with words like hope and change.

I mean, I can change things, you know? But I can only change so much. I can't change human nature.

I don't need to get into my food stamp childhood or how my only friends as a kid were the nutria in the creek near our apartment building—that just don't matter. But I do want to tell you about the day I found out what I could do. That's important, because I think it shows you where my instincts were right from the start.

It was one of those sweltering summer nights when the only good the whirring fans did was blow around the mosquitoes. Mama, she was real big on fans—we probably had a dozen scattered around our little rat-hole. Of course, it was also all those fans that made it hard to hear the guy with the knife who'd just broken the rotting door jamb on our front door.

Sometimes I wonder what would have happened had I heard him breaking in instead of what happened next. Maybe I would have tried to stop him, and he would have killed me for sure, since at a seventeen I was nothing more than a broomstick. Then everything would have been different, which means me *not* hearing him was a kind of miracle too.

But I didn't hear him. The fan on the shipping crate next to my bed—a crate that served as my dresser—roared like a jet engine. I was also suffering from an excruciating migraine. I'd gotten them all the time since I was little, but they were really bad that summer. I was lying on my back on the sheetless mattress, cradling my head, trying to will away the pain—and then, all of a sudden, Mama screamed.

It was no ordinary scream. Mama, she didn't like spiders none, and she'd scream like she'd seen the devil himself when she saw one. This was worse. It was the blood-curdling scream of somebody saying howdy to Mr. Death.

I was up and stumbling through the darkness, dashing to her room in nothing but my underwear. Kicked a shot glass next to the couch—it went skittering over the curling hardwood. Mama's door was open, and since she liked to sleep with a nightlight I saw the black man straddling her in the bed before I saw her. I also saw the knife in his hand, the blade already soaked in blood.

"Mama!" I screamed.

When the man turned, his eyes were so huge and white that I thought he must have been some kind of demon. No black man had eyes that big. Then I realized he wasn't black at all: He was a white man wearing a ski mask.

The man moved off my mother with the languid wariness of a leopard, not at all afraid of the bean-pole teenager in the doorway. It was at the moment I saw Mama's blood-soaked neck that the pounding in my head returned—much fiercer this time, a million ice picks driving into the back of my skull.

She was still convulsing, grappling at her neck, making the worst kinds of noises. The migraine brought tears to my eyes, so she and the man weren't much more than blurry shapes, but I knew she was dead. Dead and gone. The man took a step towards me, the knife held casually at his side.

"That'll teach the bitch not to laugh at a man's pecker," he said.

The iron grip of the migraine was tightening around my skull. He stepped up to me; I could smell the booze on his breath and the cigarettes on his leather jacket. The world was going white—he was visible only as a hulking silhouette. Then I felt the tip of his knife pressing against my crotch.

"Whadya think, kid?" he said. "Should I spill your balls on

the floor?"

Mama was silent now. The only sound was all those roaring fans. I don't know if it was Mama's silence, the prick of the knife, or the immense pressure behind my eyeballs, but my bladder let go. A flood of hot urine soaked my legs.

The man snickered. He pressed the knife just a little tighter, then pulled it back. "Scared little coon like you ain't worth the effort," he said.

He started for the door. I knew I'd dodged a bullet, but all I could think about—beyond the searing pain in my skull—was that Mama was dead. I was finally able to blink away some of the tears. It looked like Mama was floating in a pool of oil, there was so much blood.

That's when the migraine reached its crescendo. In my crazy life, I've been shot, stabbed, whipped, and tasered. I've been strangled. I've been punched in the face. I've had my ear chewed-off. I've broken almost every bone in my body. I've experienced almost every kind of pain imaginable, and none of it has even come close to the intensity of that migraine.

That's when the switchback happened for the first time.

Some part of me must have known what I could do, because even wrapped inside all that excruciating, mind-numbing pain, I still had room for one thought. *This hasn't really happened.* Not only did I think it, but I thought it with the kind of certainty that a person knows the color of the sky or the smell of a rose. It wasn't a wish. It was a fact, something I knew was true.

My vision swirled as if someone took a paintbrush and swirled all the shapes and colors in circles. I felt a sinking in my stomach, as if I was in plane lifting off a runway. A violent chill swept over me, gooseflesh breaking out all over my body.

Then I was in my bed.

It was that sudden, as if I'd clicked between channels on our little black and white television. I was back on my mattress, staring up at the ceiling in the dark, the fans roaring. The migraine had disappeared. I didn't know it then but they were gone for good.

I dashed through the dark, this time sidestepping the shot glass. When I saw Mama in bed alone, not a drop of blood on her, I didn't even feel relief. I knew she'd be fine. I just didn't know how much time we had.

"Mama! Wake up!" I jerked her shoulders.

"Wasssis?" she said, her breath reeking of the cheap vodka she liked so much.

"A man, he be coming! We gotta hide!"

She was still pretty out of it, but I managed to grab her hand and drag her towards the bathroom. I wanted to take her to Mrs. Delawin's apartment, but I figured he was probably already coming up the stairs. The smartest thing I did was pick up the phone along the way—one of the few times we actually had one—and dial 911.

When the woman answered, I didn't even wait to her to finish before shouting that there was a bad man in the apartment and our address.

She started to fire off questions, but I left it off the hook and pushed Mama, protesting now, into the bathroom. She didn't fuss for long, because as soon as I turned the lock we heard him banging-in the front door.

Mama started to scream, but I clamped my hand over her mouth. We hunkered down, putting our feet against the door and bracing ourselves against the toilet. We heard him skulking around out there for a while, but eventually the doorknob rattled. Mama couldn't contain herself and whimpered.

He started cursing something awful, throwing himself against the door. The wood splintered. It felt like we were trying to hold back an elephant. A gloved hand punched through the door and he grabbed for the handle. Mama screamed. That's when we heard the sirens. He must have heard them too because he tried to jerk his hand free.

Only it got stuck, and he thrashed about for a time before finally getting it loose. Mama and I held one another, both of us crying, listening to him running for the door.

He wasn't fast enough. By the time he made it to the hall, the police were already there.

THE RAIN, REALLY COMING DOWN NOW, crackled on the church roof like snapping bones. Any drowsiness that Father Holder had felt had long since disappeared. The young man's story was better than Sister Mary's coffee. That didn't make it true, of course. It just made him a good storyteller.

"Son," he said, "I don't mean to doubt the veracity of your tale, but are you saying—"

"I'm saying I'm a time traveler," Michael said. "Sort of, anyway. I call myself a Switchbacker. Never met another one like me, so I figure I've got naming rights."

"Are you sure it wasn't—"

"A dream? Oh no. I can see how you'd think that, and maybe if it'd only happened once I would have believed that, too, but I've since done it lots of times. Probably a million switchbacks by now. It's a pretty good name, huh? You can take it literally, because I go back and switch things around, but it's a little like a switchback on a road too—only this time it's time bending back on itself."

"Michael," Father Holder said, being careful how he proceeded, unsure the exact nature of the young man's delusion, "I'm not sure, well, why you're telling me this. It's … interesting. It's certainly as interesting as the tales I used to read in those old pulp magazines as a kid. But beyond that …"

"Oh, I know you don't believe me, Father. That's okay. You

will eventually, though. I promise."

Father Holder shifted uneasily on his padded bench. He was feeling cold. The thermostat was set to go off at eleven, but he didn't think his chill was related. There was something almost threatening in the young man's guarantee.

"I just don't know what you want from me," he said.

"I want you to listen."

"All right."

"To the rest of my story. That's all."

"Okay. I can do that." Then Father Holder had a flash of insight. Maybe this whole story was related to some complicated emotions the young man had regarding his childhood. Maybe there *was* some deeper issue he could tease out if he was patient. Maybe he could even bring another sheep into the flock. "Do you see your mother these days?"

"No, she died. Got AIDS."

"Oh, son, I'm sorry to hear that."

"Yeah. It wasn't surprising, though. My mother was what you'd call a working girl. I didn't know this until I was maybe nine or ten and I realized that she was having to pay for my food and clothing somehow—until then I just thought she had lots of guy friends. She was still very religious, though. I didn't see the irony in that until I was older. Methodist, though. Not Catholic." He chuckled.

There was an uncomfortable silence. Was this the truth or just another thread in his fantastical tale? The white eyes staring back at him through the mesh were wide and unblinking. For a moment, Holder wondered if there was really a young man there at all. Maybe it was just a pair of eyes floating in the darkness like fireflies.

He cleared his throat. "How about your father? Do you know—"

"Nah, let's not get into all that," Michael said. "I know what you're trying to do, and I appreciate it, but I really don't have much time." He sighed. It was not a sigh of exasperation, but one of longing. "I need to tell you about a girl. Her name's Annie. She's the reason I'm here tonight. She's the reason for everything, really. In a way, you could say Annie herself was the miracle ..."

THE FIRST TIME I met her, she was with a group of her girlfriends at the Bellagio on one of those blistering August days hot enough to evaporate the neon in the signs. I'd been in Vegas five years— at least, five years according to my biological age. In switchbacking years, I might have already been well over a hundred. I tried to keep track, but then I got into drinking and even normal time didn't mean much anymore.

I was a miserable wretch at that point—miserable and rich. If my mother would have had any idea how much money I burned up every day, mostly on hookers and booze, she would have hopped out of her grave on one foot. It wasn't always that way. When I really got a handle on switchbacking—slowly, over a couple months after that first time—I was the happiest person alive. I was happy because I realized real quick I never had to make another mistake. So long as I followed the rules, I could live a perfect life.

The rules, as I soon discovered, were actually fairly simple: I could switchback as many times as I wanted over the same time period, repeating the same hour over and over again if it suited me, watching Star Wars ten times in succession, eating an ice cream cone a dozen times in a row, but there was one big catch: I could only switchback as far back as the last switchback. So if I switchbacked five minutes, then that moment in time was as far back as I'd ever be able to go.

At first it didn't seem that big of a negative. I used my power to ace the rest of high school and get perfect SAT scores—easy as pie when you could take tests as many times as you needed. I used my power to become the star running-back despite being so scrawny. When you have a real-life instant replay, you can dodge any lineman because you always know which way he'll lunge.

Nobody caught on. They all thought I was a late-bloomer. It wasn't until my freshman year at Notre Dame, on a full-ride scholarship, that I realized the limits of what I could do.

When Mama called, she was already in the hospital, and her voice was so hoarse it didn't even sound like her own. She'd gone in because of pneumonia, but blood work revealed she had AIDS. I'd pretty much turned my back on her, ashamed of that life, but as soon as she told me her condition something broke inside me. She started crying, telling me she was only calling because she wanted me to get tested too, but I was already looking up flights on the computer.

There's no need to go into great detail about the two years I spent obsessed with saving Mama's life, but the end result was always the same. I used my switchbacking to make us a ton of money in day trading, so I was able to get her all the best drugs, but the most I could do was buy her a few months. I couldn't do the one thing that would have really made a difference—switchback far enough in time to get her out of hooking, or at least make sure she was always safe about it.

So when she passed a few days before my twenty-second birthday, I fell into a funk. I swore I'd never switchback again unless it was to save someone I loved, but of course there was no one I loved. I drifted, ending up in Vegas where I started hitting the Blackjack tables hard. I still wasn't switchbacking, but I soon burned up all my savings and like any addict surrounded by temptation, I fell into my old ways.

After five years, I was completely dead inside, a time-traveling zombie—and that's when I saw Annie sitting with her friends in the *Fontana* bar.

At first, I don't know if it was anything more than lust. But I will say that I knew the first moment I saw her, decked out in stylish, all-white denim, I thought she looked like an angel—long, curly, auburn hair; freckled, milky skin; penetrating, brown eyes. A smoky haze clouded the dimly lit room, but she might as well have been glowing. I was crossing the room to get myself another Scotch, and when I saw her I stopped dead. She noticed.

That's when I knew I had a chance. I sensed the attraction.

It was the briefest of moments and then she was laughing and smiling at something one of her friends said. It may have been a flicker in time, but my whole life changed with that look.

A band was playing on stage, but I have no idea what kind of music it was—my vision had narrowed just to her, the rest of the world a gauzy blur. Her friends, all pretty white girls in chic clothing and expensive jewelry, the kind of girls any guy would have killed to bed, were nothing but shadows. The next thing I knew I was standing at her table.

"Hi there," I said, going for the suave approach.

Annie looked at me with suspicion, a gold bracelet dangling from her slender wrist as she held her wine goblet aloft. Whatever attraction I'd seen was already gone, like a desert mirage.

"Hey, you with security?" one of the other girls said. "You find my purse yet?"

Ordinarily I might have been offended by the remark—what, a nicely dressed black man in a blue blazer couldn't just be a guest?—but I was focused on Annie. "I'm Michael," I said to her. "Can I buy you a drink?"

She had one of those expressive faces where even the slightest twitch of a muscle said more than words ever could. Perfect eyebrows arched ever so slightly. Pouty lips pursed. Her gaze shifted to her glass.

"Is there something wrong with the one I have?" she asked. There was the refinement of years spent in highbrow boarding schools in her voice.

"Well, no," I said, "I just thought—"

"You thought what? That I need another? So you're saying I'm a lush?"

"No, of course not." My cheeks felt warm. It'd been a while since I'd felt so flustered. "I just thought you might want company."

"Oh, so now you're insulting my friends?"

They all laughed—all of them except Annie. Her mouth didn't change at all, though her pupils narrowed as if she was a hawk soaring for prey and I was a rabbit that had strayed into her line of sight.

"I think maybe I'll go," I said. "My mission here is done. I've apparently convinced you I'm an idiot."

I was hoping my sheepish tone might win me some sympathy—get them to ask me to sit down out of pure pity. It had worked before. When I turned to go, a couple girls did say "Aww, don't go," and "No, stay," but I didn't hear anything from Annie. That's when I knew I'd blown my chance.

Of course, for me, there was always another.

I closed my eyes and switchbacked to when I'd just stepped up to the table, murmuring to myself, *This didn't happen, This didn't happen,* each repetition taking me another beat back in time. There was a momentary wave of disorientation, like passing through a cloud of warm air, but I'd long since learned how to never show it on my face.

"Hi there," I said, making sure to say it to all the girls this time. "I just came off a nice run and I'm feeling flush. Can I buy you all another round of drinks? I'm pretty much a Vegas lowlife, but I'm harmless."

The other girls giggled. Annie bore into me with her eyes.

"So you're trying to get us drunk, is that it?" she said.

I looked at her as if just noticing she was there—and then

held her gaze for a beat longer than necessary. "If that's what you want. I was just hoping for some good conversation."

There was more laughter. This time they were laughing *with* me and not at me. The way Annie lowered her wine glass, I could tell I'd unnerved her.

It wasn't long before I was regaling them with tales from my life as a professional poker player, and it wasn't long after that I was showing them around the strip as their personal tour guide. Annie watched me warily, but now and then I caught another one of those smoldering glances so I knew the attraction was real. I didn't switchback again, thinking I might need to rewind all the way back to the table if I blew it, and that turned out to be a wise move.

They were only there for the weekend, a rich girls' last summer hurrah before they returned to Stanford for fall term. Annie was pretty tight-lipped about herself, though she was quite free with her opinions on the fake Italian architecture and the dangers inherent in the gambling industry. Smart, tough, and beautiful, with a bit of an icy edge—I was madly in love after only a couple hours. It wasn't until she got a call on her cell phone, when we were walking under the fake sky of the Venetian, that one of her friends finally let slip who she was.

"Probably talking to Daddy," one of her friends said, when Annie was safely out of earshot, standing over by the canal. This girl, a redhead with a body to die for, was making it obvious she wanted to take me to bed. She laughed a little too hard at my jokes and found lots of excuses to touch me on the arm.

"Oh?" I said. "He keep a close tab on all his daughters?"

"He's only got one," she said. "Three sons, but she's the princess. Anything Annie wants, she gets. And a guy like him, he can get her just about anything."

"What, he in the mafia or something?"

She laughed too hard and touched my elbow, leaning in close

enough that I could smell the apricot perfume. "You're so funny, Michael. You do know who she is, right?"

"Why would I know who she is?"

"She's Annie Jackson."

"Yeah."

"Daughter of Quincy Jackson?"

I gave her a blank look. She shook her head, bemused.

"*Senator* Quincy Jackson?"

"Oh. Well, I don't follow politics much."

"Well, me either, but I figured since he was *Nevada's* senator, the name might ring a bell."

If anything, the information didn't intimidate me. It only made me want her more.

"HOLD ON," Father Holder said. It was a strangely compelling fabrication, of course, but it had taken a turn he found disturbing. "You're saying that this Annie, this girl you mentioned, was Senator Jackson's daughter?"

"That's right."

"I know her. I know the whole family. He's a good Catholic. They used to come here before they switched to the Holy Redeemer." And Father Holder thought ruefully about those generous donations that no longer graced his offering plates.

"I know," Michael said. "That's one of the reasons I came to you."

The bright eyes stared at him, unflinching. The rain went on beating its drum. Somewhere outside, a siren blared in the distance. Father Holder swallowed away the lump in his throat.

"Son, be honest with me here, did any of this really happen?"

There was a long pause before Michael spoke, and when he did, there was a new edge. "I *told* you, you'll have all the proof you need—eventually. Right now I just need you to listen."

"Son—"

"You can still do that, can't you, Father? Listen? I mean, you haven't lost your way completely, have you?"

It was if the boy and torn through the mesh and touched Father Holder's heart with a cold finger. "What?" he said.

Michael sighed. "I'm sorry. I shouldn't have said that."

"What did you mean?"

"I think you know what I meant."

"Well, well, if you think you can come into my church and insult me—"

"Save it," Michael said curtly. "You can kick me out if you want, but then you'll never hear the end of my story. And I promise you, you'll always wonder."

Father Holder simmered in silence, but he didn't say anything, and the young man started speaking again.

EVENTUALLY I MANAGED to tease out a little of Annie's personality—how she was majoring in art history because she loved art but recognized she had no artistic ability herself, how she was a sucker for children who smiled, how the icy exterior masked a heart that was easily bruised. By the time we were having dinner at *New York-New York*, the grumbling of the roller coaster muted by the thick glass walls, I'd decided I was going to do everything I could to win her.

I know how it sounds. It doesn't sound rational, but then love never is. I was grasping for something, anything, to give some meaning to my life. She was a life preserver tossed to a drowning man.

Dinner was lively—after all, my wad of cash made the booze flow freely—and Annie opened up even more. She cracked jokes about all the lewd things that happened in the halls of Congress. I talked about some of the crazy stuff me and the fraternity guys did back at Notre Dame. I even told a few tall tales of the bayou I'd learned from my childhood, something I'd *never* talked about with anyone. It was during one of our laughing fits that Annie looked at me with those piercing eyes of hers.

"So, Michael," she said, "you going to be a gambler the rest of your life?"

It was as if she'd doused a fire with a bucket of cold water. The laughter turned into a smoldering silence, and everyone looked at me uneasily.

"Well, you make it sound like I'm a hooker or something," I joked, trying to revive our easy banter. A few of the girls laughed, but Annie wasn't finished.

"What I mean is, is this what you're going to do with your life?"

I took my time, sipping my beer, trying to decide the best tact to take. I wiped the froth off my lip with a napkin. "I guess I haven't thought that far ahead. Just having fun right now. Nothing wrong with that, right?"

She shrugged. "For a while."

"You know, for someone majoring in art history, you're sounding an awful lot like my high school guidance counselor."

The redhead barked obnoxiously, but she was the only one. Annie and I were back to staring at one another as if no one else was there.

"Just curious, that's all," she said. "No need to get offended."

"I'm not offended."

"I just thought, you know, with your talent for numbers, you could put it use on Wall Street or in economics."

"Ah," I said. "You mean, in more *honest* work?"

"No, that's not—"

"Something less dirty?"

"Michael, I wasn't—"

"Because coming from a girl whose daddy works in politics,

that's a little hard to take."

I made sure to say it with a laugh, which got all the other girls to laugh too. It was a nervous laughter, though; the laughter of people wanting to release pent-up tension. Annie just glared. One of the girls said something about her own father running a garbage company, and then the conversation moved to safer ground. I made sure to laugh and crack lots of jokes, but Annie said hardly a word the rest of the evening, and I thought, oh no, I've blown it. I figured I'd do another switchback after we called it a night.

When we rose from the table, I was still trying to sort out how it had gone wrong. Annie took a pen from her purse and jotted something on a napkin, which she folded in half.

"I know you'll probably hate me for doing this," she said, "but this is the phone number of Nathan Monroe, my dad's chief of staff. He knows lots of people who can hook you up. Tell him Annie sent you." She held it out to me.

It wasn't the kind of end to the evening I'd been hoping for—I couldn't stop staring at her lips, wondering how it would feel to kiss them—but I took it anyway. We all made plans to meet for breakfast. Heading outside to catch a cab back to my penthouse at *The Mirage*, I almost threw away the napkin. If it had been given to me by anyone other than Annie, I would have. As it was, I stopped by the garbage can as I unfolded it.

It was her room number.

It's hard to describe the immense self-control it took to remain in the bar another hour and a half—an hour for her to shake off her friends and get safely to her room, and another thirty minutes so she didn't think I was *too* desperate. It turned out that was probably unnecessary, because as soon as I tapped on the door, she jerked it open, grabbed my shirt and yanked me inside.

The room was dark except for the triangle of light spilling in from the bathroom. An air conditioner moaned dully in the corner. I got only a glimpse of her wild eyes before she was kissing me—hard, desperate kisses. Her hands ripped at my clothes. We stumbled onto the big bed and it only got more wild from there.

You're a man of the cloth, Father, so I won't get into all the lurid details—but safe to say, it was the best sex of my entire life. She was a wild animal with an insatiable appetite, and it wasn't until the gray light of dawn was spilling into the room around the curtains that we finally lay exhausted in each other's arms. Her sweaty back was pressed against my chest, her head nestled under my chin.

"Well," I said, with a sigh.

She giggled. "You're not bad yourself."

"I don't think I'm going to be able to get out of bed for a week."

"Good. Mission accomplished." Then her tone turned slightly more serious. "Don't want you to think I do that all the time. You're a special case."

"Well, thank you. I think you're special too."

She murmured in pleasure and snuggled against me. I loved the way the arch of her back fit so perfectly against my chest. I loved the smell of her hair—like lavender in spring. I could have gone on holding her that way forever, but there was something nagging me.

"Can I ask you something?" I said.

"Anything."

"What you said in the bar—about doing something with my life. Did you really mean that?"

"How so?"

"I mean, is that important to you? Do you need a guy with a respectable career?"

She took a while before answering, and when she did, there was an unmistakable shift in her tone. I couldn't say what that shift was, but I could sense something had changed. The night was gone and dawn was upon us.

"Well," she sighed, "I do want a guy that's going places."

I knew she was holding back, but I didn't want to believe it. I pressed on. "Okay. So let's say I make a life change. I've … I've been thinking about it anyway. Let's say I get into banking or real estate or something. I'm pretty sure I could be good at it." My heart was pounding, and my voice was thickening. I didn't want her to know how hard this was for me to say, but it was difficult to mask when you were lying naked in bed with each other. "So I make this change. I make this change and … and I call you up. Would you, uh, would you see me again?"

"Well, of course, Michael."

"Good," I sighed. "That's good."

"I'd always see you again. I'd see you again tomorrow."

She laughed, and I started to laugh with her, then I realized it wasn't really the answer I wanted to hear.

"Oh," I said, chuckling, trying to keep it light but still probing. "You mean, for a good lay?"

"For an *amazing* lay, actually," she replied.

"So for *that*, I don't need to change at all."

"Well there is a certain part of you that needs to change, I guess."

She laughed again, but all the humor had drained out of me. She must have realized something was wrong because she turned and faced me, our noses inches apart. Her breath was warm on my chin, and her eyes were so wide I saw my reflection in them

"What is it?" she said.

"Nothing."

"Oh, come on."

"I just—I didn't want to be a one night stand, that's all."

She pressed her hands against my chest. "You're not a one night stand. I *told* you, you're very special. I want to see you again."

"Okay."

"I want to see you lots of times."

"Well, that's good. That's real good."

"Michael …"

We were so close that I couldn't hide the disappointment on my face, so I climbed out of bed. The carpet felt like walking on satin. Naked, I went to the curtains and parted them, blinking at the strip in the morning light. All that had been alive at night with lurid electricity was bland and mundane in the morning, as unfulfilling as an abandoned amusement park. It was really in the daylight—when the neon could no longer hide all that gaudy architecture and obscene extravagance— that Las Vegas was most unreal.

"Talk to me," she said.

I shrugged. "I was just, you know, hoping for more."

"I told you—"

"I heard you," I said. "I know what kind of guy I am to you."

"Michael, come back to bed. Let me *show* you what kind of guy you are to me."

I faced her. She was sitting up in bed, the sheets tangled around her legs, her breasts exposed. Even naked, she had a presence about her, something about her posture and the tilt of her chin; with the elaborate gold headboard behind her, she made me think of a queen. I felt myself responding to her, wanting her again, and I hated myself in that moment more than I ever had.

"Let me ask you something," I said. "Let's say I go back to school. Let's say I get an MBA from Harvard. Let's say I climb to the top of a Fortune 500 company. I could do it, you know. I could do anything. Let's say I'm one of the most powerful people in the world. Would I have a shot with you then?"

"Michael—"

"Annie, just answer the question."

She sighed. She pulled up the sheets over her breasts, looking down at the bed. The temperature in the room had dropped. I shivered.

"I don't know why you're making me do this," she said.

"Isn't it obvious? I really like you."

"I like you too."

"But it's not enough?"

She shrugged. "It's not about me, Michael. Not really. It's just—you know, my father. He expects me to marry a certain kind of guy."

"But I told you, I could—"

"Michael, there's nothing you can do about it."

That's when I knew exactly what she was talking about. It wasn't her words. It was the way her eyes roved my body.

"Oh," I said, a lump of lead sliding into the pit of my stomach. "Oh, I see. Yeah. I should have known. Because I'm black."

"Michael, don't say it like that."

"I'm such an idiot."

"No, you're not. You're wonderful."

"A wonderful black man."

"Michael—"

"It's okay, Annie. Really. In the old days, it was the white man who used to have a little roll in the hay with the black slave girls. Now it's the white girls who want to have a little Negro fun. I guess that's progress."

"Don't do this," she pleaded. "Really, it doesn't have to be this way."

Now it was me feeling exposed. I retrieved my pants from the floor and started slipping into them.

"Michael," she pleaded.

My hands were shaking as I buttoned my shirt. She climbed out of bed and reached for me, but I pushed her violently back on the bed. She fell on the sheets, her breasts flopping, her legs splayed, and when she was exposed in such clinical detail I wondered how I could have ever found her attractive. She repulsed me.

"Fine," she snapped. "Fine, be that way then."

I was fully dressed and slipping on my wingtips as I headed to the door. If she hadn't said anything, that probably would have been it, I never would have seen her again and I would have hunkered down in front of my big screen television and drank away my sorrows until the memory of her was just a blur. But she had to say one more thing. She had to say one more thing that cut me right to the core.

"There's just some things we can't change, Michael," she said. "No matter how much we want to, there's just some things we can't change."

That's when I decided to kill her.

THE YOUNG MAN's last sentence hung in the air like an unsheathed blade. Father Holder cleared his throat.

"I'm sorry, son, did you say—"

"I said I decided to kill her," Michael said.

He did not say it as if it was a joke or a lark. He said it with all the conviction of a man bent on murder. The rain had finally lessened enough that Father Holder could no longer hear it tapping on the roof, and their voices sounded hollow in the cavernous church. He was suddenly conscious of how alone he was with this young man, only a thin stretch of cloth separating them. He also remembered the sirens from earlier, and he felt a prickling on the back of his neck

"Son," he said, "have you done something? Have you ... committed a terrible sin?"

"You have to understand something," Michael said. "You have to understand that switchbacking is the ultimate in wish fulfillment. It's virtual reality without the virtual. Any desire I wanted to act out in real time, I could. If I wanted to steal a child's candy bar, I could. If I wanted to rape a woman in broad daylight, I could. If I wanted to cut a man's throat for insulting me in a bar, I could. But I could also rewind time so the event only existed in my memory. Is it a sin when it only happened in my own mind? How many of us fantasize about doing terrible things?"

Father Holder's mouth had gone dry. "And did you, son? Did you do those terrible things?"

Michael sighed. "No. No, I didn't. I'd like to say it was because deep down I was a good person, but I think it was because I was still afraid of something happening. Somebody with a gun shooting me before I got a chance to switchback. Dead is still dead, I think, even for me. Of course I won't know until it happens, I guess."

"And Annie?" Father Holder said. "You're saying she was just another fantasy, then?"

"Of course," Michael said.

"So you didn't really do it?"

"Oh no, I did it. It was the one time I indulged myself."

Father Holder felt as if the confessional was sinking, dropping like an elevator. He didn't believe any of this time-travel nonsense, but he was sure the young man was using it as some sort of metaphorical defense mechanism. "But you—you did this, this switchbacking thing, right?"

"Yes."

"Oh good."

"But it's more complicated than that, Father. Let me explain …"

THE KEY WAS NOT getting caught, of course. If I wanted to act out my fantasy, then it was imperative I not get caught. I wanted to feel what it was like killing Annie, but I had another motive—I wanted to watch Senator Jackson suffer.

Fortunately, since I'd been preserving my options, I hadn't switchbacked since I first met her. The first thing I did, after I stepped into that long, quiet hall outside her room, was roll back time to the moment when I was crossing through the Fontana bar. I didn't even look at Annie and her friends. I just kept walking, back into the casino. Their laughter, fading behind me, sounded like a gaggle of geese. I despised them all.

Now there was no reason for anyone to ever suspect me. Why would they? I'd never met her.

I walked home, changed into jeans, a nice, non-threatening, baby blue sweater, donned a UNLV cap and some reading glasses I never wore in public. I took a black marker and gave myself a thin mustache.

After I returned to the casino, I burned up a couple of hours at the slots until finally, at nearly midnight, I saw her stagger to the elevator with her friends. After I waited twenty minutes, I moseyed my way to the stairwell. Nobody ever used the stairwell, so I was able to climb the five flights without passing a single soul.

Cracking open the door, I peered into the hall. Some old ladies were emerging from their room and I waited until they'd disappeared into the elevator. Then I walked casually to Annie's room, keeping my head slightly lowered. For the cameras.

I tapped lightly on her door.

After a moment, she answered with a slurred voice: "Whozzere?"

"Messenger service, ma'am," I said. "I have a package from Senator Jackson."

I heard a click of another door a few rooms down, panicking me, but then Annie's door was opening and I was lunging inside, my hands already around her neck. She tried to scream but I clamped down hard. The room was dark except for the little bedside lamp, set to low. She was dressed in a white terry cloth robe, and as I pushed her onto the bed it fell open, revealing her naked flesh.

She was writhing and thrashing about, clawing at my hands and then my face, but I put my full weight on her. One of her fingernails slashed my cheek like a knife, drawing blood, and this only made me squeeze tighter. She gagged and coughed, trying desperately to wiggle free, but her years as a pampered rich girl had done nothing for her physical strength. It was less than five minutes before she finally fell still.

I checked her pulse to make sure, but she was really gone.

After I cleaned myself up in the bathroom, I cracked open the door and waited until the hall was clear, then walked as casually as I could—that was the hardest part—down the stairwell and into the sweltering August night. Nobody stopped me.

Now understand, I still pretty much expected to be caught. There were security cameras everywhere, of course. This was a major Las Vegas casino and there was no getting around it. I just figured I could try it a couple more times to see if I could get away with it.

But I wasn't caught.

Nobody came to my door.

Turns out all my preparations were unnecessary, because the security cameras on the seventh floor were on the fritz that night, so *New York-New York* couldn't even produce a grainy surveillance video. By the next morning, when the story was all over the news and I was into my second bottle of Vodka, I was already having second thoughts, but I wanted to see it through. I wanted to at least see Senator Jackson squirm.

But when he finally gave a press conference, the bespectacled little turd was defiant. At five feet seven, with a rotund frame and only a few wisps of silver hair, he was hardly an imposing figure, but as he swore he'd track down his daughter's killer he was electrifying. The whole world thought so, too, because the clip of him banging on the podium was an Internet sensation.

Sitting on my leather couch in my silk robe, balancing a cold shot glass on my belly, I thought, oh yeah, buddy, we'll see about that. The guilt was already gnawing at me something awful, but I vowed not to switchback until he managed to catch me.

But he didn't. The bastard hired all the detectives money could buy, but nobody ever came knocking on my door. Months passed. Then a year. The guilt—it was like some flesh-eating disease. I didn't know how much longer I could endure it. I didn't know how much longer I could tell myself I wasn't a killer. I figured maybe it was time to call it a win, but then the bastard did something that really stunned me.

He threw his hat in the ring for the Presidency.

I was outraged. I thought it was a pretty callous move, capitalizing on all that publicity he got because of his daughter's death, all those humanizing interviews on CNN and *60 Minutes* that painted him as this poignant, sympathetic figure. I held off switchbacking, thinking I'd at least get to see him suffer a humiliating defeat in the election.

But he didn't lose. He won in a landslide—over 400 electoral votes and sixty percent of the popular vote. It pissed me off to no end, but I didn't want to give in yet. I wanted to figure out another way to make him suffer.

The reverse happened. A month after he took office, peace talks between Israel and the newly nuclear-equipped Iran broke down. Everybody thought war was imminent—until President Quincy Jackson stepped in there. He negotiated a peace settlement that had everybody talking Nobel Prize. He was a hero to the world.

That's when I threw in the towel. Shaking my fist at him giving a press conference with the leaders of Iran and Israel on either side, I said, "You win, buddy, you win."

Then I switchbacked it all away.

* * * * *

"OH, THAT'S GOOD," Father Holder said, immensely relieved. "I'm glad you came to your senses."

For a moment, there was nothing but the stillness of the church—the creaking and cracking of the floorboards, the light wind whistling against the stained-glass windows high above them, a whisper that might have been a four-legged creature skittering through the pews. Then Michael laughed. It was not a response Father Holder expected.

"If I didn't know better, Father, I'd say you believe me."

Father Holder didn't know about that. He still thought it was a skillful fabrication, one used to mask some deeper, repressed guilt, but he didn't want to upset the young man. "I don't think you're lying," he said, and that much was true because Michael certainly seemed to believe his story.

"Ah, the qualification. Is truth in the eye of the beholder? Of course, to me, time is too."

Father Holder chose his words carefully. "I'm just … glad the story ended the way it did. It was a … terrible thing that she did, and I understand your anger. There's no happy face to put on racism of any kind. But at least you—you switchbacked away all that terrible business."

"Yes, I did," Michael said.

"Good, good. Well, I must say this has been an interesting—"

"Then I had to do it all over again."

The white eyes stared with a renewed intensity. There was no jest in the young man's words.

"I'm sorry?"

"I wish it could have ended there," Michael said. "I really do. And if it had, I never would have come in tonight. But you see, I had to kill her, Father. That was the miracle. Killing Annie Jackson."

Father Holder seriously considered bolting for the door. He was revising his earlier appraisal of the young man. Michael was obviously unhinged. "Son, perhaps we should continue this conversation after a good night's—"

"After I switchbacked and crossed through that bar again," Michael continued, "something was nagging me. It's a good thing, too. I wondered about that showdown between Israel and Iran. I mean, the world could end, you know? You start firing nukes and usually that's all she wrote. So I didn't switchback. I waited. I waited until the whole damn crisis happened again and another President tried to stop it. Only he couldn't. And then somebody fired one of those puppies and the world went to hell."

Ordinarily, Father Holder would have scolded him for invoking that word in his confessional, but he was too dumbfounded to speak. Michael shifted, his kneeling pad creaking.

"I did everything I could to stop it," Michael said. "I don't even know how many years I spent trying—over a hundred, maybe. I joined his campaign. I convinced him to run. And a couple times, I even managed to get him into office. But something about that tragedy with Annie tempered his judgment. Without it, he was powerless to stop the crisis. I did everything. I really did."

"Son—"

"I worked for other candidates," Michael continued, his voice quickening. "I became an expert in politics and elections. I got three different Presidents elected. When that failed, I became a master mediator myself, and in a couple of my switchbacks I was even there at the table—but I couldn't stop them either. I spent more years becoming a master writer and I wrote a bestseller that warned what was coming with crystal clarity, hoping if people knew the future they could prevent it themselves. That didn't work either."

"Michael, please—"

"The only thing that worked, Father, was killing Annie Jackson. So that's what I did. I went back again and killed her. And this time I let it stand."

There were more sirens in the distance, growing louder. Did somebody know Michael was here? Father Holder hoped so. He just had to keep the young man here until the police arrived.

"Michael," he said, lowering his voice, speaking gently, "if what you say is true—"

"It is, it is."

"Well, then, there's nothing I can do about the law. But if you can give yourself to Jesus—"

Michael laughed. "I knew you'd say that. You see, Father, I've been here before. You just don't remember."

"What?"

"But what I want to know is, did I sin?"

"Well, I—I don't—"

"If you believe everything I said," Michael went on, voice rising, "or if you can at least just pretend, for a moment, that everything I said will come to pass, then was it a mistake killing her? And if that was the only way to save the world, then how it can it be a sin?"

The sirens were still out there, but were they getting closer? Father Holder couldn't tell. "I—I don't know," he said.

Michael let out a long sigh, bowing his head. "Well, I do," he said. "I know it wasn't a mistake. I don't make mistakes. I don't have to. But there's always the temptation, you know? That's the real problem. There's always the temptation to switchback all this away, you know? I mean, if I can't live with the guilt of being a murderer, and I undo it all, then it *would* be a mistake."

"I see," Father Holder said, edging himself a little closer to the curtain. He was going to make a run for it.

"No, you don't," Michael said. "But that's okay. The problem is, I *know* I can't live with the guilt. I did it once and it almost destroyed me. But I can't undo it either, so I've got one choice. I'm going to book a room in a nice hotel and swallow a whole mess of painkillers. Then I'll take a nice long nap and never wake up. Since I made sure to lose a whole bunch of money at the tables today, they'll just think that was the reason."

"Son!"

"It's the only way, Father. Tomorrow morning it'll be all over the news that Annie Jackson is dead. I'm sure you were thinking those sirens were for me, but I wasn't that stupid. I was going to do this on my terms. So you'll see the news and you'll wonder about our conversation. Then you'll get something in the mail and you'll know every word I told you is true."

"What is it?"

Instead of answering, Michael rose. Father Holder was gripped with a fear that the young man was going to attack him. Michael parted the curtain, the soft yellow light outside briefly illuminating his face. He looked so young and innocent—with one exception. There was a large gash on his right cheek.

"One more thing before I go, Father," he said softly. "I'm not the only one in this confessional who's going to kill himself."

"What?"

"In all the other timelines, you hang yourself in your room."

"That's preposterous!"

"Is it? I know that you've been terribly depressed. I know that you've lost your way. Can you tell me, honestly, that you've never once thought of taking your own life? We are in confessional, now. God is listening."

Father Holder was speechless.

"I didn't come here to embarrass you," Michael said. "I came here to tell you my story because I wanted you to know it *is* possible to make a difference. Sometimes you just need someone to give you a little nudge along the way. That's all I'm doing. Giving you a nudge, because it makes me feel a little bit better about the terrible thing I had to do. Now do some good with it. And don't try to come after me. You'd never find me."

"Son—"

"One last thing. When they ask you where it came from, tell them someone left it in your offering plate. They might frown on you picking it up yourself."

"Picking up what?"

But Michael didn't answer. Father Holder listened to the footsteps retreating, the double doors swinging open, then shut. He was too stunned to do anything but sit there trembling in the darkness. There were no more sirens, but it didn't matter. He wasn't afraid because he feared the young man. He was afraid because something deep within him had been exposed, something he'd been denying even to himself.

It took him some time, but eventually he gathered himself enough to slump his way back to the rectory. He checked the news and there was nothing about Annie Jackson or her father. When he poured himself a bourbon, his hand was shaking, but by the time he'd downed his third glass, he'd convinced himself that the young man was just a remarkable storyteller. There was no proof that any of it was real.

Waking late the next morning, a fierce pounding behind his eyeballs made worse by the lancing sunlight, he wasn't even sure about the young man any more. Maybe he'd dreamed him up too.

By the time he hustled through a shave and a shower, and he was climbing the steps to his office, he was even feeling strangely buoyant. Suicidal? Ridiculous. Yes, he'd suffered from a bit of the blues, but he never would have taken his own life. That was a terrible sin.

Then he thought of his treatment center and how the goal seemed hopeless. He wondered how long he'd really be able to keep the darkness at bay.

A man without purpose was a man without hope.

Walking into his cramped office, he said a somber hello to his gray-haired secretary, Wilma. She handed him the mail. He headed to his office, flipping through the envelopes, not thinking anything of it until he came to one without a return address. His name and the address of the church were typewritten. He swallowed, remembering what the young man had said, and looked at his secretary.

"Wilma," he said. "Did you, um, see the news this morning?"

"Oh yes," she said, shaking her head. "Such a terrible tragedy. She was so young. And nobody has any idea why."

Wilma may have still been talking, but Father Holder was no longer listening. He was thinking that the young man's tale had to be a delusion, a way to justify doing something terrible. Not real. Of course not real. With trembling hands, he tore open the envelope.

There was no letter, and at first he thought it was empty—until a Powerball lottery ticket slipped into his hand.

The Bear Who Sang Opera

The bear wanted his voice back. That's what I thought he said, and I asked him to repeat it. The cochlear implant in my left ear had been acting up a lot lately—I blamed it on Targal's frequent lightning storms—and I assumed he must have said something else.

"My voice," he said. "I think someone's stolen it."

I took my boots down from the desk and leaned a little closer. "Your voice?"

"Yes, that's right."

"But you're speaking right now."

"Yes." He bobbed his big furry head. "Oh. No, I see the problem. Not my voice. My *singing* voice. I need your help getting it back. You do help people find things, don't you? That's what I heard."

His voice was deep and gruff, but he sounded sincere. Of course, I was no expert on bears, so how would I know? Maybe bears were good at lying. He was a grizzly, standing on two feet, the tips of his ears brushing against the ceiling lamp. His black tuxedo had obviously been tailor-made for him, but still it seemed small, the buttons straining to hold in his girth, bits of brown fur showing in the gaps. His massive body completely blocked the window and blotted out Targal's fierce desert sunlight. The fringes of his fur looked golden, but with the light behind him, the rest of him was shrouded in darkness. He smelled like he spent most of his time in smoking rooms, and I noticed the bulge of a pipe in his left jacket pocket.

I was thankful he hadn't tried to squeeze himself into one of the two creaky metal folding chairs that sat across from my desk. I didn't want to buy new chairs. I couldn't *afford* to buy new chairs.

"I didn't know bears even had voices," I said.

"Well, obviously I'm not a real bear."

"Obviously," I said, nodding. Though it hadn't been obvious to me. You never knew these days.

"I'm a biological-robot hybrid."

"Ah."

"I really need your help."

"Mmm. And who, exactly, has stolen your voice?"

"Well, that's just it," he said. "I said I *think* someone's stolen it. I'm not sure."

"You're not sure? How can you not be sure?"

He shrugged. Since grizzlies didn't have much in the way of shoulders to work with, it was more a flexing of massive muscles. "Well," he said, "my memories have been tampered with, too. But it just seems too coincidental that my voice module would fail the very day I left the MGC. I think—I think it's more likely they replaced it with a faulty unit and then manipulated my memory circuits so I wouldn't remember the procedure. I *know* my memory cells were tampered with. I have a surgical engineer's report for you to prove it."

"Uh-huh. What's the MGC?"

"Mortagai Galactic Circus. I sang opera for them for over five years."

I'd heard of them. They were one of the biggest traveling circuses in the known universe, and one of the most eclectic. If there was one circus where you might find a bear who sang opera, it would be Mortagai. I once dated a girl on Realta who took me to a show when they were in town—fire-breathing penguins, tap-dancing cyborgs, shapeshifting clowns, they had it all. It wasn't my sort of thing, but at the time, I really liked this girl and I was willing to go the extra mile. Funny how I couldn't remember her name. Or whether going the extra mile paid off.

"Getting old," I muttered.

"Mister Duff?" he said.

"Hmm?"

"My name is Karvo. Karvo Portano. Can you help me?"

I wanted to ask him *why* he thought they stole his voice, but I was already afraid he was crazy, and I didn't want to give him any encouragement. There was usually a surefire way to separate the crazies from the serious clients. "You realize I charge a pretty stiff fee?" I said.

"I understand," he said. "And … well, I'm afraid I don't have any money at the moment."

Bingo. "Kind of hard to hire me without any money," I said.

"Yes. Yes, that would normally be the case. But you see, Dexter—may I call you Dexter?"

"No."

"Oh. Yes, well, Mister Duff—"

"Just Duff. When someone calls me Mister, I always feel like I should be wearing a tie."

"Oh, yes. I see. Well, it's true I don't have any money. But if I get my voice back, I certainly will. You see, it was the reason I decided not to renew my contract. I'd gained a certain amount of fame for my opera, and it became apparent I had a lucrative solo career waiting for me if I decided to leave the circus. If I get my voice back, I promise you I'll not only pay your fee, I'll pay you double. I'm good on my word. Ask anyone." He cleared his throat, a guttural roar that made the hairs on the back of my neck rise. "So you see, I will have money. You just have to trust me."

I drummed my fingers on the desk, my fingers bent so my fingernails clicked on the metal. *Just trust me.* It was a line that got me into trouble back on DKP, the last planet I'd called home, which was why I had to relocate my business in the middle of the night to the little piss-pot of a planet, Targal. She'd said I should trust her. Of course, she'd said it while she was on top of me, which had given her quite the advantage.

"Your legs aren't as good," I said.

"Excuse me?"

I shook my head. "Look, I'd like to help. It's just ... I'm booked. I can't take on more than I can chew." I regretted my choice of words. Planting the word "chew" in the mind of a bear, hybrid or not, didn't seem like such a good idea.

"You don't seem so busy right now," he said.

"I'm on lunch," I said.

"I see. Have you been on lunch all day?"

"I'm sorry?"

Karvo hesitated. In the silence he seemed so much more menacing. "I've been standing out on the promenade for the last couple of hours," he said finally. "It ... took me a while to build up my courage to come in here. I didn't see anybody coming or going from your office."

"Oh," I said. It seemed a stretch imagining him nervous about anything, but what he was saying was certainly true. I hadn't had a client in nearly a month. "Well, maybe you scared them off."

"What?"

"The clients. You know, seeing a bear out front would do that to most people."

He sighed. At least, I *think* it was a sigh. It came out as more of a snort. "Duff," he said, "are we going to play this little game all day? If you don't think you can trust me to pay you, just say so. I went through a lot of stepdocks to get here. I had to avoid all the planets where my kind are considered property, which made it a pretty long trip. The least you could do is be honest with me."

"All right, all right," I said. "Let's say I take the job. What if I can't get it back? Your voice, I mean."

"You'll get it back. I've heard you're very good at this sort of thing."

"But what if I don't? How will you pay me? I don't make guarantees, you know. I do my best, but I still have to be paid for my time."

"I will pay you," he said.

"Yeah, but—"

"I will *pay* you," he said again. "If I have to work in a Alkan crystal mine doing hard labor for the next ten years, then that's what I'll do, but I'll pay you back." He learned forward, and for the first time I got a good look at his eyes. They were small and dark brown, and there was a nervousness there, an anxiousness, I hadn't expected. "But that won't happen if you take the case, Duff. I want to sing opera. It's the one thing I feared most, not being able to do what I love, and now it's happening. You've got to help me."

He was quite earnest, and I was sucker for earnestness. I was also a sucker for strong women, children in trouble, and any brandy more than fifty years old, but earnestness definitely topped the list. Helping earnest clients, when it went against my better judgment, was the reason I was broke. It was the reason I had an implant in my left ear, two mechanical knees, and a medical file that would have filled a dozen binders if printed—all before my forty-fifth birthday.

It was also the reason I could live with myself.

"All right," I sighed, "I'll take the job."

He looked relieved. "Well, that certainly—"

"I have one question, though."

"Oh?"

"Baritone or bass?"

It took him a moment to realize the nature of my question, and then he let loose with a growling chortle.

"It may surprise you," he said, "but I'm actually a tenor."

IT TOOK ME two days to catch up with the Mortagai Galactic Circus—two days of hop-scotching across the galaxy via step-docks, battling my way through hordes of sweaty tourists and a half-dozen immigration controls, further straining my already strained credit accounts, until finally I had to endure a six-hour shuttle ride to McNary Labs, the massive, one-million-worker space station that created the bulk of the military weapons for the Unity Worlds. The circus was the week's entertainment, and they were on their last night before heading out for some of the vacation planets.

I knew I'd found them as soon as the shuttle rounded the planet to the light side and I saw the station through my pea-sized window. The station itself was four connected cylinders with flat, mushroom-looking tops, thousands of square windows covering the sleek gray exterior like glowing postage stamps. There were dozens of ships docked along the tubes that connected the cylinders, but the ship I was looking for stood out like a stripper at an old woman's tea party—a massive tanker painted bright red, its hull decorated with paintings of all the circus acts and the letters MGC in glowing, tinsel-tinted silver in the center.

After we'd docked, and I'd taken a moment to get used to the one-quarter Earth standard gravity common on manufacturing stations, I rode the station's transport seeker until I reached the

Performance Hall. I got off, but none of the green-uniformed workers did.

A big burly black guy with robotic arms stood in front of the closed double doors. One of his eyes was covered with a black eye patch. "Show's not for four hours, buddy," he said.

"I'm not here for the show, buddy," I said. "I'm here to see Hiptor Mortagai." He was one of the owners, and the day-to-day manager from what I'd learned. "Tell him it's about the bear who sang opera for him. Name's Dexter Duff."

He raised an eyebrow, but he still pulled out a black com-com and relayed the message. A moment later, he led me into the hall. Up on the stage, one of two sleek vermillion dragons was scolding a skinny guy in a Middle Ages knight getup for not hitting his mark faster. The other dragon was smoking a cigarette, which looked as small as a needle in his big, clawed fingers.

We veered away from the stage, through a back door, and down a narrow hall with poor lighting. I heard voices behind the doors. The last door was open, and a small man with slicked-back hair, his back to me, was bent over a clear glass desk stacked high with pods and holoslips. He wore a dark suit with a flaring fish-fin collar. The bald spot on the back of his head glistened under the fluorescents, and the harsh light made his olive skin seem slightly green.

"Come in and shut the door," he said, without turning. "Carl, you can go."

I went inside, the thick metal walls muting out the noise. Only then did he close the paper-thin holoslip he was looking at and face me. Hiptor Mortagai was an unremarkable, middle-aged, Chinese man except for one startling feature: he had a third eye right in the middle of his forehead.

"What's this about Karvo?" he asked.

He had a five o'clock shadow and all three eyes were blood-shot. The third eye wouldn't have been so distracting except that it wandered, looking at different things in the room, and blinked at its own pace.

"He's lost his voice," I said. "He thinks someone's stolen it."

"Stolen it?"

"I know what you're thinking," I said. "But I contacted the surgical engineer he saw before seeing me. It's true that his memory cells were tampered with, and that the voice box he has is different from the one he had at his last check-up."

Hiptor closed two of his eyes—the one on his forehead remaining open, staring at me intently—and slowly shook his head. "Poor Karvo," he said. "I told him he shouldn't leave the circus. It was the best place for him. Then he got all those foolish ideas."

The third eye looking at me with the other two closed bothered me more than all three of them looking at me at the same time. "Foolish ideas?" I said.

"Yes," he said. "It was that agent of his—Swendlehurst. Creepy man. Can't stand to even look at him—those shifty eyes of his. He told Karvo he could become a star if went solo, so obviously he found another way to make money off Karvo's voice. I told Karvo ..." Hiptor trailed off, then his two regular eyes fluttered open. "What a minute! You're not here because he thinks *I* stole his voice, are you?"

I stared at him. Sometimes silence could get people to tell you things much better than any words.

"That furry bastard!" he cried. "After all that I ... How dare he! Do you know the condition he was in when I found him on that mining colony? Do you have any idea how much money I put into him to get him back to health? And I had no idea what kind of talents he had at the time. I did it all out of the goodness of my heart! Some gratitude!"

He seemed genuinely indignant. Still, he was in the circus business, which was the business of making things look genuine when they usually weren't. "You weren't mad he was leaving?" I said.

"Of course I was mad! I hate to see my friends do stupid things. He thought he was going to be a big star, and I just didn't want to see him hurt. And now, for all my concern, I get called a thief!" He glared at me, the pupils of all three eyes an intense black. "And who do you think you are, coming in here pointing the finger?"

"Nobody's pointing—"

"I looked you up, Duff," he said. "You've got quite a criminal record."

I shrugged.

"And your license is expired," he went on. "I could have you arrested for posing as a private investigator. It's a criminal offense."

"Oh, you wouldn't want to do that now, would you? That wouldn't be at all nice."

"I think you better go," he huffed.

"Just a couple more questions," I said.

Hiptor stabbed one of the buttons in the console embedded in his desk. There was a beep. "Carl, please escort Mister Duff to the door." He let go of the button and shook his head at me. "Just because I'm in the circus doesn't mean you can come in here and toss around a lot of accusations. I'm an honorable man, Duff. I've always been good to my people. Ask any of them."

"Then why didn't you want him to leave?" I said.

"Don't put words in my mouth!" he said. "I never said I didn't want him to leave. I said I didn't want him hurt."

"You didn't think he could make it on his own?"

"No, I didn't! And before you get the wrong idea, it's not because he didn't have the talent. He had talent in abundance. But he also had the worst stage fright I've seen in the two decades I've been in his business. The worst! We had this whole routine we went through to get him calmed down enough to perform. And then afterwards!" He shook his head. "My God, if you didn't praise him to the stars, he assumed you hated it, and then he'd spend a week growling and snapping at everyone. I just didn't want him going out there and get eaten alive. If he stayed here, I could protect him."

The door banged opened and there was Carl and his two mechanical arms. He jabbed a silver gleaming thumb toward the door. "Let's go, pal."

"In a second, pal," I said, focusing my attention on Hiptor. "How much money you lose when Karvo left?"

"Get out," Hiptor said. His lips were trembling.

"You heard 'im," Carl said. He reached for me, his silver fingers bent like clamps in one of those arcade game where the goal is pull out a stuffed animal.

"I'm guessing you like that fancy hand of yours, Carl," I said. "I'd hate to see you lose it."

My tone caused him to hesitate, because even a frumpy guy in worn black leather on the backside of forty could *sound* menacing if the words were backed with genuine guile. But then he laughed and reached for my arm. Leaving meekly probably would have been the smartest thing to do, but the instinct to refuse to be bullied ran too deep.

I knew if he got those metal fingers of his on me, it would all be over, so I pivoted inside his reach, right up next to him so he wouldn't be able to do anything with those arms without stepping back, and I jabbed him hard in the gut with a swinging elbow. I knew if I missed by much he would have just pummeled me, but I didn't miss. He let out a loud guffaw and doubled over, gasping.

Then I turned back to Hiptor, whose all three eyes gaped at me.

"Don't—Don't hurt me," he said in a small voice. "I'll—I'll answer any of your other questions. You can look in my books … I'm an … an honorable man …"

I smiled. "No more questions for now," I said. "Have a nice day, Mister Mortagai."

Then I turned and left. Carl was still moaning.

I HADN'T COMPLETELY ruled out Mortagai being behind the voice theft, but my gut told me he was telling the truth. On my way out, I knocked on a few doors and nobody had a bad word to say about him. Everybody also confirmed what Mortagai told me about Karvo: a great talent who was scared to death to get in front of an audience.

It took a bit of searching, but I managed to locate Karvo's agent on Naj-Naj, a developing world, once part of the Dulnari territory until the war ended a few years back. The Naj-Najs were dumb and hardworking, and their world was a goldmine of natural resources, so of course now that it was safe to invest there, money was pouring into the planet. Naj-Naj music was also the latest rage across the Unity Worlds, so agents were swarming in like blood-sucking bats.

Fortunately, there were already several stepdocks, so I was able to arrive after less than a day of hopping and without any back-breaking shuttle rides. The biggest city was called, simply enough, Big City, because that was the translation from Naj-Naj. It was smack-dab in the middle of a rain forest, the trees as tall as mountains, the air thick and humid and buzzing with millions of insects just above the field barrier poles lining the city streets.

When I contacted Swendlehurst on his listed link, I told him I'd discovered a Naj-Naj who could sing like Bing Crosby, and if he paid me a small finder's fee, I'd tell him the name. He told me he was currently having lunch at Harlo's, a restaurant on the top floor of the tallest building in Big City, and that he'd be happy to talk.

He was sitting by one of the windows, the emerald forest

stretching out to the horizon behind him. The place was crowded, mostly with humans and the wolfish-looking Dulnari, but the wait staff were all the spindly, stupidly grinning Naj-Naj.

I recognized Ned Swendlehurst from the headshot—a pasty, round-faced man with a mop of blond curls so perfectly domed-shaped that it had to be a wig. But I wasn't prepared for how massively fat he was—a flat-topped mountain of flesh in a glittery suit and a dimpled red tie, his rolls of flesh like lava flows down the triangular slope of his body.

Clinging to each jiggly arm was a burly woman in an obscenely tight purple dress, and when I got close, I realized they were twins. Each of them sported a wart on the bottom of their nose. They stared at him longingly while he ignored them, fiercely tearing into his barbecue ribs.

I stopped at the table. The women gazed at me the way cows gaze at passing hoverpods. Swendlehurst went on eating.

"So?" he said.

Red sauce speckled his double chin. I was hungry when I walked in the door. I wasn't any more.

"I lied," I said. "I'm here about Karvo Portano."

The pause was almost imperceptible, a slight hesitation before he took his next bite, but I caught it. "Mmm," he said.

"Someone stole his singing voice," I said.

He wiped the mess off his chin, finally belching loudly. "Tell me something I don't know," he said.

"Do you know who did it?"

"If I did, do you think he would have come to you?" He finally looked up at me, narrowing his beady little eyes. I disagreed with Hiptor: they weren't shifty so much as lifeless. It was like looking at doll's eyes. "I know all about Karvo's situation. It's quite sad. Who are you, anyway? Some kind of detective?"

"Name's Duff," I said. "I help people find things."

"Of course you do. How quaint." He bent his meaty mouth

down toward the ear of the woman on his right. "Look, my dear, a modern day Sherlock Holmes. Perhaps he can find your missing g-spot. Then you'd know what an orgasm is first-hand."

The woman blushed and looked down shyly.

"Hiptor Mortagai thought you might have something to do with it," I said.

He chuckled. "Of course he would."

"Well, did you?"

"Ha! You are a direct one, aren't you, Detective Duff?" He wiped his hands clean on one of the white napkins on the table. The way he did it, and the red stains left behind, made me think of someone wiping their hands after killing someone with a knife. "I know good old Hiptor has more eyes than he does brains, but I'm sure you can do better. Why would I take his voice? Do you have any idea how big he was going to be?"

"Not a clue."

His tiny eyes flared wider. "He was going to be absolutely huge! The market on Ipsin Totar alone, which devours opera like it's some kind of drug, would have made us both rich. I had him booked six months out within a few days, and a deal lined up with a major unicaster. Why would I take his voice and walk away from that?"

I shrugged. "Maybe to sell his voice to someone else."

"Nonsense! Detective Duff, making money—"

"Just Duff," I said.

"—off someone's singing is not just about the voice. It's the whole package! It's the brand that is the person! And Karvo Portano had already built his brand in the circus. The bear who sang opera! Why would I mess with that? It would have been foolish in the extreme. I did not make it to where I am in life by being foolish."

"I can see that," I said.

"And this is beside the point," Swendlehurst said, "but I considered Karvo a close friend. I love the opera! My wife loves the opera even more than me! It would be unthinkable for me to do something to harm one of the greatest tenors our galaxy has ever known!"

"Wife?" I said.

"Yes! She adores his singing! Absolutely *adores* it! He sang for us both on our ship many times! Ask Karvo."

I didn't want to tell him it was the wife part, not the wife liking opera part, that I found hard to swallow. "So you don't have any ideas on who might have taken his voice?"

He shook his head, and the rolls on his neck swayed like heavy drapes. "None! If I did, I would have gone to the furthest reaches of the galaxy to get it back! That crime was not just a crime against Karvo—it was a crime against opera lovers everywhere!"

THE REST OF THE CONVERSATION didn't reveal anything else that could help me. Either Mortagai or Swendlehurst could have been lying, and probably were, but it didn't change one thing: I didn't see what either of them had to gain stealing Karvo's voice. Even if they *had* sold it to someone else, how could that person even use the voice down the road without getting caught? A hyro—which was the laymen's term for biological robot hybrids—was an amazingly sophisticated bit of machinery, more complex even than the human body. It would have taken a team scientists to hide Karvo's unique binary signature, and of course that would have cost more than stealing the voice could have possibly been worth.

I retired to the windowless lounge on the other side, squeezing in at the black marble bar between a couple of Dulnari. They glared at me, their blue eyes glowing luminescent in the hazy, dim room. They had a musky odor that bothered lots of folks, but after the ten months I spent on the sulfur-stinking Mabokin, no odor really bothered me any more. Plus if you were going to sit near two Dulnari, it was better to sit between them, because then they couldn't do their telepathy thing.

After I warned my stomach with three shots of brandy I slouched into the corner com-com unit and punched in Karvo's number. His brown face blinked up on the screen. Instead of a tuxedo, he wore a white terrycloth robe.

"Have you found it?" he said eagerly.

"No dice."

He looked crestfallen. "A pity."

"Look," I said, "tell me something. How much money you think you would have made the first year solo?"

"It's hard to say."

"Take a guess."

He thought about it a moment, then quoted me a number. It was ten times the number I expected. So Swendlehurst was probably right. It would have been stupid to walk away from that.

"You look frustrated, Duff," Karvo said.

"Well, that's because I am."

"I wish I could offer you some kind of lead. It's just ... my memory ..."

"I know," I said. "Look, would you call Swendlehurst a friend?"

He nodded. "Both he and his wife were really supportive. Ned seemed heartbroken when I told him, and Alexia ... Well, she cried like I'd died. You don't suspect them, do you?"

Swendlehurst's wife. She'd come up twice now in the span of a few minutes. I didn't know if there was anything there, but talking to her would be better than staring at my reflection in the bottom of a glass of brandy.

"Your agent said they live on a ship," I said. "You have any idea where that would be?"

* * * * *

It turned out that the ship was right there, orbiting Naj-Naj. Karvo told me she traveled with Swendlehurst all over the galaxy because they both preferred nex-space travel over the stepdocks. He also told me they had a very loving relationship and they hated to be parted from one another for long. I thought about the two women sitting next to Swendlehurst in the bar and wondered if she knew how much loving he was really doing.

I didn't want to give her a chance to ignore me, so I rented a sub-nex shuttle—shopping around until I found one cheap enough I could afford—and piloted the creaky heap toward Naj-Naj's smaller moon, which had a popular casino. Swendlehurst's ship was a deluxe cruiser that couldn't have been more than two years old, big enough to hold a few hundred people, and long and sleek and handsome in all the ways that Swendlehurst himself wasn't.

When I was passing near it, I sent a distress signal. Any ship licensed in the Unity Worlds was obligated by law to respond to a distress signal if able. Sure enough, a young man, dark-haired and square-jawed, as handsome as any model, appeared on my monitor. It was a shot from the neck up, making his face fill the screen, which was a little unusual.

"Problem, sir?" he said.

"Navigational system's screwy," I said. "Can I dock while I make repairs?"

He gave the go ahead and ten minutes later I was popping open the connector hatch and stepping onto their ship. The air was slightly on the warm side. The young man who talked to me was there to greet me, and right away I saw why he had only shown me himself from the neck up on the com-com.

He was naked.

"Forget something?" I said.

"Sir?"

I motioned towards his body. It wasn't just a body. It was a *perfect* body, well-sculpted and well-endowed, his skin a smooth, creamy tan, not a mole or a scar on him, every muscle and contour a work of art. He looked down at himself, not at all embarrassed or ashamed, and then nodded.

"Standard ship policy, sir. You're welcome to remove your clothing as well, though it's not required of guests."

"That's all right. You're not human are you?"

"No, sir. I'm an android."

"Ah."

It figured. Unless specifically programmed to have a sense of modesty, Androids had none. Unlike hyros, they were not sentient—just fancy computers that did as programmed—and could never be considered more than property. Still, standing next to his Adonis-like body, and knowing it was all a miracle of modern manufacturing, didn't make me feel any better.

"Is Mrs. Swendlehurst available?" I asked.

He hesitated. "I'm sure I can help you with your repairs, sir. What do you need?"

"I can handle it. Can you just relay a message to Mrs. Swendlehurst? Tell her I'm a friend of Karvo Portano."

"As you wish, sir."

He strutted away, his gluteus maximus as disgustingly perfect as the rest of him. The message had the desired effect. Five minutes later, while I was pretending to poke around under the dashboard, he returned requesting that I follow him. We walked through a ship that was an elegant as any vacation cruiser, passing dozens of other androids, all identical, all naked, until a pair of double doors slid open and we walked into a cloud of steam.

Adonis lead me more over a green marble floor toward the sound of bubbling water, and eventually I saw the shape of person sitting in a hot tub. The shape turned into a woman with bright blonde hair tied up in a bun—a stunningly beautiful woman, tanned and toned, green eyes glittering like emeralds, naked slender arms resting on the granite lip of the hot tub. The frothy water reached the top of her breasts, high enough to hide most of her body while low enough to make it clear she was naked.

"Leave us, Six," she said.

Adonis bowed and walked away.

"You're Alexia Swendlehurst?" I said.

She arched an eyebrow. "Surprised?'

Already sweating, I unzipped my jacket. The air felt warm and heavy with each breath. "More than a little," I said.

"You're wondering why a goddess like me would be with a slovenly creature like my husband, is that it? Well, our relationship is complicated, but it works for us. Now, do you have it with you?"

"Excuse me?"

She sighed. "I'm sure you enjoy staring at my breasts, but I'd rather not prolong this experience more than necessary. As I indicated in my message, I'll pay you one million prime for it. But that's firm."

One thing you learn in my business is that you take advantage of whatever opportunities are thrown your way. After a moment's confusion, I realized that she thought I had Karvo's voice box and I was trying to sell it to her. It was also obvious that she had some kind of relationship with the person she expected to retrieve the voice box—but not a good enough one that she knew him by appearance.

"That's a lot of money," I said. I didn't want to lie, but I was happy to let her go on believing in something that wasn't true.

"But not enough?"

"I didn't say that."

She shook her head. "Enough games. Name your price."

"But perhaps it's the game I want to talk about," I said. "Like, what are you going to do with the bear's voice once you get it? I know you like opera. You going to keep it all for yourself, is that it? You want to have your own private talent you don't have to share?"

It was a stab in the dark, and it definitely struck a nerve. Her face hardened, her lips forming a thin line, her eyes moistening. She didn't cry, but she was obviously struggling to hold back the tears.

Then, suddenly, she rose from the water, not making any attempt to hide herself. The rest of her body was just as tan and trim and naked as the rest of her, the water running down the perfect swells of her breasts and over her flat stomach and between her legs. She was as tall and lithe as a professional free-fall player.

"Come with me," she said curtly.

She stepped out of the tub and glided away from me, disappearing into the steam. The sight of her glorious body caused a momentary hiccup in my brain, before I snapped out of it and followed her. Still, I was definitely in some kind of stupor, because when I walked through the open archway in the back of the room, one that led around a corner to an exercise room, I was in no way expecting the hard blow to the head that was immediately delivered to me.

I was on the floor before I realized what happened, tasting the rubber on the lightly-padded blue floor. My cochlear implant starting whining—a maddening, high-pitched sound. My vision went dark for a moment, returning just in time to see something large and red moving swiftly in my direction.

My reflexes took over, my forearm coming up and taking the blunt of the impact, sending a jolt of pain up my side. I rolled with blow, away from her, and ended up back on my feet—crouched, a bit wobbly, but with both hands up in a fighting posture.

"How *dare* you impugn my motives!" Alexia cried.

I blinked away the sweat in my eyes and finally she came into focus. Somehow, in the few seconds she'd been out of my sight, she'd taken the opportunity to don red boxing gloves and red boxing boots. Of course, she hadn't put on anything else, so seeing her bouncing up in down like a fighter in the ring, all those shapely, glistening curves bouncing right along with her, I felt a strange mixture of emotions: rage at being attacked *and* the most powerful animal attraction I'd felt in my whole life. Damn, now *here* was a strong woman.

"Mrs. Swendlehurst—" I began.

"His voice is a treasure!" she said, and now she was crying. "A treasure! Have you ever heard him sing *The Bolandassi's Lament*? A marvel! The only thing I wanted was to make sure the voice got back to him! That's why I put out the word I'd be willing to pay a good price for it! How *dare* you lump me in with thugs like you. Karvo's had a hard enough time as it is, getting over his stage fright, and I would never, *never*, do anything to make his life harder!"

I didn't want to hurt her. It would have been a crime against nature. "Listen," I said, "I'm not what—"

With a shriek, she jumped toward me and side-kicked hard right at my head. I ducked to the left, but not quite fast enough because she delivered a glancing blow that tore at my good ear. It felt as if someone had stabbed me with a branding iron.

More kicks followed right after that one, each one harder and more lethal than the last, and I blocked them away with my arms. My restraint quickly faded. She was good, damn good, and if not for the crazy rage that had overwhelmed her, she might very well have gotten the best of me.

But blinded by her anger, she left herself too exposed. I timed her next kick, ducking away and then grabbing her by the calf and heaving her leg upward.

She went down on her back, landing on the rubber with enough force that it knocked the wind out of her with an audible *thwump*. I thought that would be the end of it, and I took my time regaining my own breath, my heart starting to slow down, but then she let loose with another ear-splitting shriek and suddenly she was biting my ankle.

With a howl of my own, I kicked her hard on the side of the head—no restraint this time, not even a little—and as she was stunned, fell on top of her. By the time she recovered, I'd clamped down on both of her arms and had her pinned beneath the weight of my body.

"Let—me—go!" she cried. She squirmed beneath me, her wet body like an oily snake, and it was all I could do to keep her from slipping away. Her face was pink with exertion. "Six! Three! Come in here! I'm being attacked!"

"Mrs. Swendlehurst, if you'll just—"

"Nine! Four! Help, help!"

"Alexia! I'm *not* here to sell Karvo's voice! He *hired* me!"

She had her mouth open to scream, but instead, I watched her eyes re-focus on me. She blinked a few times.

"He did?" she said in a quiet voice.

"Yes!"

"Why?"

"To *find* his voice! I'm a private investigator!"

A long pause. "Oh," she said.

I felt all the tension slipping out of her muscles, her body going slack. I was suddenly very conscious of this wonderful naked creature beneath me—even through my clothes, the hardness of her in some places, the softness of her in others.

"Have you found out anything?" she said.

"No."

"But you're going to keep trying?"

I sighed. "Yeah. I'm out of ideas, but I'm going to keep trying."

I kept waiting for her to ask me to get off her, but instead, she just looked at me. Her gaze, so full of contempt just a moment ago, changed. It was still intense, but now it … *smoldered*. Her lips parted every so lightly, and I felt the heat of her breath on my chin.

"Perhaps," she said, her voice a lustful purr, "I could help pay for your services."

I felt her hips gyrate a little beneath me. I couldn't believe it. One moment she was trying to dent in my temple, and the next she wanted in my pants. Truthfully, it was damn tempting. A little guilt-free sex—her husband's behavior got me off the hook with that one—was right there for the taking. Plus I hadn't had *any* sex, guilt-laden or otherwise, in way too long.

But before I could make a decision one way or the other, three of her Adonis androids burst into the room. They headed straight for her, and I started to rise, bracing myself for another fight.

"Stop!" she commanded.

And of course, they did stop, standing as still and mute as statues, their large male appendages just inches away from our heads. I was almost off her, but she grabbed me by the scruff of my jacket and pulled me back down.

"It'd be a shame to waste this opportunity," she said.

"Uh-huh. What about them?"

"They can watch. It doesn't matter."

I laughed, thinking she was joking, but the expression on her face didn't change. Any lust I'd felt moments ago faded. Shaking my head, I rolled off her, and staggered up to my feet.

"Not me, lady," I said. "I don't make love to an audience."

She propped herself up on her arms. Watching the movement of her breasts, I was struck with a pang of regret. What a shame.

"You're walking away from sex with *this*," she said, motioning to her body, "because you have a little performance anxiety?"

After one last longing look at that very body, I headed for the door. I didn't think there was anything more I could learn from her, at least not in our present state of minds. If I stayed any longer, I knew which part of me would take control.

"It's not performance anxiety," I said. "I've just gotten better lately at self-preservation."

And then, just like that, I knew who had stolen Karvo's voice.

HE SHOWED UP at my office ten minutes after I reached him on the com-com, his fur still wet and glistening from his bath. He'd been staying at a dirt-cheap hotel, anxiously awaiting any news, and when he walked through the door, he bumped the frame so hard I heard the wood crack. He didn't seem to notice. He'd dressed so hastily that his tuxedo was buttoned wrong.

"Well?" he said.

I took my time, deciding exactly how I was going to play my cards. The key was all in the delivery.

"I found it," I said.

He let out a great big sigh, deflating at least a foot from his full height. "Thank God," he said. "Was it Mortagai?"

I hesitated. I could have told him the truth, of course, and maybe that was the more honorable thing to do. I could have told him that after I had my epiphany with Alexia, I'd gone straight to the biomechanical engineer Karvo had mentioned when he first came to my office, the one who confirmed that Karvo's voice box had been removed. With a little bit of arm-twisting, both real and figurative, I'd managed to squeeze the truth out from him: that *he* had been the one to remove the voice box in the first place, and that he still had it in his possession. He'd also erased the whole encounter from Karvo's memory banks.

Most importantly, he'd done it all at Karvo's request.

The engineer hadn't wanted to do it, but Karvo had been very insistent—hysterical, was the word he used—and the engineer had convinced himself that he was actually doing Karvo good by removing something that was causing him such distress. That was the realization that hit me while I was fending off Naked Kickboxer Lady—that somebody who had paralyzing stage fright, who had to be coaxed and cajoled and comforted before every act, somebody who had *performance anxiety* of the worst order, might go to great lengths to self-sabotage their own career so they wouldn't have to deal with those emotions.

Solving the mystery, though, turned out to be the easy part. The hard part was deciding how to give the bear his voice back in a way that would prevent him from doing the whole thing over again.

"It wasn't Mortagai," I explained. "In fact, it wasn't anybody you know. Just a two-bit thug who caught one of your shows and saw an opportunity to try to make a quick buck. He had once been an engineering student, so he had just enough knowledge to pull off the theft."

"Is he in prison now?"

"Well ... no. No, I'm afraid he's ... dead. He made the mistake of coming after me with a hyperpistol."

"I see. Where is the voice module, then?"

I reached into my side drawer and pulled out the black plastic case containing the voice module, placing it in on my desk. His mouth parted as if I'd just placed a bucket of tuna there—or, in his case, maybe an expensive plate of fresh sushi. He reached for it with his big paw, and I immediately held up my hand.

"Not so fast," I said.

He looked confused. "Is there a problem?

"No. No problem. I just have something else for you first."

I reached into the open drawer and pulled out the second

box, this one white, made of thick cardboard, and much bigger than the other one. It took two hands to lift it out and place it on the desk, and it landed there with a loud *thunk*.

"What's this?" Karvo asked.

"Fan mail," I explained. "Mortagai had been holding it for you, and they were kind enough to print it for me. But not just any fail mail. This box is all from biological robotic hybrids like you. You're quite a hero to them, you know." I watched his furry face and his dark eyes, watched how the words sank in, got traction, took root. I drummed my fingers on the desk, carefully choosing what to say, knowing this was where I really had to put on my own circus act and give my spiel the air of truth that would seal the deal. "So here's the thing," I said. "I know when you get your voice back, and the next time you walk out on that stage, you're going to feel some fear. You're going to wonder if there's another crazy out there like him, someone who wants to stop you from doing what you love. So you're going to have to make a choice. You're going have to decide if all these fans—these hyros who believe in you, who see you as an inspiration of what's possible—are worth that risk. It's quite a responsibility you have, you know. I don't want you to take it lightly."

The bear said nothing for a long time. He looked at the box of fan mail, then at the box containing his voice. I hadn't known him long, and still couldn't read his animal face all that well, but I thought I saw the conflicting emotions. I thought I saw the war within him between the old panic at having to perform and this newfound responsibility he must have felt to his fans. It was a toss-up which was going to win, and I found myself holding my breath until I saw him reach for one of the boxes.

The white one.

"Fan mail, you say?" he said.

I smiled. "That's right."

"I see," he said. He seemed to be rising, inflating with confidence and bravado right before my eyes. "I see, well, I … I'm quite touched." He bowed his head, and when he looked up and spoke again, there was a quaver in his voice. "I want you to know, Duff, that I'm going to pay you as soon as possible. I'll be back here standing in front of your desk before you know it."

I laughed. "I appreciate it. My credit accounts could certainly use a lift. But make sure you call ahead. I … may not be here."

"Oh? Where will you be?"

I looked at him, not sure how much I wanted to say, not sure how much I wanted to even admit to myself, then looked past him at the tiny sliver of window that wasn't blocked by frown fur. Over the sleek metal roofs of the city's buildings, I saw Targal's endless, barren dunes under the searing yellow sun. I also saw, out there on the horizon, a flicker of white that meant another lighting storm was on its way. My bad ear would soon be ringing.

The truth was, Karvo wasn't the only one suffering a bit of stage fright. I'd been kicked around, beaten and battered in both mind and body, and I'd allowed my own fears to banish me to this place—a place where I might die of boredom before I died of poverty. I'd done it to myself, and it was time to get back on the stage.

"Are you going to take a vacation?" Karvo asked me. "You could certainly use it."

"No," I said, shaking my head. "That's just the problem. I've been on vacation long enough."

The Time of His Life

They actually bought the little house in September, right after they'd welcomed Jared into the world, but it wasn't until the day after Christmas that Tim found the hidden room.

Life had been so nuts back then that he'd barely gotten all their crap from the apartment moved, much less put everything it its proper place. Not that life had gotten any *less* nuts now. That was the new reality Tim was slowly coming to accept. Whatever remained of his peace of mind—and any private time to himself—vanished the moment he heard his second child's piercing wail echoing off those tiled delivery room walls of Rexton Memorial Hospital.

Case in point: Half the junk they'd brought with them was still buried in cardboard boxes, either in the one-car garage or up in his studio. Between changing diapers, warming bottles of formula, and waking up at God-knows-when-early to rock Jared back to sleep, they kept telling themselves they'd go through the rest of it, but what actually happened was that they only went digging when Maggie wanted something.

"Did you hear me, honey?" she said.

He blinked up at her, from his place down on the carpet with Alexa. They'd been playing ponies—or at least, she had. He'd drifted off at some point when the ponies were having a picnic in the new barn they'd bought her for Christmas, daydreaming about that new strip he'd doodled a few weeks back. He'd planned to work on it over the break, before school reared up again, but of course that hadn't happened.

"Hmm?" he said.

From her perch on the couch, Maggie gave him the look, the one that made him feel like he was being a jerk, a certain tilt of the head and arching of the eyebrows. Even with the glare of sunset behind her, piercing through the spindly branches of the pin oaks, he could still tell she was giving him the look. She adjusted Jared, raising the bottle a little higher. The last dying notes of Bing Crosby's "White Christmas" faded to nothing. The CD changer shuffled to another song.

"Those two sconces," she said. "Could you go find them?"

"The what?"

"The sconces. You know, the ones we had in our bedroom?" When he continued to stare blankly, she added with a sigh, "The two silver things I put candles in that were over our bed?"

"Oh those," he said.

"Oh those," she said. "I think they ended up in that big Sony box."

"I have no idea where that is."

There was the look again. Any more protesting from him and she'd play her trump card, the whole I Bore Your Children routine.

Feeling weary, he kissed his daughter on her blonde head and trudged out to the garage. Frost ringed the paned window that looked out on the backyard. The cold, brittle air smelled faintly of the gasoline for the lawn mower. Rickety wooden steps led both down to the concrete floor, and up, to his studio. He checked his watch—Maggie's present to him, not real gold of course, but still nice. He wanted to make it quick, but he knew he needed to give this at least five minutes.

The frigid concrete curled his toes. The boxes in the garage were stacked high and deep. In his search, he pushed aside bikes, studded tires, and their rusted barbecue, but he didn't see the Sony box.

Upstairs, then. The room—and it was being generous calling it a room—was technically nine by twelve, but the sloping ceilings on either side made it feel much smaller. Since it wasn't connected to the house's heat, it was as cold as the garage. There were two paned windows, but the overgrown laurel bush outside squeezed off most of the light.

Still, it was *his* room. His studio. That's what they'd agreed before they'd called the broker to make an offer. Sandwiched in among all the boxes were his drawing easel, his crane light, and his metal desk. The strip he'd been working on—about a bunch of animals living by a creek, inspired by the neighborhood park— was taped to the easel. In the crimson light, he saw that a layer of dust had formed on the paper. The dust of disuse.

No time for self-pity. He didn't bother turning on the space heater. It took him only a minute to search the boxes in the room, but then he remembered the closets. There were two of them, one on each side, the doors barely four feet high because of the low ceiling.

He tried the first. There was no light, only what filtered in, and he waded through a sea of boxes in the near-darkness. No Sony box. In the second closet, he stumbled past an old Hoover, a metal sled, a kite choked by string, not one but *two* blenders, a bean bag Maggie told him he couldn't have in the house—ending up at a wall of boxes along the far wall.

It was very nearly pitch black, but he saw no Sony box. He

was about to turn around when he noticed that the boxes weren't pushed all the way against the wall. There was a gap maybe a few inches wide.

He pushed on the boxes, but they didn't budge. *Something* was back there, wedged between the exposed studs and the boxes. If it turned out it was the sconces, and he didn't check, Maggie would never let him hear the end of it.

The boxes were wedged in pretty tight, so it took some doing to move them. It was so dark he could barely see his own hands. He felt along the floor near the wall and was surprised when the floorboards near the studs were ice cold.

Now *that* was odd. A pipe right under the floor, maybe? That's when his eyes finally began to adjust, and he saw the silver gleam of something jutting from the wall. It was the size of a small apple in the middle of the unfinished plywood.

A doorknob?

Impossible. Unless his sense of direction had completely failed him, this was the exterior wall. He reached out and took hold of it—and a sizzling, burning cold shot through his arm.

He let go with a yelp. Now he was mad. Something like this should never have passed inspection. Was it a joke, or was there really a door that opened into the laurel bush?

He had to know. He rubbed his hands together, warming them, and then grabbed the knob.

The metal was so cold that it scorched his hand, but with a noisy rattle it turned to the right. There was an even louder creak and then a puff of frigid air. The shadows of the wall deepened, the hints of boards and beams melting to black. Palms outward, he reached with his hand, and his hand went deeper, still deeper, his elbow now where the wall should have been.

Tim felt the first pangs of fear.

Part of him wanted to venture farther inside, but caution held him back. He wished he'd brought a flashlight. He touched the floor inside the opening—plain, rough floorboards, no colder than the ones beneath his feet. It was definitely a room. A hidden room.

He also had the feeling he wasn't alone.

The door creaked. He felt a rush of air—a stale, putrid odor, like the last breath of a dying man. He jerked his hand back just as the door slammed with a dull thud.

HE SCRAMBLED DOWNSTAIRS. His heart was still pounding, and sweat trickled down his back. Maggie was now on the floor playing ponies with Alexa. Jared sprawled on a blue blanket, fixated on the rattle in his chubby fingers.

"You'll never guess what I found," Tim said.

Maggie looked up. "Did you find the sconces?"

"What? No. But I—"

"Darn it, Tim. Did you *really* look for them?"

"Maggie, I looked."

"Sometimes you don't look very hard."

"I looked! I looked!"

"All right, you don't have to yell. I'll look myself later."

He tensed. Translation: They're out there, but you were just too incompetent to find them. The thing was, she was probably right. But he didn't want to fight. He wanted to tell her about the room. He crouched next to her.

"Maggie, you won't believe—"

"Man, you stink," she said. "What were you doing up there? And what happened to your *watch?*"

"Huh?"

"Look at it. We're going to have to take it back."

He looked at it. Sure enough, the hands were frozen. Five, ten minutes ago maybe, they'd stopped.

* * * * *

THAT WAS WHEN Tim decided, rightly or wrongly, that he wouldn't tell Maggie about the hidden room—at least not yet. There was still some part of him that suspected, irrational as it was, that if he shared his discovery with her that it might not exist anymore. They'd trudge up there and it would be gone. Or if not gone, then ordinary. Explainable. His broken watch would have been a co-incidence, nothing more.

It was the same feeling he'd gotten as a boy when he'd spotted what appeared to be the end of a rainbow in the cherry orchard behind his house, and when he'd dashed inside to retrieve a back-pack for the gold, his ever-serious father had sat him down and made him suffer through a lecture on optical illusions. By the time he'd snuck back to the orchard, the rainbow had been gone.

So he waited. He waited while Maggie found the sconces in a box in the garage, raising them triumphantly upon her return. He waited through spaghetti and meatballs, Alexa in the tub, Dr. Seuss, lights out, and Maggie trudging off to bed with a yawn. He was usually the last one up anyway, letting his exhausted mind turn to putty while watching basketball or some stupid sitcom—and feeling guilty because, exhausted or not, he could have been be up in his office working on the new strip.

But this time he wasn't tired at all.

When he stopped to retrieve a flashlight from the kitchen, the digital clock on the microwave showed it was 10:05. He noted the time because if he was up past midnight, Maggie might come looking.

Climbing the stairs, he felt like he did as a kid when he'd snuck out of his room on Christmas Eve to sneak a peek at his gifts. The temperature in his office had dropped to near-freezing; he felt the cold hardwood through the thin soles of his slippers. He flicked on not only the overhead light, but the light attached to his easel as well, turning the lamp to face the closet door.

The little flashlight was not as strong as he remembered, but it was a far cry better than bumbling in darkness. When he got past the boxes, and shined the light on the back wall, he saw the doorknob at once—a dull scratched silver, the kind of simple knob usually found on a closet door.

It didn't make sense. He swept his flashlight over the entire area and saw them—hinges. They were the same silver color as the knob, deeply recessed and attached to the studs. Peering closer, he finally saw the door. The perimeter was hard to see because of the way the lines blended into the patterns of the pressboard.

An optical illusion. Like the end of a rainbow.

Had the previous owner put it in? The house had been vacant for a year, the property slouching through probate after the old widower who'd lived there passed, and he didn't get the sense that the grandson had spent much time in it.

Tim realized he was stalling. Gritting his teeth, he grabbed the knob and twisted. The chill seeped into his skin like arctic water and he let go the moment he shoved the door. The opening was utterly dark, as if the air itself had been painted black, yet when he aimed his flashlight inside he was surprised at how easily the light penetrated.

The unfinished floorboards extended to untextured drywall not more than six feet away. He pointed the light to the right and saw gray metal shelving, packed with slim leather volumes in various shades of brown and red.

Crouching under the doorframe, Tim stepped inside. Something cold and slender like a wet strand of hair brushed his cheek. He yelped and jumped back, jerking his light up. When he saw that the object of his dread was a metal chain attached to an exposed bulb, he let out a strangled laugh. The ceiling was low, perhaps not even seven feet, made of the same unfinished drywall.

He gave the chain a yank and was pleasantly surprised when the light came on, emitting a low buzz. Now he saw the room in all its glory, a cramped space with no windows. The first thing he laid eyes on was the metal desk, up against the wall to his left. A green felt swivel chair, yellow stuffing protruding from a tear along the bottom, was parked in front of it. Except for a brown banker's lamp, there was only one other thing on top of the desk. A book.

Not a book like the slender volumes on the shelves, however. It was also brown leather, but it was both thicker and smaller, with gilded silver edges. The whole room couldn't have been more than eight feet by eight feet, so a single step took him to the desk. One glance was all it took to know what book it was—the title embossed in huge gold lettering on the cover

The Holy Bible.

He found no writing inside, no name or inscription. The thin parchment felt wrinkled and well-used—not at all like the one Bible he owned, a gift from his Baptist grandmother which still crackled the few times it was opened. Inside the desk, he found a half-dozen magnifying glasses and two pairs of reading glasses. That was it. The rest were just empty drawers.

When he checked the leather volumes on the shelves, he saw at once the purpose of the magnifying glasses. The books were filled with stamps, nicely preserved in Mylar sleeves, of every size and denomination. Marveling at the number of volumes, he guessed there must have been nearly a million stamps.

He was standing there, inspecting an orange Cuban stamp that pictured Fidel Castro, when he was suddenly struck with the feeling that he was not alone. A chill ran up his spine. He glanced back at the door, but no one was there.

The feeling passed, and he shrugged it off as the understandable jumpiness of finding something so strange. He knew he'd been gone long enough that Maggie might come looking for him, so it was time to leave. The door had a lock on the inside, the simple push-button kind, and he made sure it was unlocked.

Returning to the kitchen, he braced his hands on the countertop. His heart was only now starting to slow. His shirt was soaked with sweat, and he blinked several time to clear the sticky sheen over his eyes.

That's when he saw the time. 10:07.

According to the clock, only two minutes had passed since he'd gone upstairs.

AT FIRST, TIM didn't believe it. Despite other clocks in the house confirming that was indeed the time, it took him a couple more experiments before he was convinced of what he suspected in that first moment—that time had stopped while he was in the hidden room.

It was agonizing waiting until the following night, but there were no good opportunities before then. He waited until the kids were in bed, when he and Maggie were watching some stupid reality show, then told her he wanted to look for some old Beetles and Bailey books he thought were in one of the closets upstairs. He checked the time before he went up—8:47.

The room was just as he'd left it. He stayed for ten minutes, leaving the door open so he could hear Maggie coming. He'd brought a little digital clock, a cheap plastic thing he'd gotten when they'd subscribed to Time magazine a few years back, and he watched the minutes pass.

The clock didn't stop inside the room, which worried him, but as soon as he stepped back into the closet the screen went dead. He clicked some of the buttons and jiggled it, but it was gone. Heading downstairs, he had to consciously avoid running. Easy now.

Before he even got a look at the kitchen clock, Maggie's first words told him everything he needed to know.

"Wow," she said, "that was fast."

It DID NOT take Tim long to realize the implications. While there might have been people in the world who would have called up *60 Minutes*, Tim did not think this way. Instead, he realized what it meant for him personally—that he now had all the time in the world to do the one thing he loved most.

It took until the following weekend before he had a block of time big enough to get the room situated. When Maggie took the kids to her parents' for a Sunday brunch, he begged off, complaining of an upset stomach. Then he dashed to the local art store and picked up a new easel and adjustable lamp—paying with cash from when he'd sold some graphic novels to the used bookstore a few weeks earlier. Maggie might not notice missing art supplies, but she would have certainly noticed the disappearance of the easel and the lamp.

Retrieving his toolkit from the garage, he set to work on the easel. He left the door open, still not quite trusting the room's special properties. But he got the easel constructed without interruption. There was a spare outlet behind the desk and he plugged in the lamp. He wondered briefly about the electricity, where it was coming from, then decided to shrug it off. When you received a gift, sometimes it was better not to know where it was bought.

The room finally arranged to his satisfaction, he set to work finishing the panels. When Maggie still hadn't returned, he drew four more. Without a clock this time, he had no idea how much time passed, but eventually his bladder needed relief, so he headed downstairs.Not more than fifteen minutes had passed since he'd gone upstairs.

That's when he knew he was about to have the time of his life.

* * * * *

THE NEXT THREE WEEKS were pure bliss. The drawing pads filled by the dozens. Soon the walls were decorated with his creations—not just in pen and ink, either, but in bright oils too. At first, he thought he'd bring a clock, to track how long he worked, but then he realized how pointless that was. Why would he need to track the time in a room where time did not pass?

Instead he simply worked until he didn't feel like working. Not only did he accomplish a great deal, he was always there for his family. Alexa needed a story read to her? No problem. His turn to make dinner? Sure, he'd make it every night of the week. Changing Jared's diapers? Bring it on. He had his hidden room now, and it made him want to work harder at being the model husband and father.

Of course, there were some problems, but they were all surmountable. His beard didn't stop growing while he was in the room. Maggie noted it one day, telling him he'd better buy a new razor because she'd seen him shaving that morning. So he took his electric razor upstairs, shaving before he left the room. His sleeping rhythms soon got out of sync so he dragged a cot and some blankets upstairs and built in some nap time. He brought snacks and water bottles so he wouldn't have to stop to eat. The bathroom breaks were the toughest. He actually thought about bringing up a little portable potty, but he just couldn't bring himself to do it. Better to slip downstairs occasionally.

He indulged in his sojourns at every opportunity. In-laws over for dinner, the father-in-law getting a bit obnoxious with his Republican monologues? Tim suddenly announced he'd left the lamp on in his office and that he'd back in a minute. And he was—a five hour minute. The Vice Principal breathing down his neck? Tim came home for lunch—Maggie was always happy to see him—and also took some time for himself upstairs.

Sometimes it was days before he returned to work.

There was always time.

There was time for everything.

IT WASN'T UNTIL the end of that third week that he got that feeling again he wasn't alone. He was putting some finishing touches
on three dozen Cold Creek Gang strips, ones he was readying to
submit to one of the syndicates. He paused to admire his work—
he really was getting better, no doubt about it—when the air grew
heavy.

All at once he felt edgy. Loneliness gnawed at him, a desperate sadness. He was absolutely sure that he was being watched,
that there was somebody right behind him. Slowly, he lowered
the pen, waiting for some tell-tale sign of an intruder—a whisper
of breath, a scratch of clothes, *something*. The person was right
there. He sensed it. They were going to get him.

He spun around in his chair.

No one was there. The door was closed, just as he'd left it, but
it was unlocked. In fact, he hadn't been locking it at all, and he
realized what a mistake that had been. Not because of a possible
intruder but because of Maggie. What if she wandered up here?

His mouth dry, his skin cold and clammy, he crept to the
door. There was still this feeling that there was somebody out
there, somebody with a terrible need to get inside. When he was
close enough, he punched in the lock. It made a loud click, like
the sound of a gun being cocked. It was only then that he realized
he'd been holding his breath, and he let out a long, shuddering
sigh.

That's when the door rattled.

He very nearly jumped out of his slippers. He was close
enough that he not only heard it, but saw it—the jiggle of the
knob, the slight slippage of the entire mechanism, loose in its

socket. Every muscle in Tim's body turned to ice.

The rattle lasted only a second, and Tim thought maybe that was it, maybe the person had given up and gone away. Then the knob rattled again, much harder this time, a violent shaking that threatened to rip the whole door off its hinges—and it went on and on, growing stronger, a swelling hurricane of violence.

"Hey!" Tim cried.

The rattle stopped. Tim felt his pounding heart in every square inch of his body—on his tongue, behind his eyelids, even under his fingernails.

"Who's there?" he said. "Maggie, is that you?"

No answer. He had an awful foreboding that the person/thing/creature/whatever on the other side was about to burst down the door. The seconds passed. He remained frozen. The doorknob didn't rattle.

"Go away," he said, his voice shaking. "This is my room."

Finally, the feeling passed, and it was as if someone loosened a vise gripping his skull. But another feeling took its place. It was the feeling that things had changed—either the room, or him, he wasn't sure.

Things would be different. He didn't know how, but they would be different.

IT WAS A COUPLE DAYS before Tim braved the room again, but to his great relief, nothing rattled the door. Not that day, or the next, or any of the days to follow. From time to time, he still had the feeling that he wasn't alone, but it was fleeting, and he was soon so engrossed in his work that it hardly troubled him.

The work—that was all that mattered. He focused his whole being on the cartoons. But when he finally showed Maggie the strips, he encountered a problem he hadn't anticipated.

"Wow," she said, marveling at the artwork laid out on their

kitchen table. The kids were asleep, and the house still smelled like the Swedish meatballs they'd had for dinner. In the bathroom, water streamed into the tub. She pushed a strand of her hair behind her ear and leaned closer. When she did, the fold of her terrycloth bathrobe fell open, revealing a hint of breast. Ordinarily, this would have stoked some desire within him, but he felt nothing but the urge to close her robe for her. "This is amazing," she said. "I love the coke bottle glasses on the otter. Very cute."

"Thank you," he said, beaming.

"I'm very impressed. I didn't even know you were spending much time on this."

He didn't like the way she said the word *time*. It made him suspicious. "What do you mean?"

"Well, all this stuff—it's a lot. You're never up in your office for more than a few minutes. Have you been working on it at school?"

"Oh," he said, his mind racing. "Yes. I've—I've worked at it on my lunches. And while students are doing projects. You know, here and there. Got to find the time somewhere." He laughed nervously.

She looked at him, eyes narrowing.

"What?" he said.

"You," she said. "It's like you're not telling me something."

"Maggie, don't be ridiculous."

"Is something going on?"

"No!" The blinds in the living room window were open, and the gaping darkness suddenly bothered him. He went to them and closed them. "I hate that we leave these open all the time. Anybody could be out there watching."

"Why would somebody be watching?" Maggie asked.

"What? This is silly I'm going upstairs."

Maggie shrugged. "Okay. You'll be down in three minutes

anyway."

Tim didn't answer. He was afraid his voice would betray him if he did. His whole body was shaking.

HE MADE several changes. The first was that he made sure to spend a little longer in his actual office before coming downstairs. The second was that he decided that he would be much more careful about how much, if any, of his work he shared—not just with Maggie, but with anyone. It would raise questions, he saw that now. Those questions could lead people to finding out about the hidden room, and he couldn't have that. More important even than becoming a professional cartoonist was protecting his secret.

This was *his* room. If other people found out, they'd want in, and it was a small room. There wasn't space for anyone else. Even worse, the publicity might bring in the media hounds—and after that would be the religious nut jobs, the paranormal investigators, the skeptics. It would all be ruined.

Unfortunately, matters only got worse with Maggie. She complained that he was distracted. That their sex life was in the toilet. That when he was with Alexa or Jared, he looked like he wanted to be somewhere else. The fights were something terrible to behold—shouting until they were red-faced and hoarse. More than once he raised his fist before catching himself. He'd never hit her before, but he was coming so close, and he saw something in her eyes he'd never seen before—fear.

He knew this was because of the room. He knew he was spending too much time in there—days in a row, weeks even, with only the briefest forays back into a world in which time passed. He was becoming disconnected with his other life. He had to pull back. He had to pull back or he was going to lose himself.

It was Alexa that finally drove this point home. He finished reading her a book—which one, he'd forgotten by the time he slid it back on her shelf—and turned out the light. When he leaned over to kiss her forehead, he saw how beautiful she was in the near-darkness: his blonde angel, with flawless olive skin and big brown eyes. He felt the clench of the bittersweet love that only a parent can know, the strange concoction of adoration and grief.

"My little princess," he said.

"My big daddy," she said, smiling up at him.

"Do you know how much I love you?" It was their little game.

"Lots and lots?"

"Oh yes. There aren't enough lots to say how many lots I love you."

He kissed her forehead, the flesh so tender and soft. He turned and she kissed him on his stubbled cheek. It reminded him that he'd forgotten to shave before coming downstairs—something that had been happening more frequently. When he leaned back, he saw great concern in her eyes.

"What is it, sweetie?" he said.

"Daddy, why is your hair getting gray?"

It was a cold blade straight to the gut. His mind raced, trying to come up the appropriate response, something to put her heart at ease, even though he knew *exactly* why his hair had been going gray. How much time had he been spending up there? How much *older* was he than he should have been? A year? Two? *Five?*

The shame that washed over him made his knees wobbly. He may not have been robbing his daughter of precious minutes with her father now, but he was taking years from her on the back end. Would he even be there to see her graduate from high school? It was the first time he realized that though the hidden room was giving him time, it was also taking it from everyone else.

"Oh, just getting a little older dear," he said to her, hoping she wouldn't notice the strange quaver in his voice. "Nothing to worry about." And he thought to himself: Enough. This is it. It ends now.

But of course it didn't. He spent more time up there than ever.

IN THE WORLD of his hidden room, everything felt right. Tim created piles and piles of cartoons—not just his Cold Creek Gang, but four new strips. He soon ran out of room and began clearing out the stamp books, thinking he'd stash the money in the room for emergencies. Then the proprietor at the local collectible shop asked a few too many questions and that was the end of it. Tim put them all in boxes and left them outside the local Boy's and Girl's Club one morning. He felt good about that. It was one of the few things in recent days he felt good about.

For in the real world, the world where time stops for no man, life continued to unravel. The fights between him and Maggie grew worse, and then they stopped altogether—replaced by a terrible, hateful silence. He started home from the neighborhood park one day, telling himself Alexa wouldn't miss him, she was playing with some neighborhood kids on the swings—and only caught himself when he was halfway home. At school, parents complained. They said their kids told them that their art teacher often disappeared for half the class, claiming he had to go to the bathroom, but then someone spotted him driving away from the school. The Principal told him if it happened again, he'd be suspended.

He was only five minutes away, he figured. He could be back in minutes. They would never know.

When he looked at himself in the mirror each morning—and morning was a relative term, because he was so out of sync with the reality of night and day—the person who gazed back at him was not himself. It was a gray, gaunt, ghost of a man, with hollowed eye sockets and skin liked parched sand. He knew the hidden room was destroying him. He knew it, and yet he felt powerless to stop it.

It was only when he came home from school one day—at lunch, planning to spend more time upstairs—and found Maggie packing suitcases, that some tiny remnant of self-preservation finally sparked inside him.

"What's this?" he said.

She looked up from the rainbow of tightly-packed socks, and he saw, for the first time, that she had changed too. She was painfully thin, her eyes like dull marbles, her skin looking like it might flake away like an old, paper mache doll left too long in the sun. The first pink buds of spring spotted the rhododendron outside the window. Out in the living room, where the kids were parked in front of the television, Dora the Explorer was counting to ten in Spanish.

"We're going to my parents," she announced.

It took a few seconds for the implication to hit him. The world pressed in on him, the pressure increasing as if he were in a diving bell, sinking fast into the dark sea. His throat constricted, and when he tried to say her name, it came out a sputtering cough. He took a step toward her and she held up a hand.

"Don't," she said.

"But, Maggie, please—"

"I'm not arguing. I don't know what's happened to you, but it's not good for us here anymore. It's not even safe."

"I can do better."

"You've said that before."

Had he? He vaguely remembered fragments of conversations about his behavior, telling her he was just in a funk, that things would improve, but they all had the fuzzy qualities of dreams. She zipped up the suitcase and moved to the next one.

"You need help, Tim. You're need to call that number I gave you."

"I'm not on drugs."

She pressed down on her shirts, flattening them. "I wish I could believe you."

"I'm not on drugs!" he cried. "I'm not drinking or anything like that! Have you smelled it on my breath? Have you found pills? Have you found *anything?*"

"Shh! For God's sake, the children!"

"Maggie—"

"Please don't. *Please.* I've made my decision. Now you need to make yours."

All three suitcases were zipped up. She was really he going. He couldn't believe she was really going. He saw that her eyes were watery, and it gave him hope. She still cared. She hadn't stopped caring.

When she started for the door, he dropped to his knees and begged her to stay. She tried stepping around him and he hugged her legs. He thought, if he just he held on tight enough, she wouldn't go. She cursed him and tried to tug her legs free, but he didn't loosen his grip. Then she slapped him hard on the side of the head. It rattled him enough that his eyes watered and ears rang, but he held fast. She slapped him again, sobbing, but he wouldn't let go. If he let go, he knew he would die.

"Okay!" he cried finally. "Okay, dear God, I'll show you! I'll show you everything! Please don't leave! I need you! I need you to save me!"

OF COURSE, she was suspicious. Why wouldn't she be? It sounded like the mad ravings of a drunk or a meth addict. *I've got a room where time doesn't pass.* But after he pleaded with her to just give him a chance, and she agreed with an exhausted reluctance, it only took a couple demonstrations for her weariness to be replaced first with amazement, then with a mixture of anger and sympathy.

"*This?*" she said, running her hand along the portfolio books that packed the shelves. "This is what you've been doing all this time?"

He nodded. He saw her considering, processing, judging. Was it relief he saw or something else, something darker? His paranoia briefly got the best of him, and he imagined her bringing another man up here. How would he ever know? Then her eyes welled up, and he thought, this has to be it. If he didn't do it now, he never would.

"I know what we need to do," he said. "Do you trust me?"

She looked at him, all the fatigue showing on her face like the spots and divots on an old mattress.

"I need you to trust me," he said.

"Tim—"

"Please, Maggie."

"The kids are downstairs. I need to—"

"No time has passed for the kids. Please, it will only work if you trust me."

She closed her eyes, hugging her chest, and rocked a little on her feet. "All right," she whispered. "I'll trust you. This one time."

"Good," he said, "I won't fail you. How much gasoline do we have in the garage?"

IT WAS SEVERAL MONTHS before they were able to locate a suitable replacement—another cottage, this one down by the river—and another month after that for the deal to close. The insurance company raised a few eyebrows about their story of the raccoon knocking over a camping lantern in the garage, but they didn't hold up the money. By that first Saturday in July, Tim was wheeling the last of the boxes down the ramp of the U-Haul. It was amazing how much stuff they'd managed to accumulate in the few months they'd lived in the hotel.

A warm breeze swayed the Douglas firs surrounding their property, briefly giving him a glimpse of the sloping roofline of their only visible neighbor. From the garage, Maggie emerged from the maze of furniture and crates with a glass of lemonade. He parked the hand truck and took the drink gladly, pressing the cool glass against his sweaty forehead.

She wore a pink cotton sundress that bared her arms, and he saw how her skin was freckling like it did when she spent a lot of time in the sun. A few months ago, he wouldn't have even noticed. It made him happy, noticing.

"Both kids down?" he said.

She nodded. "At the same time. Miracle, isn't it?"

"Quick, let's make a run for it."

"Not very funny."

But she smiled and it was not a wan smile or a forced one. It had taken months for her to smile that way again. There was still doubt and suspicion that occasionally flashed across her face like an emergency broadcast message, but he hoped that would go away in time. He'd have to earn it. He knew that.

He took a drink, savoring how the cool sweetness relieved his parched throat. She was still looking at him.

"What?" he said.

"I thought, you know, that you might want to come inside."

"Why?"

Her gaze strobed his body, and when she looked up at him again, there was a certain glimmer in her eyes.

"Oh," he said. *"Oh."*

She smiled impishly, then turned and sashayed her way back to the door—sashaying being the perfect way to describe that seductive movement of her hips. When she got to the doorway, she gave him a single glance over her shoulder, all by itself enough to set his arousal on fire. He placed his glass on a stack of boxes and started after her.

On his way through the garage, he passed the plastic jug of gasoline for the lawn mower, the one he'd picked up just that afternoon from Target. It would be a strange irony if the house burned down on accident. Since this house came with a good sized shed, he grabbed the can and huffed it outside, to the backyard. It would only take a second.

He waded through the tall grass and slid open the creaky metal door. He saw some old plywood sheets, some moss-covered paving stones, and a rusted garbage can, stuff the previous owners had left behind, and he set the jug just inside the door. He was turning to go—the image of Maggie stretching out on their bare mattress buzzing in his brain—when a queer feeling overwhelmed him.

He was not alone.

It was unmistakable. There was no other feeling quite like it, and Tim was seized with a quench of terrible panic. Not now. It couldn't be happening now.

Everything inside him told him to shut the door, but he had to know. The plywood sheets, the way they were leaning against the back of the shed—something could be behind them. It was possible.

His sweat turning cold, he inched his way to the back of the shed, shuffling over the sawdust and dirt that coated the concrete slab. The shadows deepened. The air was thick and humid, choking him with each rapid breath. He grabbed the sheets—there was three of them, each not more than an inch thick—and with a shaking hand leaned them away from the wall.

There was a doorknob.

It was the same silver knob, scratched, loose in its socket, that he knew so well. A small whine of protest rose up, and Tim froze, thinking some animal was in there with him before he realized that *he* was making the sound. No. No, it wasn't fair. This wasn't giving him a fighting chance.

But even as he thought this, he watched his hand move of its own accord, the fingers closing around the knob. The cold seared into his flesh, but he didn't care. It was waiting for him. His room. He could step inside and once again have all the time in the world.

There was a loud click, and he flinched.

There was *someone* on the other side! He jerked the knob, but it was locked. The searing cold spread up his fingers to his arm. Then the anger washed over him and he began to jerk the knob back and forth. He'd break it down. It was his room.

"Hey!" someone cried.

The idea that another person had taken over his hidden room only increased his rage. He let go of the knob, searching for something that could help him get inside. His gaze fell upon the mossy paving stones and he grabbed the top one and hefted it high over his head. They couldn't have it. The room was only for him.

"Who's there?"

Tim gaped in horror at the door. The voice—he knew it now. It was unmistakable.

"Maggie," the voice said, "is that you?"

That's when Tim remembered—that day, soon after he'd found the room, when someone rattled the doorknob. Now, impossible as it seemed, *he* was the one on the outside.

"Go away," the person on the inside said, voice trembling with obvious fear. "This is *my* room."

He saw himself then as if from a distant camera—this crazed lunatic, eyes ablaze, a square stone held aloft. He saw the full reality of what he was, of what he would always be, no matter how many houses he burned or where he went in life. The room would always be with him. There was no running from it.

For a few precious seconds, he stood paralyzed, a man poised to dive into an abyss more dark and deep than any he had ever known. It beckoned to him just beyond the door.

Then, with a convulsive shudder, he lowered the stone and placed it on the stack. Despite the heat, he trembled. There was no running, this was true. But there *was* turning away. He could turn. He could be strong enough—today, now. That was all that mattered. Being strong enough now. He could find some time here and there. He could carve it out like everyone else.

It took all the strength he had, but he turned.

The Problem with Polly

It wasn't that Nathan Randall disliked cats, but the notion of *liking* them hadn't ever crossed his mind either.

So when he woke to Beethoven's *Sonata in F Minor* playing from his alarm clock, stretched out his arms, yawned, and opened his eyes to find this raggedy, tortoise-shell cat—an odd jumble of black, tan, and orange fur that made it resemble a gremlin of sorts—staring down at him from atop his dresser, it was cause for concern.

"And what do you think *you're* doing?" Randall said.

The cat blinked.

Randall had a carefully orchestrated schedule. A five-minute obstruction would mean five minutes out of his breakfast of tea and biscuits, his brisk walk around the park, his reading of the Wall Street Journal, or, worse, tardiness at the Department. He realized that he had left the kitchen window ajar exactly six inches, for it had been a cool evening with a slight breeze, and that this creature must have admitted itself onto the premises through those very six inches.

He rose from bed—swiftly, for Randall abhorred laziness—
and threw on his robe. The cat watched in its own detached way,
glancing once at Randall, then drifting its gaze to something else,
a smudge on the wall, perhaps, that excited it to the same degree.
As Randall looked closer, he noticed that the cat wore a purple
collar with a gray metal tag. It was his first sign of good news.
Careful not to get too close, he peered at the inscription.

POLLY

DO NOT IRRITATE
DO NOT AGITATE
THIS FINE FURY MAGISTRATE
OF FELICITY.

SHE'S ONE TO STAY
SHE'S YOURS EACH DAY
IF YOU REGARD HER, AS YOU MAY
WITH AFFINITY.

Randall half-suspected that the cat was someone's practical
joke, but since he had no enemies, or friends for that matter, he
could think of no one who would want to do such a thing. It
didn't matter. Regardless of where the animal came from, he had
little time for such foolishness. He realized that cats have claws
and those claws, when properly used, could inflict pain. Yet each
passing moment was another crimp in his schedule. So without
knowing quite what he was going to do, but knowing he had to do
something, he reached for the cat.

In one instant the cat transformed itself from a harmless fluff
of fur into a screeching, hissing incarnation of the devil. Its back
arched, fangs protruded, eyes bulged, and tail shot up. Do not
irritate, the tag had warned. He saw why.

Now Randall may have been stubborn, but he was no fool who rushed in, so he wisely decided that his hand may not have been the best object in which to shoo away the pugnacious pest. His copy of Dostoevsky's *Crime and Punishment* lay at his beside, and it being a hardback and at least ten inches in length, might suffice as an instrument with which to prod the cat. This seemed promising in theory, but as he tried it out, poking at the cat, the little creature simply retreated farther back atop his dresser. It hissed defiantly, then proceeded to clean its paws.

"So it's going to be that way, is it Polly?" Randall said.

He realized that he could solve his problem now, taking whatever time was needed to get the job done, or simply abandon the effort and hope that the cat let itself out. When the cat found that there would be no bowl of milk for its empty stomach, it would seek out another, more yielding host down the street. This is the course of action Randall chose, and later, if he could have done it again, he certainly would have tried harder to rid himself of the cat at that very moment.

For when he returned from his shave and shower, steam rising off his robed body, he found not one cat peering down at him from atop the dresser, but *two*. Two tortoise-shell cats. They sat side by side, identical in every respect right down to the collars and the tags, watching him with the same feline mixture of indifference and indignation. Now Randall knew that he was the target of someone's joke. But who? Who would go to the trouble? Not his boss, for the man may have regarded Randall with reserved contempt, as most people in close contact with Randall did, but he had never overtly harassed him, nor shown any sign that he would. He barely had ten words a day with anyone else at the Department. He never talked with his neighbors.

"Who put you up to this, eh?" Randall asked.

The cats yawned in unison and turned to contemplate the lint on the curtains.

It didn't matter. Randall never intended on owning one cat, and he certainly wasn't going to be running a hotel for a whole lot of them. He retreated to the hall closet and retrieved his broom. *She's yours each day?* Not a chance.

He swatted at the twin felines and felt a thrill of satisfaction when the two leapt from their perch and scurried out of the room. He pursued them into the living room, brandishing his weapon as a bloodthirsty conquistador might.

"Run, you little pests! Run! Ha, ha!"

He swatted at their retreating tails. In an instant, the two cats had traversed the distance to the kitchen window. With one last slap at them, Randall succeeded in forcing them outside. He leapt to the window and threw down the sash. Arms raised in victory, he watched the cats disappear under a gap in his wooden fence.

Feeling altogether good about his masculinity, and his heart thundering away in his chest as it hadn't in years, Randall turned back to the bedroom. In one flicker of a cat's whisker, his enthusiasm changed to despair. For there in the living room, lined up across his couch like a row of Roman sentries, were the cats. Not two cats. Not three cats. *Four cats.* Quadruplet Pollys. He felt not anger now, but something else, a darker feeling far removed from his experience.

Dread.

"Now let's think this through," Randall said, although he was talking more to himself than to the cats. "We can work this out."

The cats blinked, eight eyelids snapping in unison, like multiple camera shutters capturing his image.

"I'm going to get dressed for work, you see," Randall said. "Yes, that's exactly what I'm going to do, for I can't be late. I'll leave you to do as you wish. You can think about me. Yes, you can evaluate me for a time, you see. As you can probably tell, I won't be much of a friend to you. Here, I'll even leave the kitchen window open if you should decide to go."

With that, he returned to the bedroom, doing his best to avoid the green eyes of his visitors. His situation did not improve. In the bedroom he found four *more* cats on his dresser, and from the way things had been developing, he knew these weren't the same cats from the living room. In a moment, his suspicion was confirmed, for the cats from before appeared in his doorway.

Then they meowed, and it was like the blast from a trumpet.

Shaken, Randall proceeded to get dressed. As the eight watched him, he slipped on his trousers, his perfectly dimpled tie, and his suit jacket. He had a simple plan now. He would ignore them. He would get in his car and go to work. When he returned, they would hopefully have left through the window. No time or appetite for breakfast, he grabbed his car keys and his brief case and headed for the garage. When he saw his car, however, he knew he wouldn't be leaving any time soon.

It was filled with cats.

Eight of them, it appeared. They covered the driver seat, the steering wheel, and the dash board of his gray sedan. Randall felt himself losing it. A burning sensation rose up his neck to his forehead.

"Get out of there, vermin!" he shouted.

Eight more cats appeared in the back seat, whiskered faces pressed up against the windows. He opened the garage door and found a blockade of cats—*sixteen* of them, he counted quickly—preventing him from leaving. Like a group of finely trained soldiers, they began to march toward him. The car door popped open and those cats streamed into the garage, joining the others. Their dark fur was like a river of oil flowing in his direction.

He slammed the door and retreated into the house, only to find that the situation inside had worsened. The cats were too many to count. Cats on the refrigerator, the breadbox, the microwave. Cats sitting on the furniture, hiding under it, and hanging from the sides. Cats clawing their way up the curtains. Cats on cats—two or three deep in some places. He could no longer see his carpet there were so many cats. The shedding hair from so many cats filled the air with thick black smog and Randall choked and wheezed just to get a breath. He ran for the front door, but when he threw it open, *more* cats poured into the house, blocking his way.

Shielding himself with his briefcase, he retreated in the only way he could—back to his bedroom, for there were yet no cats in that direction. The door to the garage crashed to the floor and those cats piled into the house. The smell of cats now was overwhelming. Several had already defecated. Others were coughing up hairballs. When they saw that he was moving away, they moved after him—slowly, like a dark, blubbering mass of furry lava.

"Get back!" Randall cried.

They arched their backs and hissed, and it was the most frightening sound he had ever heard, like a million bees buzzing through his house. He turned and bolted for the bedroom and he heard them stampeding behind him. He slammed the door and pressed against it with all his might, but he could feel the pressure building on the other side like a mighty tidal wave, and in an instant the door gave way. His back pressed against his bed, he warded them off by swinging his briefcase, but then they had torn that away from him and he stood before them, exposed.

Randall fell to his knees. "What do you want from me?"

Fangs out, claws protruding, the cats moved in.

"Please," Randall begged. "I'll do anything."

Several cats in front of him vanished.

What had happened? A cat in front of him was close enough that he could read the inscription on its tag, and the last word of that first stanza—*affinity*—made him realize what he had to do.

"She's one to stay," Randall said. "Of course. *One!* Regard her with affinity."

He wasn't exactly sure how to treat a cat with affinity, but he knew the things most of them liked. He reached out and petted one of them and more of them vanished. He scratched another behind the ears and the crowd thinned again. They began to purr now, hundreds of them, and if he didn't know better he would have thought it was the first tremblings of an earthquake.

"Good kitty," he said, petting still more. "You're all such good kitties."

Still more cats disappeared, until he could actually see his carpet. He waded through them to his kitchen, for he had an idea of how best to treat a cat like a king. Using the biggest bowl he could find, he poured them nearly an entire gallon of milk and set it down in the middle of the herd. The feeding frenzy lasted only a few moments, and when the milk was gone, only one cat remained.

One scrawny tortoise shell cat. Licking her paws. Ignoring him like only a cat could.

"Hello Polly," Randall said. "Would you like some more milk?"

It was on that day that Nathan Randall became a proud cat owner. He was vigilant in his care for her, never forgetting to put out her food or change her litter box, for if he did he always found that her twins would soon appear. In the mornings, she watched him from the bathroom counter while he shaved, and curled up on his lap while he read the paper. He had to shorten his morning walk by five minutes so as to leave plenty of time for her each morning, but he gladly did so.

It even helped him make conversation with his neighbors and coworkers. For instead of having nothing to say, he now talked about his cat, as all cat owners are prone to do, regaling others who listened with polite attentiveness to his cat's exploits. He didn't even care when their eyes glazed over.

All My Invisible Friends

Danny was definitely my favorite. This is not something you admit to children, of course. There are no favorites—or at least there shouldn't be—among parents and child psychologists. But I would be lying if I said Danny *wasn't* my favorite. He was my favorite the moment he walked into my oak-paneled office, sandy bangs blocking his watery blue eyes, and flashed me a buck-toothed smile. It may have been that smile. It may have been that I knew everything he had been through in his six short years and I still believed that smile was authentic. You get pretty good at reading smiles in my line of work, and Danny had one that jacked you straight into his heart.

That's why, six months after I met him, it was so hard to tell him I couldn't be his therapist any more.

"But why?" Danny asked.

The grandfather clock read three minutes to five. I had deliberately waited until the end of our session to break the news. Danny slouched on the blue bean-bag chair across from me, legs outstretched. The snow once lodged in the treads of his tennis

shoes—brand new Nikes, a birthday present from his foster parents—had turned into a puddle on my hardwood floor. The setting sun, breaking through the blinds to our right, filled the room
with a warm orange glow. Pulled up next to him was another
bean-bag chair, this one for his invisible friend, Nick.

I swallowed. I knew it was going to be difficult breaking the
news, but I didn't think I would have had a coal-sized lump in my
throat. The question was there in his voice even though he hadn't
said the words: *Did I do something wrong?*

"It has nothing to do with you," I explained. "It's me. I just …
need a break for a little while."

Danny looked glum. He didn't often look glum, and it was an
odd expression to see on his face. He looked at the empty bean-
bag chair, then back at me. "Nick wants to know if it's 'cause of
your wife dying," he said.

The question, and how plainly it was put, made me feel a pang
of grief. There were things I told my children and then there were
things I withheld. I had told Danny I was married, that my wife
was a child psychologist like myself, and that we had no children
of our own. I had not told him how June had been battling brain
cancer for the last two years, or how she had finally succumbed to
it two months earlier. I had not told him how it felt to be alone at
the dinner table night after night, or how I sometimes broke into
fits of helpless sobbing at something as trivial as finding a pink
sock behind the couch.

Even a month earlier, his comment may have caused me to
feel a surge of anger, but that was mostly gone. What was left was
a hollowed-out place inside of me, and a depression that had only
deepened with each passing week.

I leaned back in my swivel chair, the springs squeaking. Nick
had been with Danny since I started with him, and I knew it was
no cause for concern. Most children let them go by his age, but
then, most children hadn't been through what Danny had been

through. "Who told Nick this?" I asked. My voice had gone dry.

"Nobody," he said. He pointed at my cluttered desk. I never sat behind it when I was in session. I had found it was one barrier I could easily dispense with.

"You don't have the picture on your desk no more," he said. "The beach one. The picture of your wife. So Nick tells me to ask Phil if you are okay and Phil says your wife pass away. I saw this long time ago but I didn't say. I know you feel sad, Dr. Tom. It's okay to feel sad, like you always say." He leaned forward, hugging his bony knees. He liked to wear shorts even in cold weather. "You can talk to an adult doctor and they can make you better and then you can come back and talk to me again."

He nodded at me as if he had given me all the advice I needed, and now it was up to me to follow it. You can think you've mustered all the necessary defenses, all the protections you need to prevent the onslaught of grief from overwhelming you, and then in an instant they're thrown aside and you're roiling in the storm again. All it took was a kid who had lost his father to a car wreck and his mother to a drug addiction—but for some reason could still occasionally smile—to cast me back into the sea.

"Well …" I said, trying to find my barriers again. "Well … You're—I mean, Nick is very perceptive, Danny. Very perceptive. Um … Phil is right. June passed away."

"And you're sad?"

"Yes."

"But you'll get better."

"Yes. Yes, I'll get better. I … It'll just take some time." I smiled, trying to sound more confident in this answer than I really was. "I just don't think I'm a very good therapist until I deal with some of these things. And I think you deserve the very best."

He smiled at me. "There's nobody better than you, Dr. Tom."

"Thank you, Danny. That means a lot."

"Nick wants to know when you'll come back?"

"I don't know." I shifted uncomfortably in my seat. "I'm going to be honest with you, Danny. I may not come back. I may decide to do something else."

"Oh."

There was a moment of silence. Out in the reception area, I could hear Phil, Danny's foster father, talking to my receptionist.

"Well," I said, leaning forward and smiling at Danny. "It's time for you to go, I think."

"Okay," he said, his face downcast. He looked at the empty bean bag chair. "Nick has a question.""All right."

"He wants to know ... He says something bad might happen to me, and he wants to know if you'll take care of him if it does." Danny looked at me, his eyes watery. "Can you look after Nick if something bad happens to me, Dr. Tom?"

The question made me hate myself for doing this. I considered briefly just seeing Danny and quickly dismissed the idea. A clean break was what I needed.

I stood, helping him to his feet. I put my hands on his slim shoulders and looked down into his eyes.

"Listen to me," I said. "Nothing bad is going to happen. You're going to see a very nice man named Doctor Edward."

"I know ... but can you still promise? Nick wants you to promise. He doesn't like being alone."

There was a tap on my door. I glanced at the smoked glass, saw Phil's silhouette, then looked at Danny. This line of questioning was bothering me. I would have to tell Edward about it.

"Promise?" Danny said.

If I'd had more time, I would have probed deeper, trying to find out why Danny was persisting on this idea of something bad happening to him. But I felt tired, defeated. In the end, I just wanted him to leave happy.

"I promise," I said.

* * * * *

THE SNOW WAS GONE in a matter of days, but then the onslaught of rain began. Snow never stayed long in Rexton, a medium-sized town in the lush Willamette Valley, but rain was another matter. That winter, it rained nearly every day from December until March, not a hard, brief pounding, but a steady drizzle interrupted by the occasional glimpse of sunshine. I spent most of those months holed up in my riverside condo, watching cable and listening to the rain tap against the metal roof. And it was raining the night I got the call from Danny's foster mother.

"Oh, god, Doctor Morris," she said. "It's Danny. He's missing. He never showed up for school and we can't find him anywhere."

To hear the panic in her voice, you would never guess that Danny was not her biological son, or that he had only been in her care a year. On my muted television, a few burly security guys on a late-night talk show were preventing two women from tearing each other's hair out.

"Calm down, Mrs. Clark," I said, rising from the couch. Even as I gave her this advice, I felt my own panic rising. All I could think was *he was right. Dear God, he was right.*

"It's just not like him," she said. "He's a good boy. He always calls—"

"When—when did you last see him?" I asked.

"This morning. He walks to school." She started crying. "It's only a block away. We just never thought—"

"And you called the police?" I glanced at the clock in the kitchen. It was a quarter to nine.

"We called *everybody*. Oh Jesus. I just thought, maybe you would know. He really liked you. Maybe you would know a place, you know, where he would go if, if, if …"

"Did you call Dr. Johansen?"

"Yes. He hasn't seen him either, and he has no idea where he would go. Oh, God, what if ... what if somebody—"

"There's no point speculating on what-ifs," I said, though my own mind was racing through those very possibilities. "Perhaps he's hiding. Sometimes children do this. I'll wander around the school and some other places. Maybe, if he sees me, he'll come out. But you keep calling around, all right?"

She thanked me profusely and we hung up. I'd put on a brave front for her, but the truth was, I wasn't at all confident in my theory. She was right. Danny just wasn't the type to disappear.

Still, I had to do *something*. I put on my overcoat and my fedora and headed outside to the parking lot. The rain, a fine mist, was visible only in the yellow bubbles of light surrounding the street lamps. The moist air dampened my cheeks.

I was halfway to my Acura when I saw the boy leaning on the pine tree near my car.

For a moment, I thought it *was* Danny and I pulled up short. As he stepped out of the shadows onto the asphalt, standing at the fringes of the light from the street lamp, I saw it wasn't him. He looked like Danny—skinny, blond, wearing shorts and a t-shirt— but he was taller and broader. He had strange proportions, with a head too large for his body, and hands and feet the size of a man's even though he couldn't have been more than ten. He walked toward me.

"Hello," I said, "can I—"

That's when I realized the kid wasn't all there. At first, I thought he was hard to see because of the mist, but that wasn't it. The kid was fading in and out, as if he was cast onto the air by a flickering projector. I blinked away the moisture in my eyes, but it made no difference. The cars and the trees were dimly visible through his body.

"Doctor Tom?" he asked.

His voice made the hairs on the back of my neck rise. He sounded just like Danny. He stopped a few paces away from me, close enough that I could see a phosphorescent blue halo surrounding him. A wind picked up, shaking the trees, and his body rippled away before returning again.

"Yes," I said.

"We need to get Danny," he said

"Yes."

"He's all alone."

"Where—where is he?"

He stared at me. His eyes, too, were out of proportion, nearly twice as large as a normal person's. He didn't blink.

"He's all alone," he said again.

I was trying to think of what to say next when the kid turned to my Acura. He circled around to the passenger side and looked back at me. Slowly, I walked over to the driver side, looking at him over the roof of the car.

"Who are you?" I asked.

"Nick," he said.

It took a moment for the name to register, and then I remembered: *Danny's invisible friend*. When I spoke again, my heart was beating loud in my ears.

"Where do you want to go?"

"I'll show you."

As I unlocked the door, the keys jangled in my shaking hand. I was going to unlock the passenger side when I glanced over and saw that he was already sitting on the leather seat, the handle of the door visible through his body.

"Go," he said.

He never gave me an address, but as we drove, he told me where to turn. Ten minutes later, we were on an old country road, my headlights cutting through the inky blackness. The windshield wipers squeaked across the glass. The car jostled from the occasional pothole.

"Turn here," he said.

We turned onto a narrow gravel road that wound ts way through an apple orchard. The trees looked like they hadn't been tended to in years. At the end of the road there was a dark, tiny farmhouse with broken windows and a gaping hole in the roof. Next to this was a barn which was missing its front doors and most of the boards. I turned to Nick for confirmation and saw that he was already outside, standing in the beams from the head-lights.

I grabbed the penlight out of my jockey box—the only flashlight I had on me—and trudged over the muddy ground. I followed him behind the barn, where the stink of manure and rotting wood was in the air. The batteries in the penlight were dying, and the pale, thin strip of light was just enough to keep from tripping on the lumpy terrain. Nick, however, was growing brighter as we walked, so that when we finally stopped by a pile of junk—rusty folding chairs, bicycles missing wheels and seats, aluminum window frames—he looked as solid as me.

He pointed at the ground.

"What is it?" I asked.

"Here," he said.

"What do you—" I began, and then I realized what he meant. Shining my light where he was pointing, I saw that the mud there had been freshly tilled.

"Are you … Are you saying …?"

Nick stepped up close to me, his blue halo glowing brightly. Without a word, he suddenly thrust both his hands straight into my chest, his arms disappearing up to his elbows.

A burning pain swept out from my stomach to my fingers, making my ears buzz and my hair stand on end. The world went temporarily white, and then images and feelings surged through me, hot and electric, one crashing on top of another in a kalei-doscope of memories—Danny talking to me, Danny pointing a green squirt gun at me, Danny smiling at me on top the jungle gym. I saw and felt it all as if I had lived it myself—Danny's whole life from whenever he created Nick through the funeral for his father, in the hospital with his mother, happy times with his foster parents, talking with kids at school, talking with me, talking with my colleague, Doctor Johansen. Every secret wish and painful longing he had ever shared with Nick was now my own, and it all came in one furious rush until the last memory, the one that was brighter and hotter than all the others: Danny, bound and gagged with duct-tape, next to this very barn, him kneeling next to a hole in the dirt. Though the night was black, I could see it all in chalky outlines, as if it was a still life rendered on dark paper with a white pencil. Now I was no longer standing next to Danny, I was him, afraid and alone, and I looked up into a night sky, blinked away the rain, and saw the man standing there, leaning on a shovel, sleeves folded up to his elbows, a small flashlight clamped in his mouth.

Dr. Edward Johansen.

Oh, God, Edward, no ...

And then I was crying, not Danny but me, alone on my hands and knees in the dark. My nose was inches from the dirt. I was clutching the pen light but it had gone dead. I had let him down. I had failed him.

Nick was gone, and I didn't need to look around to know this. He was inside me now. I would look after him. Oh yes, Danny, I would look after him for the rest of my life.

I cast aside the penlight, and, still sobbing, dug my bare fingers into the cold, wet earth.

DANNY WAS DEFINITELY my favorite. I would be lying if I said otherwise. He changed my life before and after his death, but I didn't know just how much until a few weeks later.

After the police dug out Danny's body, after Edward's arrest, and long after the funeral, I was at the grocery store picking up milk, cereal, and a few cans of soup when I saw a barefoot black boy in blue overalls standing in the frozen foods section. He looked about seven. The melody of an old Beetles song played faintly above us. It was late, nearly one in the morning, and the store was deserted. It was the only time I left my condo. It was the only time I could stand to face the world.

I knew from the first glance what the boy was. The blue halo surrounding his short black hair. The transparency of his brown skin. I never thought I would see these signs again, but then, I hadn't been looking.

I stepped up to him. He looked at me with a mixture of trepidation and longing.

"Are you lost?" I asked him.

"Yehsur," he said.

"Where are you from?"

"Missoura, sur."

"That's a long ways. Where's your friend?"

He looked down at his bare feet. "He gone, sur. Long time now."

I knew exactly what I had to do. I put my plastic basket on the tiled floor, then knelt in front of him. "My name's Thomas," I said.

"Cal," he said, shuffling his feet.

"Nice to meet you, Cal. Do you want me to look after you?"

He nodded. I held out my arms and he stepped into them, moving inside of me, bringing with him all the memories and emotions of a man who had been dead for nearly fifty years.

OPEN HIGHWAY stretched out before me, long and straight, nothing but open prairie and grazing cattle on both sides. The sky was blue except for the horizon, where a bank of gray clouds hovered over the distant mountains. I was somewhere in Montana.

Everything I owned—everything I hadn't sold or donated—was in the motor home with me. I was done with therapy, at least the kind where I sat in a swivel chair and made notes on a clipboard.

There were many more like Nick and Cal out there, some abandoned because the need for them was outgrown, some deserted when their creators died. I had already found dozens on my way across Oregon and Idaho, wandering, lost and alone, and I knew I would find dozens more. I would go on looking until I found them all. I would do it for Danny. I would do it because it gave purpose to my life, and having a purpose was one way out of despair.

I still felt the terrible pangs of grief now and then, both for June and for Danny, but it wasn't as bad as before.

I was no longer truly alone.

All my invisible friends were with me.

The Android Who Became a Human
Who Became an Android

The last time I saw Ginger, she was sporting two breasts instead of three. Personally, I thought her breasts were perfect before, but I know that with some guys you could never have too much of a good thing.

When I stepped out of the shower, she was sitting there on the edge of my bed, decked out in a silky red number with a slit up the side that showed plenty of her long legs and a plunging neckline that definitely revealed too much of a good thing. Steam wafted out from the bathroom and rose from my bare skin. I was naked except for the towel around my waist. Outside my tinted, floor-to-ceiling window, a constant swarm of Versatian hoverpods hummed and whizzed past, everybody in a hurry to get somewhere on a planet where everybody supposedly came so they didn't have to hurry.

"I need your help," she said.

No hello. No how have you been. No sorry for breaking

your heart, emptying your credit account, and taking off with your ship and your entire twentieth-century holodisc collection. The last time I saw her, I was stepping into a shower. Now, five years later, I stepped out of one and there she was.

"You have a strange sense of irony," I said.

"Huh?"

"Never mind. How'd you get in here?"

She shrugged. "Bribed the desk clerk. I'm pretty sure he thought I was a hooker."

"You *are* a hooker," I said.

She made a *tsk-tsk* sound. "That was another life. I'm a respectable woman now—married to one of the richest stepdock manufacturers in the known universe. And you can kindly stop staring at my breasts, thank you very much. It's not *that* uncommon."

"Sorry. You know, I *am* working here. I didn't ask for you to barge in on me."

"You're working? In a place like this?"

"I'm checking the security system for the hotel."

"Ah," she said, and waved her hand dismissively. "Since when does Dexter Duff stoop to grunt work like that?"

"A lot of things have changed since you ran out on me, Ginger."

She made a pouty face, sticking out her lower lip and making her eyes wide. In the old days, I found that look irresistible. Now it just looked childish, which was probably what it had been all along. "Oh, dear," she said, "you sound bitter. I was hoping that was all water over the bridge."

"Under the bridge," I said.

"Whatever. Look, if you want to take me to bed, let's do it, and then we'll get all the tension out of the air."

"You just said you were married!"

She shrugged. "It's not like he'd care. He doesn't care about anything anymore. That's part of the problem."

"Oh, I feel so sorry for you. Let me get you a Repsiter harp and you can earn some tokens down on the tramspace."

She sighed and stood, smoothing out her dress. "Look, are we going to do it or not?"

"I'd rather lay down with a pair of blood-sucking Mornala tree worms. At least they have *some* emotions, even if it's just fear and no-fear. That's more than I can say for you."

"I bet if you drop that towel," she said, "we'd find out you really think otherwise. There's some things a man can't hide."

I snorted derisively and headed for the built-ins, the drawers sliding out of the wall before I got there. The tile floor felt cold against my bare feet. I dressed quickly, mostly because I was afraid my body *was* going to betray me despite my best intentions. My towel slid off before I'd managed to get my pants all the way on, giving her a damn good view of everything I had to offer. Or didn't.

"God, what happened to you?" she said.

It took me a moment to realize she meant the scars. "You know my line of work, Ginger."

"Yeah, but you never looked like that back then."

I slipped the shirt over my head and straightened the collar. "I was younger back then. These days, I don't always manage to duck when I should be ducking or dodge when I should be dodging."

"Maybe you should get into another line of work," she said.

"Maybe you should slither back under whatever rock you came out from under," I replied.

I glared at her. She looked back with her practiced look of placid bemusement, like she was humoring a small child. Still glaring at her, I handprinted the safe next to my bed, pulled out my laser pistol, and checked to make sure it was fully charged. It was. Then I checked to see if her expression had changed upon seeing me holding a weapon. She still looked at me like I was a two-year-old. I slipped on my shoulder holster and placed the pistol in it, then donned my leather jacket and my boots. Only when I started toward the outside door did she finally speak up.

"All right," she said, "I'll tell you what I want."

I stopped, not yet turning around. "You know, no matter what you tell me, I'm not going to help you."

"Even if I paid you?"

"Especially if you paid me."

"Even if I paid you an *awful* lot?"

"Even ... Even then."

My hesitation had only been for a second, long enough to think about the sad state of my credit account and the freeze-dried food cubes that had served as meals the past few months, a moment of weakness that lasted no longer than a blink of an eye, but she sensed it like a spider senses a twitch in its web.

"Darling," she said, her heels clicking on the tile floor, her voice drawing nearer, "you do understand that I am a *very* rich woman now. I can afford to pay you ten times your normal fee."

"I wouldn't do it for twenty."

"Then I guess I better make it twenty-five."

I had no idea what she wanted me to do, or whether I'd be willing to do it once I found out what it was, but even for a small job, it would have to be a lot of money. I'd been trying to get my act together for quite a while, and there was always something that set me back. Usually that something involved a trip to a medical ward. This could have finally gotten me my own ship. Maybe even a couple robots to take care of the small stuff.

She touched me on the shoulder. I tensed.

"Duff," she whispered, "was it really all that bad?"

"Yes, Ginger, it was."

"All of it?"

I thought about it. There'd been other women after Ginger,

some who'd broken my heart just as badly—for some reason, that seemed to be a recurring problem—but she had been the first, the one who'd made me afraid to ever let my guard down again. "If you stayed up all night reading a multivid," I said, "but the ending was so horrible that you threw the vid across the room, do you remember that the vid was good enough to keep you screening until that point? Or do you just remember how you felt at the end?"

"Hmm," she said, a bit of a purr in her voice, "I was never one for reading. I always liked my pleasures a little more … real."

When she said his, she ran her hand up my inner thigh. It would have been easy to give in, but there was no way I was going to let her get the upper hand with me, and I knew if we got anywhere near the bed she would definitely have the upper hand. She'd been a AAA sex professional, after all, certified by all the top prostitution boards and trained by the Sisters of Desire, the masters of erotic pleasure on New Saturn who only took in sixty-nine pupils each year.

I spun around and grabbed her shoulders. "Stop it," I said. "You're not doing this to me again."

"Ow, darling, you're hurting me."

My fingers pressed into the soft flesh of her arms, but I didn't loosen my grip. We stood close enough that I saw the flecks of gold in her emerald eyes—something new, something else she'd done to herself since we'd been together. We stood close enough that her breath was hot on my face. My heart was pounding.

"Listen," I said, "if I do anything for you, it will be purely for money, got it? I don't want you mentioning our past again. It's just business. We've never met. I'm just Dexter Duff, private investigator. You understand? Am I getting through that thick skull of yours, *darling?*"

She blinked up at me. "So you're saying you'll do it?"

I sighed. Same old Ginger. You could talk and talk but she always picked out what she wanted to hear. If I ended up working for her, I knew what I was getting into. She was a liar and a cheat and she was good at getting people to do what she wanted even when they knew what she was."I'll listen," I said, but I felt like I'd already agreed.

THE TRAMSPACE was always crowded in the morning, but I was in no mood to travel any farther with Ginger than necessary. A flurry of hoverpods docked and departed all around the giant transparent tunnel, a quarter mile across. The main concourse was filled with every life form and non-life form imaginable—humans, Dulnari, Hasians and plenty of four-armed Veratians in their spiffy, white uniforms directing tourists to different excursions, not to mention all the robots and androids carrying people's bags. Beneath the invisible walkway—it was like we were all walking on air—dozens of massive, white cruise ships floated in the sleek emerald waters of the Versatia's famous ocean.

We were lucky, and found a table at a bistro not far from the transport tube. The smell of coffee and toasted bagels made my stomach grumble.

"It all started when—" Ginger started.

I held up a hand. "Not until I get my coffee."

When were finally seated at a corner table, in a glass bubble overlooking the ocean, I kept her waiting until I'd buttered my bagel and put cream in my coffee. She clicked her fingernails on the shiny black countertop.

"All right," I said.

"Really? I have your permission to speak now?"

"Don't push your luck, kid."

She smiled. "Kid? You haven't called me that since you met me on the asteroid mining outfit where you stopped for repairs."

"Should have left you there, too. Those miners have probably really missed your services."

She made a clicking sound of displeasure with her tongue. "Now, now. All right, so where do I start? I assume you know that my husband is Vergon Daughn—"

That made me pause mid-bite into my bagel. "Vergon? Of Vergon Enterprises?"

She sighed. "Don't you follow the news at all? My wedding four months ago was all over the vids. Yes, that Vergon. A decade ago he built a fledgling stepdock company into a massive corporation, employing over a million people on thirty-three different planets."

She was right that I didn't follow the news much, but I did know a little about Vergon Daughn. When she'd mentioned being married to one of the richest stepdock manufacturers in the known universe, he definitely wasn't who had come to mind—for one specific reason. "Um," I began, "isn't he … an android?"

"That's right," she said.

"You're telling me you married an android?"

"Uh huh. I wasn't the one who liberated him and paid for his humanizing—some old bag who'd owned him did it before she died. But I definitely saw a good thing and went after him. Honestly, he didn't stand a chance when I came along. He proposed within six weeks."

I stared at her a long time, soaking all this in. My main complaint about Ginger had always been that she wasn't born with the normal set of emotions as other human beings—like the ability to empathize with someone other than herself—and here she went and married somebody who didn't have any emotions at all. Oh, androids could fake them, and some faked them so well that they could pass for human unless they walked under a bio scanner—but it was all an act. It was why, according to the laws of the Unity Worlds, even a liberated android still didn't possess the full rights of a biological sentient—or biosen, for short. They would always be considered property. Now property could have a lot of rights, just like intergalactic corporations were property but still had plenty of rights, but it wasn't the same.

Of course, there were lots of bleeding hearts of every race and planet who argued that liberated androids should be conferred with the same rights as biosens, but so far the law had been firm. Mostly this was because it was backed by hard science: androids may have been some of the most sophisticated machines every devised, but they were still machines.

Finally, I burst out laughing.

"What's so funny?" she said.

"You wouldn't understand," I said.

She offered up her trademark pout. "It's not like I'm some lonely heart who bought an android to be my lover. He's liberated and humanized—he could have chosen anyone, and believe me, he had plenty of women after him. It was love at first light."

"First sight."

She frowned. "If you understand what I'm saying, why do you always have to correct me? It's one of the things that always irritated me about you."

"If you're irritated," I said tersely, "you're welcome to leave at any time."

"Oh, no. No, darling. I'm sorry … It's just this whole thing has me so upset. Forgive me, okay? I just didn't get all the schooling you did. I've had to teach myself—after you taught me a lot of things, that is." She sighed. "Anyway, to get back to what I was saying, it was love at first sight. But then Vergon went and screwed things up by becoming human."

I was lifting the coffee cup to my lips, and in my surprise, I spilled some on the table. "What?"

"Oh, I have your attention now? Right before our wedding, he surprised me by showing up at our rehearsal dinner fully human. He showed himself off to our guests by bringing a handheld bio scanner with him. I was … shocked, to say the least. It's called the BIP—Biological Imprinting Procedure. You grow a biosen in the lab, then use microlasers to imprint the same memories and thought patterns as the android."

I mopped up the coffee with one of the paper napkins. I'd heard about the procedure, but the last I knew it was still in the research and development phase. There were also all kinds of ethical issues surrounding it. "Is that procedure now authorized by the Unity Worlds?"

"Of course not," she said. "It's going to be a lifetime before that happens, if ever. But if you have enough money, you can make things happen. And once he was human, what were they going to do? The bioscans all show him as human, and he made sure to confer all the legal rights on his human body of ownership in Vergon Enterprises just to make sure."

"Why?" I said.

She grimaced. "To please me, of course."

"What?"

"He said he wanted to love me for real. He said—he said—" She stopped, and there were tears brimming in her eyes. "He said I might not know the difference, but he would. He would know that he wasn't feeling it, even if he was showing it."

I wasn't quite sure I bought her sudden display of weepiness. "Seems understandable. Do you blame him?"

"No! I don't blame him. But he's ... not the same, Duff. You may not believe this, but I loved Vergon the way he was before."

"You're saying the procedure didn't work?"

She took one of my napkins and dabbed at her eyes. "Oh, no, it worked," she said. "It definitely worked. The human Vergon had all of the android Vergon's memories. He'd made the body to look like him, too. At first, he even acted like him. But ... he started changing. He acted moody all the time. He fell into a deep depression. It hurt his company—it began to go downhill. Then—then we had this awful fight. I told him I wished he'd never done it. I told him I loved him more as android." She sniffled. "I guess that confirms everything you ever said about me ... I really am awful deep down."

I resisted the urge to take hold of her hand, and it was a powerful urge. "So what happened?"

"He went back to being an android."

"He did?"

She nodded. "He did the procedure in reverse—had another android body made, too, since he'd destroyed the original just to be safe. He made a big speech to the press, saying he'd planned to do it all along, that he wanted to test the laws that limited his rights, but I knew the truth. He was doing it to make me happy."

"So what's the problem?"

She looked up at me, eyes misty. "The problem," she said, "is that he's gone."

"Gone? As in, dead?"

She shook her head. "I hope he's not dead. Right after he did the procedure and gave a press conference, he vanished. He told his attendants he was going to use the restroom, but when they went to look for him, he was gone. It's been almost six weeks."

"An android using the restroom?" I said.

"Yes, the attendants realized later how stupid they were. They'd just gotten used to him being human and forgot."

"Have you hired other investigators?"

"No," she said, "I'm afraid to."

"Why? With your money, you could hire droves of them. That would increase your odds of finding him."

She shook her head. "You don't understand. I told you his company is going downhill. It's even worse. There's this other corporation, Granger Holdings, that's trying to take it over. Because the stock price is down, they're making a run at it. Without Vergon around to steady some nerves, the stockholders are starting to sell out. The thing is, Granger does exactly what

Vergon does—make stepdocks. They just want to eliminate the competition. So if they get control of it, they'll just sell off all the equipment to recoup their losses and then fire all the employees."

"What does this have to do with hiring some private investigators?"

"Because I can't trust anyone!" she insisted. "Already, I'm pretty sure I'm being followed." She glanced over her shoulder, peering into the hordes of people passing along the concourse.

I didn't see anyone but tourists. "Why?"

"Why! Because they don't want me to find Vergon, that's why. They want to keep the stock price low, and if he shows up, it will probably jump. The shareholders would wait to see what the brilliant Vergon Daughn is going to do. No, I'm afraid whoever I hire will really be working for them. I need somebody I can trust."

"And you trust me?"

She nodded. "Iconic, isn't it?"

"*Ironic* is the world you're looking for, I think. And yes, it's very ironic."

"Iconic, ironic, whatever is it is, I need your help, Duff. I can't do this without you. I want to find my husband."

I said nothing.

"And if you won't do it for me," she said, "do it for the million employees of Vergon Enterprises that will lose their jobs. Do it for them. That's why, even if he's dead ..." She hesitated, closing her eyes and steadying herself before continuing. "Even if he's dead, I need to know. At least the company could appoint a new CEO, which the board doesn't want to do until they know for sure he's gone. Maybe then we could still save the company."

It was quite a tale. It would be easy enough to check, so I assumed it was true, but that didn't mean I trusted her motives. But I was curious why a man—correction, an android—like Vergon Daughn would up and disappear, putting all his years of hard work in jeopardy. If nothing else, I could find Vergon just to satisfy that curiosity, and maybe, just maybe, I could end up doing some good while I was at it.

And, of course, get paid *really* well.

"All right," I said, "I'll find him for you."

"Oh good!"

"But I want the money up front."

In the end, it was she who clasped my hand, giving it a reassuring squeeze. "Of course, Duff. Whatever you want."

Looking at her, her eyes wide and her lips parting slightly, I remembered her whispering those very words to me late at night between satin sheets. I remembered and tried to put it out of my mind.

Money.

I was doing this for money.

The credit showed up in my account within ten minutes of Ginger passing through the stepdock back to the Vergon Enterprises headquarters on Palfacia Prime. It was twice even the outrageous amount I'd quoted to her, with so many zeroes in the number that I actually brought up the bank on nexlink to verify it wasn't a mistake. Ever after the holorep assured me that the deposit was, indeed, accurate, I still procrastinated for the rest of the day before finally calling up my hotel client and asking him if I could take a hiatus for a couple weeks for personal reasons, assuring him I'd come back and finish the job. I somewhat hoped he'd say no, but he didn't.

Finally out of excuses, I set to work finding Mr. Vergon Daughn, the android who became a human who became an android.

The first thing I did was get in touch with the bio-mechanical engineer who performed the human-to-android transference, who, it turned out, was the same one who'd performed the BIP and made Vergon human in the first place—a tall and spindly Dulnari named Bwer Fwer. I tried him on the vid first and was told by a pert blonde—so bubbly she had to be an android herself—that he'd see me that afternoon if I could come to his office.

His clinic, Mind-Body Technologies, was located on one of the oldest and richest planets in the Unity Worlds. It was a gaseous giant named Jellon with a trillion inhabitants and well over a hundred stepdocks, so there was no need to take a ship or shuttle at any point. But I'd been poor too long to take a direct step, so it still took two hours of hopping across the galaxy and fighting through crowded immigration controls to get to the gleaming black tower that contained his office.

After waiting in his lobby for *another* two hours, being asked by three different blonde android secretaries why I was there, I wasn't in the best of moods when a fourth bubbly blonde finally showed me to his office. He was rising from his desk, a dark and wolfish figure with skin like elephant hide. Even in a sharp blue suit and red tie, he still came across as more than a little menacing, but I let loose with all of my built-up irritation anyway.

"If this is how you treat people who have appointments," I said, "how do you treat everyone else?"

His beady eyes flared briefly, but it was the only outward sign of emotion. Right away I knew he was no ordinary Dulnari, because an ordinary Dulnari would have leapt across the table and gone for my throat at the slightest provocation.

A decade earlier, the Dulnari had been a major threat to the Unity Worlds, in a bloody war that lasted nearly thirty years, and even now there still weren't many of them who held anything but the most mundane jobs. This was partly due to how much the war had set them back as a race, but it was mostly because of the nature of the Dulnari themselves. Because of their telepathic connections to one another, in concert they were incredibly intelligent, but individually they weren't much smarter than low-grade AI floor sweepers. How one could ascend by himself to become a brilliant engineer—one Vergon was willing to risk his life with—was hard to believe.

"Mister Duff," he said, extending his hand, "I'm sorry to keep you waiting. I was conferencing with several senators and they were being quite stubborn about some of my requests."

It was the first time I'd shaken hands with a Dulnari. His four-fingered hand was smaller than my own, but his skin was tougher and thicker. There were lots of folks who still wouldn't shake hands with a Dulnari, veterans of the war or victims of their atrocities, but I didn't fall into either of those camps. The need had simply never arose.

"It's just Duff," I said. "I would have been happy to talk to you over the vid, you know."

"Yes, that would have certainly been more convenient," he said, "but I felt it was necessary to talk to you in person." He froze for a second, and it was like watching a hiccup in a vid feed. "Yes, yes, quite right. Most unusual."

"I'm sorry?" I said.

"Hmm?"

"What's unusual?"

"What do you mean?"

It was like he didn't know what he'd just said. Some form of schizophrenia or stepdock madness? I'd also never heard a Dulnari speak in such an articulate manner, especially in Unity Worlds Prime. He motioned to one of the two seats across from him. It was then, when he slightly cocked his head to the side, that I noticed something black and electronic behind his ears, tiny lights flashing red and blue.

"You have an implant," I said.

"Yes," he said, showing no sign of offense. "The ones I make now are much less crude, completely internal, but mine is now so integrated into my biological processes that it would extremely problematic to move it."

"Is that why you're ..." I began, not knowing quite how to phrase the question.

"Smarter than your average individual Dulnari?" he finished for me. "Yes. My implant contains a hundred mature Dulnari intelligences. All AIs, of course, but my mind sees them no differently than the real thing ... The flaring is quite unusual this time of year."

"Excuse me?"

He blinked a few times. "Hmm?"

"You said something about the flaring being unusual this time of year."

"I did? Oh, yes. The side-effects. You see, though the implant gives me the intelligence of a small Dulnari group mind, I have not yet perfected the natural filtering process that works with a real group mind. So I may occasionally say things not intended for you. I apologize for this in advance. Please, be seated."

I did, and so did he. The three windows behind him displayed a gorgeous view of the city's skyline, but everything else about the room was absolutely sterile: a desk with a built-in monitor and keyboard, three chairs, and nothing else. Not even a couple holovids on the walls.

"I never intended to spend much time here," he explained.

"I'm sorry?" I said.

"This room, I see the way you're looking at it. I always intended it to be mostly for show. I'm a lab rat, Duff. That's where I'd like to spend most of my time, and where I did spend most of my time until my company was bought out. Then the new owners made certain changes that forced me into more of a ... diplomatic role." He said the last two words with a sneer, and for just a moment I thought of the wolf in the Red Riding Hood fairy tale, dressed up in human clothes and pretending to be something he wasn't.

"Hobnobbing with senators, you mean?" I said.

"Exactly. It's dreadfully boring … Multivids are on sale in Setifine … But you don't care about any of that. Let me tell you why we had to meet in person. When Ginger Daughn first questioned me about all of this, I was absolutely convinced that her husband's disappearance had nothing at all to do with his procedure—or at least, that nothing in his procedure directly caused it. It went perfectly. Every test confirmed it … the low-g yoga is best after breakfast … If he disappeared, it was either his own choice or because he was abducted, not because there was some defect in the transference that modified his personality." He shook his head. "Now, I'm not so sure."

His non sequiturs were annoying, but I was getting better at ignoring them. "What do you mean?"

He clasped his slender hands and leaned his long snout on them, closing his eyes for a moment before answering. "Our equipment has been tampered with."

"What?"

He opened his eyes and looked at me. "It's why I had to have you come here in person. I don't know who to trust … The headaches go away in a few days, Kylor tells me."

I pretended he hadn't made the headache comment. "You sound like Ginger," I said. "She didn't know who to trust either."

"Honestly, I'm not even sure I can trust you, Duff. However, one of the reasons you were kept waiting was that we were performing scans of your responses to our questioning. There is every indication that you are truly here investigating Vergon Daughn's death."

"You gave me a lie detector test?"

He nodded. "Three of them, in fact. I'm sorry about that, but I had to be sure … A hangover is no cure for happiness."

"Who tampered with the equipment?"

"If I knew that," he said, "I probably wouldn't need your help."

"What was done?"

He clicked his fingernails on the desk. Dulnari fingernails had the same look and texture as volcanic glass, so the clicking sounded vaguely like tinging wine goblets. "It's hard to say. It turned up on a deep diagnostic, meaning it was somebody who really knew what they were doing ... I don't play MateMax at the Laztor, no."

"What happens to the human body?"

"It was disposed of. I personally attended to its incineration."

"You ... killed him?"

"Oh, no. That would be murder according to Unity Worlds law, even if that's not technically what it is. No, he committed suicide, which is entirely legal here on Jellon. He had several witnesses from the press there. He wanted absolutely no doubt that the new android Vergon Daughn was the only Vergon Daughn. Otherwise there could be sticky legal issues ... I see that this idea makes you uncomfortable, Mr. Duff."

"Well, yeah," I said. "I mean, to the human Vergon Daughn, it was still like dying wasn't it?"

"No," he said. "It wasn't. To you, to most biosens, even to me to a minor extent, a reverse BIP would seem like death ... I hear the fruit is quite delicious ... Few humans would be willing to do it. But to an android, a perfect copy is a perfect copy, indistinguishable from the original in every sense."

"If you say so," I said. "Who bought you out? The company, I mean."

"Oh, just one of those intergalactic corporations that owns a little bit of everything. They're called Granger Holdings. I'm sure you've never heard of them."

"Actually, I have," I said, trying to hide my surprise. "And they bought you out *before* you turned Vergon back into an android?"

"Yes. It was between when I performed his BIP and when he came back for his reversal. I explained to him that I was no longer allowed to perform the operation myself, that it all had to be automated by robots because Granger wanted to roll out the process for mass production, but he said that if I at least oversaw the operation, that would be enough … why, are you allergic to peanuts?"

"Could somebody have altered the new Vergon android in some way?"

He nodded. "That is quite possible. In fact, that is what I fear most … Shakespeare was not a bad writer, for a human … I fear Vergon has gone a bit insane, or his memories have been tampered with in some way, and if you do find him and this is proven correct, then Mind-Body Technologies will be blamed for it rather than whoever tampered with the equipment."

"Ah," I said, "I'm beginning to understand."

He looked at me with his dark, penetrating eyes. "Do you? I'm asking you to be discreet in your investigation, Duff. And of course, I'm willing to pay you handsomely for your discretion."

"In other words, if I find him, and he's out of his mind, you want me to lie."

"Oh, no. Not lie. That would be unethical. Just delay the truth until we can make certain that we have enough evidence to present what accurately happened. We're doing more diagnostics, but it could take a while … Dulnaris have no need for shampoo … How much credit would you require?"

Somehow I doubted they were performing more diagnostics. What was more likely was that they wanted to doctor the evidence, if not outright manufacture it, so that no one would ever think they were to blame.

"Zero," I said.

"Excuse me?"

"I only work for one client at a time, Bwer Fwer."

"I see."

"But I will tell you this. If I find him, and he's crazy, I'll definitely let you know."

He frowned. "That's very kind of you... My mother-pod still thinks I'm unmodified."

"Give my best to your mother-pod."

"What?"

I left without answering.

THE NEXT TWO DAYS were a series of dead-ends and wrong turns that left me increasingly frustrated. Deciding to stay on Jellon until I had another lead, I spent most of the time on the vid in a cheap hotel—old habits die hard—talking with various associates, friends, and employees of Vergon Daughn. The picture that emerged was of a cautious, quiet, and extremely logical android who became an even more quiet, cautious and logical man, somebody with no hobbies other than the one he'd developed fairly recently—keeping the three-breasted woman in his life happy. Otherwise, he spent all his time working.

Even his personal attendants couldn't offer anything useful, except to say he seemed even quieter and more withdrawn after he became a human. I was trying to get a handle on where a slightly deranged Vergon Daughn might go, and it would have been helpful if I had hobbies, interests, or favorite places to get me started.

Then, on the third day on Jellon, it came me: maybe he hadn't left at all.

Maybe he was still there.

Like everyone else, I'd assumed that because Vergon Daughn was a genius with technology, he would have found a way to fool the security scanners at all the stepdocks or spaceports. But even without the scanners, that would have been incredibly risky. No, the most *logical* thing to do would have been to stay on Jellon itself, exactly because everybody knew he could get off-planet if he wanted.

But where would he go? Someplace hospitable for androids, so perhaps one of the large cities where there'd be plenty of power grids and high-traffic nex-links. I started to make a list of all the underground contacts I knew in the biggest cities, people who could point me in the right direction, when I realized I had it all wrong.

Vergon wouldn't go to a big city. He was too smart for that. He'd go someplace nobody would expect an android to go.

The good news was that most of Jellon was highly developed, so there were really only a handful of places an android wouldn't be able to survive long without returning to civilization—the Harlo Desert, the Three Seas of Kinl, and Nelsani Rainforest. In fact, he wouldn't have been able to get far in any of them without some sort of guide. If my theory was right, I just had to find the guide.

I downloaded a list of travel agents and other tourist operations to my handheld, then headed out into the crowded streets, past booths of loud-mouthed vendors of every race imaginable, the air alive with sizzling grease and pungent spices. I was about halfway to the nearest stepdock when I had the distinct feeling I was being followed.

In the elbow-to-elbow crowd, I was barely able to lift my arms, but I managed to round a corner and duck into a shadowy alcove. I hung back, the crowd drifting past like a river choked with debris. I watched, waiting, looking for a reaction of some kind from somebody, and then I saw it.

A muscular blond human in a black trench coat picked up his pace and rounded the corner.

I dropped into the crowd and followed. When I rounded the corner myself, we came face-to-face. He'd been running, and he pulled up short. His face was expressionless, but it was still frozen in place.

"Hey, buddy," I said, clamping down on his arm, "I want to have a word—"

My fingers might as well have been made of tissue because he tore out of my grip as if was nothing. Then he was running, nimbly dodging through the crowd, sprinting away at such a speed that he was halfway down the street before I managed to even shout after him.

"You! Come back!"

It wasn't one of my most original moments. But by the time I'd thought of something better to say, he was already gone.

IT WAS GOING on three weeks when I wandered into the bamboo hut at the outskirts of the tiny village of Gonoa, one of five villages at the foothills of the Nelsani Mountains. Outside, the rain sliced into the vegetation like a machete. Even after the door swung shut, the downpour still filled the hut with a roar.

I was tired and cranky and about to give up. Of course, I'd been feeling that way for the past week, and still I found myself pressing on to the next destination. The only problem was that I was running out of destinations. I'd searched every dune of the Harlo Desert, all three seas of the Three Seas of Kinl, and a good chunk of the Nelsani Rainforest.

Racks of hiking and hunting gear packed the hut. The popular, flared canoes hung from the ceiling. Twangy harp music—annoyingly popular on Jellon—played from speakers mounted in the corners, and the only good thing about the rain was that it mostly blotted out the music. The musky stench of the rainforest, the smell that got into everything and stayed there like a bad houseguest, hung heavy in the air.

Nobody seemed to be around. I pushed past some brown

repel coats and some anti-grav moccasins and found a counter for vacation booking. Nobody was there either, though there appeared to be a room behind the counter, obscured from view by beads. There was a smell too, wafting out from the back room, a tangy odor that immediately brought water to my eyes. It smelled vaguely of lemons.

"Hello?" I said.

A dark-skinned man, bald on top but with a thick black beard below, pushed through the rattling beads. He carried a bundle of yellow rope, coiled in a circle. He wore a camo vest that bared his muscular arms. His skin was mocha brown, except for the jagged, pink scar on his right shoulder. There was a bit of silver in his beard, but I wouldn't have tried to guess his age. He could have been thirty or fifty.

"Welcome to Nelsani, good man," he said, exhaling a hint of smoke from his nostrils, and that lemon smell got stronger. "Are you here for a tour? If you book today, I can give you—"

"I'm actually here looking for someone," I said.

"Oh?" he said.

"Yes. I'm looking for an android. He's quite famous, actually. His name is Vergon Daughn. Maybe you've heard of him?"

The man stared at me as if I'd spoken in another language.

"I have reason to believe he's on this planet," I went on, "and that he might be in a remote location. Maybe he came to see you, or maybe you heard of him passing through."

He simply stared, blinking.

"Any help would be much appreciated. His wife is very worried."

He might as well have been a statue. I felt like strangling him. I might not have been able to do it, he was a decent-sized fellow, after all, but I was willing to give it a shot. It would make life more interesting for a while at least.

"Did you hear me?" I said.

"I heard you," he said. "I'm trying to decide whether to help you."

My hopes soared. Finally, a breakthrough. "You've seen Daughn?"

"Didn't say that. But I might be able to help you."

"How?"

He placed the rope on a hook behind him, turning his back to me. "That depends on how much the information is worth it to you."

I gritted my teeth. "You want a bribe?"

"That's such an ugly word," he said. "I was thinking more … payment for services rendered." He turned and looked at me, and I could tell by his expression that he wasn't jerking me around. He really felt he could help me.

"How do I know if your information is worth anything?"

He shrugged. "I guess you'll have to pay me to find out. It's no big deal to me either way. Now, excuse me, I've got to take care of some chores—"

"All right, all right," I said.

I downloaded some credit to his account. He told me he knew somebody who could take me to him. I downloaded some more credit. He told me the person was him. I downloaded an obscene amount of credit and he told me to be outside in ten minutes.

THREE HOURS of hiking later, we pushed through a wall of blood-red Tasid vines and into a clearing. It had rained only for the first hour, and baked us in eyelid-sticking heat for the next two, but such was the humidity that my clothes still felt sopping wet. I'd even bought the best rain gear my guide's shop had to offer, but it hadn't made a whit of difference.

The feathery branches of the mushroom-shaped Vidi trees

blocked all but a few glimmerings of sunlight, sunlight that reflected off the mirrored exterior of a tent in the center of the clearing. It was covered in solar panels, I realized, and of course that made perfect sense. Weak as the light was, it would probably provide just enough charge for a single android.

My guide—he told me his name was Asif Phoenix, and that was the only thing he'd said despite my repeated questioning—gestured to the hut. I nodded, too out of breath to answer. He, on the other hand, didn't even look like he'd cracked a sweat. I wondered how many years he'd been trekking up and down the mountain.

"You in there, Vergon?" I said.

It took a moment, but the flap in the tent opened and then there he was—Vergon Daughn, in the flesh. Or in the silicon-plastic compound, as it were. He wore a camo outfit much like my guide's, except that Vergon's covered every inch of his body. He was shorter and less imposing than I'd expected from his holos.

"How did you ..." he began, and then he saw Asif. "Ah, so how much did he pay you?"

"Enough," Asif said.

"So much for loyalty," Vergon said.

"You didn't pay me to be loyal."

"I see. In the end, it's always about the money, isn't it?"

Asif said nothing, simply standing there looking imposing. Vergon turned to me.

"Did she hire you?"

I nodded.

"I thought as much. My other thought was that you were an assassin sent by Granger Holdings, but if that were the case, I would most likely be dead by now. Who are you?"

"My name's Dexter Duff," I said.

"Well, Mister Duff—"

"Just Duff."

"Duff, then. Fine. Do you have any idea why I'm here?"

I looked at him carefully. He didn't seem insane to me, though I'd been wrong about those sorts of things before. How could you tell if an android was insane, anyway? He could have been hiding from Granger Holdings, but the most likely reason Granger Holdings was out to get him in the first place was because his own erratic behavior had allowed the company's value to plummet. That left the conclusion I'd come to after mulling it over for a few weeks.

"I don't know why an android would be interested in a woman like Ginger," I said. "I don't know why an android would be interested in *any* woman, to be honest. But I figure you wanted to know what it was like to love her for real. Except when you got what you wanted, maybe you realized love wasn't all it was cracked up to be. Maybe you even realized she didn't love you so much after all. You see, I know Ginger. I've known her for years. I don't know if she's capable of loving anyone. And when you figured this out too, it left you so heartbroken you didn't want to go on feeling that way anymore, so you went back to being android."

He said nothing for a while, intense eyes boring into me, studying me the way a scientist might examine a specimen under a microscope.

"You're a perceptive man, Duff," he said finally.

"No, I just learn from experience. I fell for her once too, you know."

He nodded. "She has a special kind of charm. Everything you said is correct, though I am not here because I am heartbroken."

"No?"

"Of course not. I am here because I became convinced shortly after the wedding that Ginger intended on killing me."

It was a possibility I hadn't considered. "Why would she do that? You're her ticket to riches and fame."

"No, Vergon Enterprises is her ticket to riches and fame. Besides, that's not what she wants. It's power."

"I don't see why that would make a ..." I began, and then I did see it. Vergon Daughn may have made Ginger rich, but Vergon Enterprises could make her rich and powerful. The problem was Vergon himself. *He* was the one calling the shots. But once they were married ... "I get it," I said. "Once you were married, she could bump you off and then she'd inherit the company."

"Exactly. Of course, it would have been easier if I had remained an android, since so few planets grant us the same rights as biosen. She could have deactivated me any number of ways. When I became human, it made her job more difficult, which gave me just enough time to escape."

I shook my head. As well as I'd known Ginger, I should have seen that angle long before now. "I feel like an idiot," he said.

"Don't feel bad," Vergon said. "Ironically, I didn't recognize this possibility myself until I was a human. As an android, I kept giving her the benefit of the doubt, assuming that her unusual behaviors were due to the irrationality of her human emotions. But once I, myself, had human emotions, I could see that she herself lacked them—or at least any beyond greed and desire."

"I should never have come here," I said.

"No, you shouldn't have. It's quite likely you were followed."

I thought of the android who'd tailed me weeks earlier. From time to time, I'd had that feeling again that I was being followed, though I'd never seen him. "So you don't really think Granger Holdings is after you?"

"Oh, I do," he said. "That's what complicates matters. I came here until I could figure out a way to divorce Ginger, but my absence left an opening for Granger to move in. Now I'm in a predicament. I honestly came here to protect the more than one million people who work for me. But whether my wife gets control of the company or Granger, those employees get hurt either way."

My wife. I felt an odd pang of jealousy and I didn't know why. It was just a job, of course, one that paid better than any job I'd had before, but no matter how well a job paid, I never set out to hurt an innocent person if I could help it. Was Vergon Daughn innocent? Was *I* innocent? Both of us had stupidly pursued a woman incapable of any kind of real love, and for that, we probably deserved whatever punishment we received. But I felt a lot more empathy for him than I might have felt for someone else.

"I'll do whatever I can to help," I said.

He looked at me. "I'm going to speak to her. Perhaps an understanding can be reached. I have to assume there's at least a shred of decency in her."

"All right," I said, skeptical.

"But I'm still concerned she's going to try to kill me. Will you come with me?"

"Of course."

With that, he pulled out a com-com and called for a pod to pick us up off the mountain. Twenty minutes later, we were on our way to the spaceport. Asif watched us lift off, his face as stoic and remorseless as when I'd first met him.

WE FIGURED the stepdocks would be more heavily watched than the spaceports, so the plan was to leave the planet by ship. At my suggestion, Vergon bought an evening ticket at the spaceport closet to Nelsani, and then we landed the pod and rode a bakak-pulled buggy three hours to a much larger spaceport. The concourse was crowded and noisy, packed with every life-form imaginable, and we hung out in the bar until a few minutes before the flight to Palfacia Prime was scheduled to leave.

Then Vergon bought us two tickets and we hurried to the security lines, ending up behind a couple of hairy and stinky

Srendians. It was like standing behind a blue carpet that had been soaked in formaldehyde.

He looked at me. "You were in love with her?"

"Yeah."

"Why didn't you marry her?"

I shrugged. "I would have, but she ran out on me. I guess I wasn't rich enough or powerful enough for her."

"You were fortunate then."

I laughed, though he reacted in surprise, as if he hadn't meant it as a joke.

"There's one thing I don't understand," I said. "Bwer-Fwer said there was a problem with the transfer process. Do you know what happened there? He was worried your mind got scrambled, but you seem fine."

We got to the front of the line and he handprinted the ticket-checker. Androids didn't have fingerprints like humans, but they did have unique digital signatures; the machine beeped and said his name, his flight time, and his departure gate. An older human couple ahead of us craned their heads around. So it'd begun: He'd been recognized, and I'd only feel better once we were airborne. His flight and identity verified, Vergon was about to step through the security tunnel. He looked at me, dropping his voice to a whisper.

"The only problem that I know of—" he began.

But I never learned what the problem was. There was an electric shriek and the center of Vergon's chest exploded in flames.

He crumpled over, and a blue wave of fire enveloped his body, eating it up, turning it into nothing but dust. It was a plasma bolt—there was no way to stop it from completely disintegrating him. People screamed and stampeded. My shock lasted only an instant, and then I turned and saw the attacker fleeing—the blond android who'd pursued me earlier, dressed in the orange and red flowery garb of the local monks.

I took off after him. He was much faster, but he made the mistake of glancing over his shoulder at me. In the meantime, a sweeperbot rolled into his path and he tripped. I was on him in a second, my laser pistol jammed up into his chin. His eyes remained passive; he might have been watching a food processor churning out cheese.

"Tell me who you're working for!" I cried.

Beneath my legs, his chest felt warm and getting warmer. He closed his eyes, and I realized what was happening, rolling off of him just before his body exploded.

I WOKE UP in the spaceport's infirmary, two shiny medical robots tending to my wounds and a dozen green-uniformed police waiting in the wings. I had a few nasty cuts on my face and arms, and a minor concussion, but otherwise I'd been lucky. It was nearly four hours before I was able to convince the police I had nothing to do with Vergon's death, and then they were gracious enough to let me out a back door so I could avoid the hordes of media gathered outside.

I left the spaceport and walked under a blazing sun to a little hole-in-the-wall diner, sequestering myself in the com-com unit at the back. It smelled like piss and smoke inside, and even through the glass door I could hear the wince-inducing Nelsani harp music playing from the diner's speakers.

Ginger answered my page within ten seconds. She was in the back of a plush pod, the seats dark leather, and her glittering, silver outfit looked like it was made of diamonds. The camera was angling from a low viewpoint, giving her three breasts the appearance of an imposing mountain range.

"You killed him," I said.

She looked puzzled. "Whatever are you talking about, dear? Did you find Vergon?"

"Don't lie to me, Ginger. I'm sure you've seen the news by now."

At my saying this, she turned to her right and punched something out of my view. She said nothing for a moment, then sighed.

"How sad," she said, and she didn't sound sad at all. "He meant everything to me."

"Like hell he did. You killed him."

"That's quite an accusation, Duff. You have some proof of this?"

"I'll get some."

She smiled primly. "Oh, I don't think so. You can't prove something that isn't true."

"Ginger—"

"Now if you'll excuse me," she said, "I've got a company to save from takeover. And with me in charge, you better believe things are looking up for Vergon Enterprises." She looked at me levelly. "Because I'll do whatever it takes to get to the top. You know that, Duff, don't you?"

"Damn it, Ginger—"

"In fact, I always like being on top." Her smile turned coy. "Maybe you should come visit me and I'll show you exactly what I mean. I guarantee that by tomorrow we'll see eye for an eye on this."

"It's eye *to* eye, you idiot," I said, and punched off.

I was shaking, and I wanted to smash something. Ginger had won. That wasn't even the worst part. The worst part was that for just an instant, a tiny flicker of a moment, I'd actually thought about taking her up on her offer. It made me feel more lousy than I'd felt in my entire life.

It was only then that I realized why I'd taken the case at all. Crazy as it was, I'd secretly been hoping I could win her back.

* * * * *

RETURNING TO VERSATIA, I threw myself into my work checking the hotel security, hoping it would help put the whole mess with Ginger out of my mind. It didn't. I found myself following what was happening with Vergon Enterprises and Granger Holdings with great interest, secretly praying that Granger would put Ginger out on her ass. Granger might still put thousands out of work, but at least Ginger wouldn't gain from it.

I'd always been of the atheist persuasion—I'd seen too much to believe in any sort of almighty God—but what happened next was enough to challenge my conviction. *Somebody* must have heard my prayers, because Granger got control of Vergon Enterprises within a month. Not only that, but the way the deal went down left Ginger out in the cold with only a few million credit in her pocket. A few million was certainly nothing to sneeze at, but it was less than one-hundredth of one percent of what her estate had been worth before Granger took over. She was all over the vids threatening to sue, insisting a great injustice had been due, but all the legal experts said there was nothing she could do.

More amazingly, Granger didn't break up Vergon Enterprises. They *expanded* it. People didn't lose their jobs. They got raises. New stepdock deals with planets coming into the Unity Worlds fell into place, almost as if Granger had been holding back on making those deals until the takeover was finished. If Vergon was still alive, he would have been incredibly happy at how it had all turned out—*if* he could have felt happiness, that was.

That's when I figured out what had really happened.

THE RAIN FELL in torrents, slicing into the thick Nelsani jungle. I stepped into the hut and lowered my hood. Despite the weather, the little shop was bustling, the aisles full of customers browsing the gear. I found Asif at the counter, handing a box of shoes to a hairy Srendian and her hairy child. I waited until they shuffled away.

"Busy day," I said.

He turned in my direction, smiling the plastic salesman's smile, but when he recognized me it faded.

"You," he said. "I'm surprised to see you here again."

"Really?" I said. "I guess you don't think very highly of me then."

"I'm sorry?"

"I mean, if you thought more highly of me, then you might fear I'd figure out your little secret ... Vergon."

To his credit, he didn't even blink. But then, that only confirmed my suspicion. We stared at each other in the crowded room, the murmur of customers all around us. The rain crackled on the roof. I'd deliberately spoken softly enough that the customers perusing the gravboards over in the corner wouldn't hear me.

I stepped forward so we were even closer, dropping my voice to a whisper. "Don't insult me by denying it," I said.

He said nothing for a long time, then nodded. "How did you know?"

"A couple things," I said. "Your name, first of all. Asif Phoenix? As in, the phoenix that rises from its own ashes? It was a little too cute."

"Right."

"And then there was how you didn't even break a sweat scaling up the mountain."

"Of course. I should have been more careful and installed sweat glands."

"It was pretty clever," I said. "I never would have put it together except how things went down with Granger Holdings and

Vergon Enterprises. When I realized it was exactly the way you would have *wanted* things to go down, I understood why Granger Holdings bought out Mind-Body Technologies, and I also knew what the problem Bwer-Fwer mentioned was. It wasn't a problem at all. It was just that you couldn't quite cover all your tracks. You created a second android, didn't you? You created two Vergons."

"No," he said. "There was only one Vergon Daughn and he died. It had to be that way for my plan to work. I am Asif Phoenix. That is my identity."

"But you have Vergon's memories?"

"Yes. For all intents and purposes, I *am* Vergon. I only changed my identity in the physical sense. Inside, I am still the same person."

"A person who happens to covertly control an ownership stake in Granger Holdings?"

"Yes."

I nodded, amazed at the brilliance and audacity of his plan. Once he'd realized that Ginger would kill him to get what she wanted, he knew that the only way to stop her was to actually die and then have another company take over and force her out. She would have gotten at least half of his net worth in a divorce, which would have probably destroyed Vergon Enterprises in the process.

"Why not bump her off yourself?" I asked. "That would have been a lot easier."

"Easier, yes," he said. "But I'm not that kind of android, and despite what Ginger is, I am still concerned for her welfare. It's why I left her with some money. I could have easily left her broke and heavily in debt. I didn't want to hurt her. I just wanted to prevent her from hurting others."

"Sounds like love to me."

"Call it what you will."

He reached behind the counter and brought up a handheld,

punching a few buttons on the tiny black keyboard. "So how much do you want?"

"Excuse me?" I said.

"I assume you want me to pay you for your silence."

"Oh no, I didn't come for that. I just came to satisfy my curiosity. And to say 'well done. ' Your secret is safe with me."

He nodded. "Thank you. I will always be in your debt."

"Only one thing I don't understand."

"Yes?"

"Why didn't you stay human? You could have transferred your essence into another human rather than an android. Did you decide that you liked being an android better than being a human?"

"No, that wasn't it. In fact, despite what I said to the media, I quite liked being a human. And I see nothing wrong with an android who decides to become one. Or vice versa."

"Then why?"

He looked thoughtful, and I wondered how much of it was in the look and how much was in the thought. After all, that android brain of his was a million times faster than mine, and any answer he'd thought of would have taken a nanosecond. The rest was just for show. Or was it? Maybe there were some things you could wrestle with for one second or for a million and it wouldn't make a difference.

"I'm not sure I could adequately explain my decision," he said.

"Try me."

"Well, perhaps it would be best if I just summed it up with a simple colloquial expression ... Ignorance is bliss."

One of the customers looking at the gravboards wandered over, asking for help, so he didn't get a chance to explain. That was okay. He didn't need to. Androids, after all, couldn't feel anything. They couldn't feel the enormous pain of being hurt by someone they loved. In that sense, I envied him. He could say that he'd loved Ginger once, but the memory of it no longer stung.

And if I wasn't so squeamish about trying to separate the essence of me from my human body, I might have asked him if he could make me an android too.

Stone Creek Station

While cleaning out my office, I pulled the old Rand McNally atlas off the shelf and the book fell open to the two-page spread of the United States. I closed my eyes and made a blind stab at the map; when I looked down at the book, my finger had fallen in the middle of Oregon. The problem was that when I lifted my finger, there wasn't a town there, just a mountain range and some lakes.

Still, I was determined to follow my method, so I turned to Oregon in the atlas, and located on the more detailed map the spot where my finger had fallen. There were a couple of small towns in the area, but one caught my eye: Stone Creek.

It was impulsive. It was insane. It wasn't anything like me at all—always deliberate, always cautious. But that was the point. If you're serious about starting over, you can't trust yourself to make a clean break. I could never stay in Denver, not on the heels of a failed marriage, and every place I thought of to start over reminded me of Anne. Didn't we have a cousin who lived in Palm Springs? And Everett—that was near Seattle, where we went with her parents on that cruise up to Alaska ... I needed something fresh, something new, and the only way to get it was to give myself over to lady luck. For once in my life.

Two weeks later, I was coaxing a ten year-old Honda Civic up through the Cascade Mountains, my possessions distilled to a box of books in the trunk and two suitcases in the backseat. The last round of budget cuts at the university had finally forced me to do what I should have done when the ink was still drying on the divorce papers, but I wouldn't miss the job. Teaching aspiring journalists had been a way to pay the rent, nothing more. After weaving my way along the main highway for an hour, tall pines lining both sides, I came upon the hand-carved wooden sign that read, "Welcome to Stone Creek." By then, the sky had melted to black and a full moon rose over the trees.

I passed a Ma and Pa grocery store, a post office, a gas station with a single pump, and a garage with a sign above it that read, "Bob's Auto Repair," except that only half the letters were visible because the sign was coated with rust. All of these places were closed. There was also a diner called the Wooden Spoon, and by the light shining through the closed blinds, and the dozen dirty pick-ups and SUVs in the parking lot, I assumed it was open.

On my way to the door, I shivered and stuffed my hands in my leather jacket. With the blinds down, there was no way to see inside, but I heard a man talking loudly. I reached to open it and saw the sign there had been turned to "Closed."

I hesitated, then shrugged and turned the knob anyway.

When I stepped inside, the bell over the door ringing, a dozen old men turned to look at me. The decoupage tables had been pushed to the edges of the room, leaving an empty space in the middle of the black-and-white tiled floor where chairs had been arranged in a circle. One of the men, a thin fellow with vanilla-colored hair and a stooped posture, was standing; the others were all in their seats. In their faded jeans and wrinkled plaid shirts, they had the look of ranchers or hunters, a few wearing cowboy hats. They were all white and old, between seventy and eighty I guessed, faces and hands wrinkled and liver-spotted.

A radio played faintly from the kitchen. Sinatra, it sounded like. The room smelled faintly of cooking grease. They looked at me as if I had just walked in naked.

"Can I help you, son?" the one who was standing asked.

"Um, yes," I said. "I'm looking for …"

This was when I noticed that two of them had shotguns on their laps.

"Yes?" the one who was standing prodded.

"Um, for Graber Inn," I said.

The one who was standing looked at a guy three to his right, a small, white-haired man who shifted in his seat. He had a long, pinched face, a tuft of white hair on his chin, his glasses tinted. He wore a tan vest over a white shirt, a square bulge in his front pocket that must have been cigarettes. He wasn't one of the ones with a shotgun—shotguns I was carefully watching to see if they moved from their owners' laps.

"I'm John Graber," he said, his voice soft and crackling like a radio tuned to a weak signal.

"Are you the owner?"

He nodded. "We're closed, though."

"Permanently?"

"Just for the weekend. Renovations. Been scheduled for months. You didn't call ahead?"

"No," I said, laughing, unnerved at how everyone was staring at me. "Is there anywhere else I can stay?"

Graber frowned and looked at the man who was standing.

"Most of the town's closed for the weekend, son," the man who was standing said. "Best to head back to the highway."

"Oh," I said. "Well, see, I really want to stay in Stone Creek."

"Why?"

I knew I should have gotten out of there, but the more they wanted me to leave, the more I wanted to stay. Looking back, I'm not sure why I was so determined to start with Stone Creek, except that it was something to grasp onto when nothing else in my life seemed worth grasping. "I'm … a travel writer," I said, "and I'm doing a story on small towns."

"Not much here worth writing about," Graber said.

I laughed. "My editor says differently."

One of the men with a shotgun, a burly fellow with a double chin, cleared his throat. He had the kind of mean-ass stare that would have made children wet their pants. "Come back next weekend," he growled.

"We really have no place to stay," Graber said. "The Inn is a mess."

"Oh," I said, backing toward the door, deciding to see just how far their lack of hospitality would go. "Well … I've got a tent in my car. I'll just camp in the woods for the night."

"This ain't no state park," the man with the shotgun snapped.

I nodded. "Yeah, well, what the government doesn't know can't hurt them, right?" I waved, turning toward the door. "It's not too cold. I should be all right."

"Wait a minute," Graber said, sighing.

"John—" the man who was standing said.

"It's all right, Larry," Graber said. He looked at me. "I do have a room you can stay in."

"We shouldn't do this," the burly man with the shotgun said.

"I won't be any trouble," I said. "Just a bed and some clean sheets is all I need."

Others were starting to speak, and Graber held up his hand to silence them. "Go left on Bogs," he said, "through the town, and stay on it for five minutes. You'll see a yellow mailbox. There's a key under the Buddha statue."

"John—" the burly man with the shotgun said.

"Let it be, Fred," the tall man said. "You go on now, son. We're having a … a town meeting here, that's all. Might be a couple of hours before John comes back."

"Sure," I said. "Sorry to intrude." I nodded at Graber. "Thanks for making an exception."

He nodded. Most of the men were frowning at me. I headed outside, feeling a little bad about lying to them. The moon was bright enough that I saw my shadow on the gravel. Getting into the Honda, I saw a crack appear in the blinds.

I eased the car onto the main road. I was planning on heading to the motel when I felt the itch. It's the itch that every reporter feels when he senses a story. My first instinct was to ignore the feeling, which was what I usually did. But seeing the old guys back in the diner reminded me of Dad. He would have been about the same age. Dad had been so happy when I decided to follow him into journalism, and equally as disappointed when I told him I didn't think it was something I was cut out to do.

"You won't guilt me into this," I said aloud.

I drove a little farther, to the edge of town now, then remembered something he had said to me shortly before he died, and about six months before we stopped speaking to one another. He had discovered that I had been in Honolulu a year earlier, when Senator Brown's daughter lost her legs to a shark on Wakiki Beach, and he wondered why I hadn't gotten the story. When I told them I had been on vacation, he had wrinkled his nose in that distinctive way that made me feel like used cat litter and said, "A good reporter is always on the job." In all my life, I could never remember Dad saying he was proud of me. Never once did he pat me on the back and say I was doing well. It was always, "You didn't get that ending right," or, "Is this really the truth of the story?"

A good reporter is always on the job.

"Shit," I said, and took a hard right into the parking lot next to the auto repair shop. There was some space behind the building, where my car would be out of sight from the main road, and that's where I parked. When my headlights fell on the dumpster, a black and white cat sprinted through the hole in the chain link fence.

I walked briskly back to the diner, staying in the shadows. I circled around to the parking lot side, to the last window. Heart pounding, I cupped my ear against the cool glass. There was a conversation going on, one voice lapping right up against another, but I could only make a few words.

"… train … last time … make sure of it …"

"… why can't we … a few of us …"

"No! The risk …"

"… got to be this way …"

"… easy for you …"

"… we agreed … vote stands …"

This went on for ten minutes, but I never could get a good sense of what they were talking about. Suddenly the voices stopped and I heard what sounded like chairs and tables scooting along the floor. The front door rattled, the bell rang, and I ducked behind the building. The shadows were so deep there it was like stepping into a black cloud. I banged my shin against a gas meter and I had to bite my lip to stop myself from making any sound. I massaged my leg, expecting any moment a cacophony of voices, a slapping of backs, a see you next time, Bill and Bob and Lou. But instead I heard only the crunching of feet on the gravel. Then this noise stopped, the door closed and then there was only the sound of the pines stirring in the breeze.

I remained absolutely still.

"You all ready?" one of them said. I recognized it as the voice of the tall one—Larry.

There was a murmur of ascent.

"All right, then," Larry said. "No sense waiting. Got good

moon."

I heard them walking on the gravel again, and then it changed to the duller sound of them walking on asphalt, the footfalls moving away. Cautiously, I peered around the corner and saw them walking down the center of the street, two or three abreast. Several had flashlights trained on the ground. I watched them as they walked to the edge of the town, and I wondered if this was some sort of ritual that concluded their meetings, a pleasure stroll before getting in their cars and going home to their wives. I expected them to turn and head back, but instead they kept walking, not along the curve of the road, but straight into the woods.

Afraid they would reappear, I hesitated, then decided *what the hell*. I reached the woods perhaps a minute after them. Winded, my sweaty shirt sticking to my chest, I lingered there until my heart stopped pounding in my ears. A thick wall of ferns blocked my passage. I heard the crackle of twigs and dry leaves in the distance, and I plunged through the ferns.Moonlight breaking through the gaps in the trees allowed me to see a narrow trail, tall grass crowding the way. I was wondering if I might have lost them somehow when I heard a murmur of voices directly to my right, off the trail. I turned in their direction, having to force my way through a wall of prickly bushes whose branches scratched at my exposed face and neck like sharp fingernails, and then I was in the open again.

The canopy of pine trees blocked most of the light, but I made my way by targeting the occasional spot of moonlight, one after another. I heard the voices, and this time they were louder and more distinct, so I slowed, careful to watch where I stepped. I came upon a dry creek bed a dozen feet across, pines crowding both sides like spectators at a parade. Leaning out into the open, I saw flashes of light up ahead, in what appeared to be the middle of the ravine.

Watching the lights, I became aware of a peculiar shape up

ahead, in the middle of a circular area that must have once been the pond that fed the creek. It was some type of house. As I approached, I saw a flat area out in front, a long, narrow deck. Then I saw the two dark bands stretching in front of the structure, and suddenly the shape made sense. It was a train station. The dark bands were train tracks—tracks that only extended as far as the edges of the creek bed.

"Hold it right there, mister," a voice said behind me.

I slipped forward into the ravine, and had to sit to stop from going down. When I turned, one of the old men from the diner was standing there, a bald, heavy-set fellow in overalls, a shotgun in the crook of his arm. I was relieved to see he wasn't pointing it at me.

"Damn," he said, shaking his head. He had a slightly protruding forehead, his eyes lost in shadows. "Larry thought he heard something, but … What the hell are you doing up here?"

I swallowed. "Well …"

"Guess it don't matter now," he said. "Come on, head down there toward the others."

"Look," I said, "I didn't mean anything. I'll just go. I'm—"

"That ain't gonna happen now," he said. "Don't make me ask again."

Frowning, he shifted the shotgun in his arms. I walked down into the ravine, him trailing behind. The bottom of the creek bed was littered with rocks under the grass, and my foot came down painfully on them more than once. As we neared the other men, I saw them turn on the platform, heard the hollowness of their footsteps on the wood. When they shined their flashlights on me, I could only see them in silhouette. I stopped when I reached the train tracks—real train tracks, shiny and new.

"You were right," the one behind me said.

"Damn, son," Larry said. He was standing in the middle of the bunch.

I wondered just how the hell I could get out of this situation. "Look, I … called my editor on my cell phone before I came up here. She knows where I am. I was just … just looking around, and—"

"Calm down," Larry said. "We're not gonna hurt you. It's just unfortunate you're here, that's all."

"He can't be here when the train comes!" It was the burly guy with the shotgun. Fred.

"What do you want do want to do?" Larry snapped. "Shoot him?" When Fred didn't answer, he said, "None of us here are killers."

"But the vote …" It was Graber, the Inn owner.

"The vote is the same," Larry said.

"But he might talk," someone else said, a man who hadn't spoken before. "People might come looking."

Larry was silent a moment. "Well, we'll just have to trust he'll do the right thing. Come on up here, son. Train might be here at any moment, and there's something we need to tell you. Point your flashlights away from him, boys, so he can see."

Train? Wondering just what kind of pack of loonies I was dealing with here, I stepped over the tracks and climbed onto the platform. With the flashlights directed away, I got a better look at the station in the moonlight, and I marveled at the craftsmanship. There was a ticket window, several benches, and a sign hanging from chains with shiny brass letters: "Stone Creek Station."

"Did you guys build this?" I asked.

"Yes," Larry said.

"Why?"

Before he could answer, a far-off whistle pierced the stillness. Everyone backed up, fanning out along the platform. I turned along with them, hearing other sounds now: the churning creek of wheels, the screech of brakes, the hiss of steam, getting louder. I expected a joke, a guy with a boom box maybe, but then I saw a black oval appear above the end of the tracks to my left.

Thinking it was something in my eye, I blinked several times, but the spot didn't go away; instead, it grew in size, blotting out the forest behind it. A light appeared in the blackness. The screeching became deafening, the whistle came again, and then a shape emerged from the rift.

I saw a headlight. Black chrome. A smokestack.

A train.

The steam-driven locomotive pulled to a stop in front of us, smoke rising from the stack, a single red passenger car in tow. A band of yellow lights extended along the top edge of the passenger car. The interior was lighted, and I saw the shadowy silhouettes of passengers, perhaps a dozen of them, sitting at the windows.

At first, I thought perhaps the windows were tinted, but I realized with a cold chill that it wasn't so: I could clearly see the green-felt seats and the yellow walls; only the people were fuzzy to me, borderless, their distinctiveness washed out and grayed. It was as if each of them wore a black nylon netting stretched tight over their bodies.

A door at the rear of the passenger car opened and these dark apparitions filed onto the platform. I backed away, but the others stood their ground. When the figures reached the group, each of them stopped in front of a different man.

"Son?"

I felt the hairs on the back of my neck rise. I knew the voice even before I turned and saw him—a lanky, sixty-year-old man with big hands and a full head of gray hair, his gold-rimmed bifocals low on his nose. He was dressed in a white, button-up shirt left open at the collar, red suspenders, and pleated brown slacks. It was what he usually wore, except sometimes the shirt was blue instead of white. He was wearing it the last time I saw him, when I told him to go to hell.

My mouth went dry, and when I tried to speak, my throat

constricted so that the word came out as more of a gasp.

"Dad?" I said.

Even in the moonlight, he seemed solid, as a real person should. He definitely didn't look like the apparitions that had emerged from the train; then I saw that there *were* no more apparitions. All of them had become real people, men and women alike, some old, some young, even a child or two among them. They were talking to the men from the diner.

"How have you been doing?" Dad asked.

"Fine," I said, swallowing.

"And Anne?"

I didn't answer. What was I supposed to say? We got divorced, Dad. She cheated on me and she had ever reason because I was never much of a husband. That what you wanted to hear? I learned from the best. You didn't teach me much, Dad, but you certainly taught me how to fail at being a decent human being.

But I didn't want to ruin the moment. Something amazing was happening, and I didn't want to ruin it. I tried to bottle all the bitterness inside.

"She's fine," I said.

"Good, good, glad to hear it," he said, though he didn't sound like he cared all that much one way or the other. "What paper are you working for now?"

The fear I'd felt seconds earlier was gone, replaced by a rising irritation. I didn't like the direction the conversation was going. It was falling into a familiar routine.

"Various places," I said.

"What paper?"

"Did I say I was working for a paper?"

"No reason to get angry."

"I'm *not* angry," I said, though clearly I was. And then everything I'd been pushing down deep inside broke free. "What, you want to hear that I'm out of work? Well, it's true. I'm a bum.

I was certainly never good at being a reporter, but you already knew that, didn't you? It probably makes you happy seeing how miserable I am now, doesn't it?"

"Don't be ridiculous," he said stonily. "How could you think that of me?"

I turned away. A mild sense of panic swelled up inside me. I didn't know what was happening, but I sensed that it was an opportunity that might never come again. Here was a chance to mend things, and I didn't want to squander it.

"I'm sorry," I said, turning back to him. "I'm sorry about what happened, you know." My throat was tightening. It was hard to get out the words. "Really, I'm sorry. I'm sorry about not speaking to you. About not coming to the hospital. But you understand, don't you? I couldn't ... I thought I was a failure in your eyes."

"I only wanted you to live up to your potential," he said.

I don't know what I expected him to say, but that certainly wasn't it. I opened my mouth to answer, then shook my head and laughed at the absurdity of it all, us repeating the same lines we had said dozens of times before, now, in this place. Wasn't this supposed to be one of those fairy tale moments when the father realizes how wrong he has been to the son, when he apologizes and asks for forgiveness, when all past hurts are healed and all past wrongs are put to rest?

"I don't believe you," I said. "You're dead, and you still won't change."

"I only wanted the best for you," he said.

"Why couldn't you just tell me you love me for who I am?"

"You shouldn't need me to say such a thing. You should be stronger than that."

It was then that I realized that no amount of hoping or expecting or wanting could get someone to be other than who they were. People may change or they may not, but they had to do it on their own. And once they were gone, even that possibility died, too. All you could do was come to terms with the memories—to accept the choices you made and make the best of them. For the first time, I also realized that I had been doing my best my whole life to fail as a journalist, because I had been sure I could never be as good as my father.

The train whistle sounded.

Dad was opening his mouth to say something else, but I didn't give him another chance to hurt me. I grabbed him and hugged him. I couldn't have said whether he felt like my father, because I couldn't remember the last time I hugged him, but he felt as I imagined he would: thin and frail, a man who was much bigger in print than he was in real life.

Then, as I turned to smile at him, his image faded and became shadow-like. My arms slipped through him as if he was made of air. I saw his head dip as he nodded at me, then he joined the other apparitions filing toward the train. Some of the men around me were weeping. One by one, the shadow-things climbed aboard, slipping into their seats, a few waving hazy arms, a few pressing cloudy faces up to the glass. The engine churned to life, the wheels turned, and with a screech the train lurched forward and disappeared through the dark spot on the other side of the tracks.

When it was gone, I turned, and there were all the men gathering around me. There was happiness. There was grief. I saw hope and despair. Life was complicated. I realized that death should be no different.

"How long have you been doing this?" I asked.

Larry, looking drained, stepped up to me. "I'll answer all of your questions," he said. "But first you got to promise you'll help us with something."

"What's that?"

He looked at his friends gathered around him, then back at

me. A stiff breeze rifled through the trees, making the sign hanging above us creak.

"Help us destroy this place," he said.

THE NEXT DAY, armed with cans of gasoline and a dozen fire extinguishers, we returned to Stone Creek Station. The place didn't seem so impressive in the harsh light of a noonday sun. Within an hour, we had burned it to the ground.

They told me they had woken ten years earlier, all with the same vision: to build the station in this specific place in the woods, and to be there on a full moon in November. Why the vision came to these particular men they didn't know, except, they figured, all of them had recently lost somebody important. Each of them saw that person when the train appeared. Every year, they had returned to the station, a few of them dying off along the way, until ten years had passed. Though they had been old men when they started, at least they had been living. Now they had spent their whole year waiting for the next time the train appeared.

They could either keep clinging to the past, or finally get on with their lives. Wait any longer, they realized, and there would be no lives left.

So the vote was taken, the ayes had it, and I was there when the vision was turned into a smoky ruin. When I told them who I was, the truth this time, they said it was fate that had guided my hand on the atlas. They said I was there to share this truth with other people, so they could see there was no good in wanting the memory of someone you love to come to life. Because all that you regretted before, you would still regret when that person went back to being a memory again.

I insisted I was no longer a reporter. I told them it wasn't something I wanted to do. And they said if that was true, then why did you follow us?

So here I am, back to journalism. I may never win a Pulitzer, but I'll also never ignore that itch again, the one I feel when I'm on to a story. One last thing: If you take the time to open an atlas, you may have trouble finding Stone Creek, Oregon. Although I said I'd write about what happened, I also promised I wouldn't reveal the real location or their real names. I did visit a real town in a real state, and it may have been Oregon, but it also may have been Washington or California or Idaho. Hell, it may have been on the East Coast. I'm not saying. But I got the story. I got it for me. Dad may not have liked the way I told it, but it was the truth the way I saw it, and I'm finally okay with that being enough.

Deep Down in the Diggyback

The beast with two heads came at night and stood outside her brother's window. He came after the coughing stopped and their parents had gone to bed. He came whether it was rainy or windy or still.

"Sammy," Derrick would say, his scratchy voice hard to hear above the droning furnace, "Sammy, I see his shadow."

Each time it happened, she threw her sheets aside and ran into his room, following the nightlight to his bunk bed. There her brother would be waiting, the sheets pulled back. She would join him in bed, even though his parents said *no, you never know what you can give him, pneumonia maybe.* Together they would stare at the blinds.

"He's big, bigger than a horse," he told her one rainy night, "and each of his heads has two horns. He's always whispering but they're words I can't understand, another language maybe. Sometimes he scratches the glass with his fingernails. Mostly he just stands there. He lives in the Diggyback."

The Diggyback was what the kids of the neighborhood called

the forest of pines at the end of the street, a forest a mile long that separated their neighborhood from the one beyond it. It was thick with ferns, ivy, and other plants. Kids dug there for buried treasure, which was how it got its name. But they would only go so far. There was a dark, foreboding place deep down in the Diggyback that made you cold just to look at it.

"Have you seen him?" Samantha asked. "I mean, other than his shadow?"

"Once," Derrick said, gulping. "Once I saw him. We came home late that one time from that doctor in Chicago. Remember? It was late and I was sleeping in the car and Daddy brought me in and put me in bed. He forgot to close the blinds and since I wasn't awake I couldn't remind him. So then I woke up like I usually do and I was coughing. And the first thing—the first thing I saw, when I was coughing, was *him*. Standing in the window. He was whistling. High and low. Up and down."

Samantha remembered his screaming, how loud it had been. "What did he look like?" she asked.

"He was ..." Derrick started, but then he shook his head and pulled his blanket up to his nose.

"But what did he—"

"No, no," he said, shaking his head. "But ... but it's good that you're here. He always goes away when you're here."

So she stayed ready, because she never knew when the beast would visit. At school, she was always tired, and when she wasn't tired she was angry. Her parents made her speak to the short man in glasses who held up shapes and said "Tell me what you see." It was always the same: the beast from the Diggyback. Derrick's coughing became worse, and no amount of whacking him on the back would make it go away. The mucus got thicker and gooier. He went to lots of doctors. The pill bottles in the bathroom were always taking up the counter space and falling on the floor. She tried to stay ready, she always did, but then came the night when he was eight and she was twelve. She was so tired, her eyelids couldn't stay open.

She woke to a screech of a window sliding open and the clatter of blinds being pushed aside. She heard a word—she thought it was her brother's voice saying "Ssss," as in the beginning of her name—but then it was cut off. She lay there stiff in bed, frozen with fear, and then there came a whispering from the other room of strange words. *Dibidy bibidy deoxyribonuclease ... Pamma wamma pancreatic ...*

She sprang out of bed and ran into the other room, hollering to scare it away. When she got there, his bed was empty, and the blinds were swinging. A cold breeze tickled her neck. She caught the shuffle of footsteps on the grass, a *paddy-pad-pad.*

She grabbed her slippers and her pink robe, then dashed back to her brother's room. When she climbed out the window, her foot caught on the window sill. She fell in the damp grass, her nose full of the fertilizer her father had spread on the lawn only yesterday.

The houses were still. A cat meowed several houses down. The air was cool on her skin. Standing there on the grass, all but naked to the breeze that shook the birch trees hugging her parent's yard, she felt afraid.

Then, a faint whistle: *high-low-high.*

She looked up and she saw them, passing through a pool of yellow lamplight down the street, the shadow of the beast, and next to him, grasped by the beast's burly hand, the matchstick-thin boy unmistakable to her even in silhouette.

"Derrick!" she shouted.

"Sammy! Sammy!" he cried.

The creature, as tall as the one-story houses around it, tucked her brother under his arm and ran for the Diggyback. For a moment, she saw the color of its skin, green and brown, like swamp water speckled with bits of mossy bark. The lamplights led right to the Diggyback, but that's where they stopped and the real darkness began, giving way to tall pines swaying in the night.

She followed the beast, her slippers slapping along the pavement. She heard a chuckle that was deep and lippy, like the chuckle of her great-grandmother before she died when she took off her teeth and put them there in the jar next to her bed. Her Momma would tell her to say nighty-night, Grandma, and Samantha did, just as she was told. Her great grandmother would laugh that awful toothless gurgling laugh with saliva dripping over her cracked lips. The beast's laugh was like that only worse, the scariest sound she had ever heard.

While she ran, she remembered what they talked about only two nights before when they were hiding under the covers, their faces damp with perspiration.

"Do you think he's real?" he asked.

"Who?"

"God."

Samantha had decided long ago that there was no God, at least not a *kind* God, because no kind god would ever do this to her brother—not to someone as good and gentle as Derrick. And if he was a *mean* God, what was the point in believing in him?

"Yes," she lied. "Yes, I do."

"I think there is, too," he said, "but he's lost. He's out there somewhere, but he can't find his way home."

The dogs around her started barking, their howling rising up out of the silence, little ones, big ones, joining in a chorus. It was dark, no moon, no stars. She heard the thumping of the beast's feet. She reached the edge of street, the last lamp like a gatekeeper to the Diggyback. She heard rustling in the tall grass, and she hesitated there, afraid to go farther.*High-low-high.*

She charged inside, the muddy ground squishing under her slippers. The grass whipped at her ankles and her arms. She was into the trees, and the light receded behind her, just a spot now, then a dot, then hardly anything at all. The smell of the air had a tang to it, a bite, that nipped at the insides.

A call, faint: *"Sammy!"*

She pressed on and came to the place where she felt cold. The trees arched, canopy-like, over an opening into a thick wall of ferns. All the kids, when they came to Diggyback, would point at the dark place through the ferns and say that's where they buried 'em, that's where they died, that's where the evil spirits and ghosts and goblins hunker down in the bushes and wait for kids to come inside, the kids who are only looking for berries or spiders or slimy-slick snakes—and then, *bam,* the bad ones spring up and snatch the kids in their mouths and slurp 'em down. In all their days near the Diggyback, Samantha had known only one who went even part way into the bushes—the boney, white-faced kid that she loved with all her heart, her Derrick, who would go up to edge of it and stick his fingers into the deep of the shadow. Only for a moment, just a beat, and then off they would run, all the kids, as if the devil and all the demons of hell were nipping at their ankles.

Last one out is a rotting corpse! Last one out is gobbled up and gone!

But that's where his voice had come from, so she pushed through the ferns, and stood there a moment, the silence cutting her down the middle like a knife.

High-low-high.

It was not far now. Steeling herself, she ran into the cold place, calling his name. Her own name came back to her like a faint echo. She pushed through the bushes, going deeper into the darkness of the Diggyback. Soon she saw a light coming from this place, a blue, flickering, phosphorescent light, and the more she walked, the brighter it became.

When she pushed through into the light, she saw its source— dozens of children perched on the sides of a grassy knoll. Only the children weren't really there at all, because she could see through them as if they were nothing but smoke over a fire. When the breeze came, they blew with it before coming back and settling.

There in the center of the children, at the edge of a pond, stood the beast with two heads. He cradled her brother under his arm like a rolled-up newspaper. The light was pale but Samantha could see the beast well enough. When she was in the hospital visiting her grandmother, she once had the opportunity to look upon a man in the next room who had been horribly burned. The nurses were changing his bandages and she saw him in all his ghoulish detail—the blackened skin, the disfigured face, the sores spread over his splintered body. This creature was uglier.

He was big but not muscular, his rolls of fat covered with red scabs. His belly was round, bulging like an oil drum. His heads were a mismatch of parts from other animals. One head had buggy frog eyes, a wolf's snout, the ears of a rabbit, and a black, tangled beard that grew in all directions. The other had a buzzard's beak, the sad eyes of a horse, and long, braided white hair. Both had two bone-colored horns tipped with red. There was something about the second head, the one with the white hair, that made him less fearsome—a certain gleam in the eyes.

"I want my brother," Samantha said, approaching.

The black-bearded head threw back his head and laughed. The white-haired head looked at her with pity. That's how Samantha thought of them from that point on—as black-beard and white-hair.

"Let me go!" Derrick shouted. "Let me—"

The beast placed his huge hand over the boy's head, silencing him. Only Derrick's eyes were visible between the cracks in the beast's fingers.

"Please don't hurt him," Samantha pleaded.

She was only a few steps away. The smell was awful. She wasn't sure if it was from him or the pond, but it was like the stench from the refrigerator when there was something rotting in there, only a hundred times worse.

"What are you?" Samantha said.

"Staphylococcus Aureus," black-beard said.

"I don't understand," Samantha said.

"Pseudomonas Aeruginosa," white-hair said.

Samantha realized that it was speaking in that other language, the one they couldn't understand. She thought it sounded familiar. Like how the doctors talked when they talked with Mommy and Daddy.

"I won't let you take him," Samantha said.

Impulsively, she ran forward and seized her brother's hand. Black-beard, chuckling, merely looked down at her. Samantha couldn't pry her brother her lose. Derrick was looking drowsy, his eyelids halfway closed.

"Let him go!" Samantha cried.

Black-beard bared his fangs, and out between the cracks in the teeth came the foulest air, dark like soot. She fell backwards, landing painfully on her bottom. The smell was fouler than the dump when she helped her father take the leaves there.

"Don't ... please. . ." she said, feeling suddenly drowsy. The air was making her tired, and she struggled to remain awake.

"Please, please," black-beard said, mocking her.

He turned and took a step toward the pond. He had one leg in the murky water. Her brother lay limp in his arms, his eyes glassy, his skin as white as the paper Samantha used before she drew the pictures for the funny-looking doctor. She could hardly move. She didn't want the beast to get away, but her strength was gone.

"Ibbidy dibbidy do!" white-hair cried, his head turned in her direction.

She managed to get up. The beast was at the water's edge. She threw herself on his leg and attached herself like a shackle.

Her elbow plunged briefly into the water. It burned. Not hot or cold, but more like a feeling, like a horrible hurt when someone said something mean to her. Her nose was just inches from the surface of the water, and she saw in the water's reflection not her face, but the face of wizened old woman, hair like yellow wax, flowing in gooey strands over a deeply-lined face. The movements of the face matched her own. She shut her eyes, forcing it out of her mind.

The beast shook his leg, black-beard cursing her, but Samantha held on. The blue-glowing children floated down to the water to watch. They stood in a ring, their faces brighter than the rest of their bodies.

Samantha held on. She held on even while the leg kicked, while black-hair screamed, his wolf snout snapping just inches from her face. Above, through the web of trees, she saw a brightening in the sky. Any moment now and she was sure she would lose her strength.

Finally, with a roar from black-beard, the beast tossed Derrick on her, and the two of them tumbled back on the muddy bank. Breathless, she looked up to see the two-headed beast sinking into the pond.

White-hair shaped his lips into an O, and then produced the whistle Samantha had heard earlier.

High-low-high.

Then, white-hair smiling, black-beard sneering, the beast sank beneath the surface of the pond. She waited until the ripples died, then, with the other children watching, she picked up her brother. He was as light as a pillow.

She passed through the ferns and back into the street, the streetlights going dim under the first light of the dawn. In her arms, Derrick did not stir, and she feared he was dead.

"Almost home now," she said to him. "Almost home."

When she returned home, and had him in his bed, his eyes

finally fluttered open.

"I'm alive," he said.

"Yes," she said, and held him close. His body was getting warmer. She held him for a long time, held him for as long as she could, held him because she was afraid that someday soon, when she was sleeping, the beast would come again.

"How long until he comes back?" Derrick asked.

"Longer," she said. She realized that she wasn't answering him at all, but talking to someone she didn't believe in, someone who was lost, maybe. "A lot longer," she said, and tried to make herself believe that if he was real, he would find his way home.

The Human Addict: A Dragon's Tale

If I had only eaten one, perhaps Great Sire would have been lenient. If I had only gone to him after that first one, he might have told me to incinerate all traces of my transgression and speak no more of the matter.

But I had not stopped at one.

"Humans!" Great Sire cried, puffs of smoke rising from his nostrils. "You're telling me you're addicted to eating *humans?*"

He crouched at the back of the dank cavern, three tiny females preening his purple wings. A roaring fire kept the darkness at bay and cast his enormous shadow on the cavern walls. He was the biggest of the dragons, in both girth and wingspan, though he was more fat now than muscle. Although it would have been a death-wish to say this to him, I doubted it was even possible for him to take to the air. If not for his position as leader, which demanded that he be fed and cared for without any effort on his own, he surely would have starved.

His enormous body took up so much of the cavern that I

could barely get my wings out of the freezing rain. It was just as well, because I didn't wish to get closer. No dragon had worse breath than Great Sire—and that was saying something, since dragons, as a whole, had very bad breath indeed.

"I believe so," I said. It had taken great courage on my part to make this admission. Dragons didn't need to eat but once every full moon, so gluttony was considered the worst of our crimes. There was not enough food on the planet for dragons to be gluttons. If a dragon was caught indulging, the punishment had to be severe.

In most cases, death.

For all except Great Sire, of course. The leader was expected to indulge; it was the way he showed his status. There was no irony in this. It was merely the way of things, just as the way of things had been for millennia not to eat humans—a food source considered beneath us.

"But, but," he sputtered, hot spittle flying out of his mouth and spraying me in the face, "they're so—*scrawny!*"

One of the females giggled.

"I know," I said.

"I could understand lions, perhaps. At least they have tails." Tails were considered a delicacy to dragons, though most of us believed lions were too majestic a creature to be eaten. "But humans—they're just skeletons with bits of hair attached to them. What could you possibly find addictive about them, Larka? They're disgusting!"

I flicked a tongue between my jagged teeth. My mouth was watering at the mere mention of them. I imagined their bones snapping in my jaws. "I don't know," I said. "I just—do."

"How many have you eaten?"

"Um … hundreds."

"Hundreds! In the last year?"

I hesitated. "In the last month."

He glared at me, then rolled onto his side so that the females could clean his scaled belly. Outside, the rain pounded on the mountainside. My soaked tail had grown numb. I could feel the water hardening into ice on my scales.

"Well," he said, "you've put me in quite a predicament, Larka. I mean, you, of all people—a dragon whose job it is to *catch* the overeaters. To bring them to justice. To mete out punishment. That you yourself would be an overeater, it's a great blow to dragonkind."

"I understand," I said.

"And to have it be *humans*—that's more embarrassing than anything else. You can't shake a tree without a few humans falling out. What's the challenge in that? How about unicorns? Or trolls? If you were addicted to eating them, at least you could face your punishment with your pride intact. But humans . . " He shook his big head, his ruby eyes blazing bright. "Have you tried to quit?"

"Oh yes," I said. "I've tried everything. I've tried to limit myself to one a day, and that failed. I tried weaning myself off humans by switching to monkeys, but they didn't satisfy me. I even tried wearing a patch of human hair on my body, thinking the smell of them might be enough, but it only increased the craving." I sighed. "And what I really worry about is how they're changing. They seem to be getting smarter."

"Smarter?" he said, chuckling. "Come now, these are humans."

It was dangerous to contradict Great Sire, but I needed him to understand. "Well … they used to do nothing more than just lurch around with hunched backs, grunt a little, and eat whatever food was handy. Now they walk upright, build their own caves, and even tie together trees so they might travel on water. They used to throw rocks at me when I chased them. Now they throw sharpened sticks. One even penetrated my scales the other day, drawing blood."

"So what are you telling me? Are you afraid they might kill you?" I could tell he was suppressing a grin, his jagged teeth protruding over his leathery lips.

"It's more than that," I said. "I'm afraid they might kill all of us."

His laughter was so sharp and loud that all three females leapt off him, briefly taking to the air like buzzing flies.

"Absurd!" he cried.

"But Great Sire—"

"Speak not another word of this nonsense!" he bellowed.

Such an order meant the conversation was over. My real fear was that hatred of dragons, sparked by my own behavior, would run so deep in humans that when the day came when they were capable of wiping us out—and I had no doubt that day would come—they would surely do so. It was the real reason I had come to him with my problem. I didn't want to die, but I didn't want to be the reason dragons were destroyed either.

But I said none of this. I merely bowed my head.

The smoke poured from his nose, choking the air. He settled down finally, and the little females returned to his side.

"Here is what I will do," he said. "I cannot sentence you to death—not for humans, a food so common and dirty. I would not be able to live with myself. But I can't let you go on devouring them either. So you will go to the Far North, where it is icy and cold and no humans live. There you will stay until you no longer crave them."

"And if the craving never goes away?" I asked. Dragons were a long-lived bunch, and we were slow to change—if at all.

He rolled away, turning to face the cavern wall. The flickering fire made his shadow shimmer like a ghostly thing. "Then you will stay there forever," he said.

* * * * *

So I WENT NORTH. It was a long journey, and ice so coated my wings toward the end that I nearly couldn't fly. Finally, I reached the desolate, snow-covered icebergs, where darkness reigned for half the year. I had been there a few times in my journeys as a scout, my first job among the dragonkind before my promotion, but only briefly.

I used my fire to burrow deep into one of the mountains of solid ice. There I spent most of my time, venturing out only once every few months to feed on fish or fowl. Once I spied a mermaid in the distance, a close relative to the humans, and I had to flee quickly to prevent myself from consuming her. I got the shakes bad the first few nights, breaking into a sweat, but then they passed.

Still, the craving remained, so I stayed.

I have no idea how long I was there. Since dragons have a lifespan of tens of thousands of years, we do not experience the passing of time quite the same way humans do. I know only that the sun rose and set many times. A few months, a few years—it was hard to say, especially in my maddened state of mind.

My craving for human flesh stayed with me. It finally dawned on me that it would never go away, that it was just as much a part of me as my wings or my fire, and that I couldn't so much beat it as control it.

I felt I *had* controlled it, but there was one only way to know for sure.

I had to put myself around humans again.

RISKING THE WRATH of Great Sire, I made the long journey back to warmer lands, returning to my leader's mountain dwelling. The peaks were covered with snow and the sky was as gray as ash.

I expected him holed up in there with a dozen females, keeping warm.

But the cavern was empty. By the looks of it, it had been so for some time—there were no bones or scales.

I searched all over, looking for dragons of any kind, and was dismayed to find none at all. I saw no unicorns, trolls, or any other fairy creature. Humans, however, had spread like weeds in the ensuing years, and their little brick and wooden houses dotted the countryside—a huge improvement in their living conditions.

The craving was stronger than ever, a pulsing need fiercer than hunger or the desire to mate, but I did not give into it. The humans behaved much as they did before I left, shrieking and fleeing at my presence.

I tried to stay among the clouds, but I finally grew frustrated at not finding any of my kind, and swooped down on a gray-haired man fishing at the edge of a river. Up close, they looked different now. Not as hairy, and they seemed to enjoy wearing the skin of other creatures.

I landed in the shallows, splashing water on him. The water was cold, but was nothing compared to the water in the north.

Gaping at me, he dropped the rod he had been holding.

"Have you seen any dragons?" I asked, and then realized as soon as the words were out of my mouth that he couldn't possibly understand me, since I was speaking Dragontongue.

He said something in a language I also didn't understand, then turned and fled.

I realized if I never learned the human tongue, then my chances of finding out what happened to my kind were slim. Even though it was a terrible temptation, I kidnapped the old human and took him to Great Sire's cavern. I fed him and brought him water. He was terrified at first, but when he saw I wasn't going to kill him, he gradually relaxed. From him, I slowly learned to speak his tongue.

He had not seen a dragon, he told me, in over thirty years. The dragonslayers had killed them all, so far as anyone knew.

"But I am pleased to see you, dragon," he said stroking my side. "I saw one as a boy, and I always thought that killing you was wrong."

It is impossible to describe how depressed and angry I was at hearing this news, how ridden I was with guilt. Had I been the cause of all this? I was tempted to gobble up the old man, but my restraint won out. Plus I was pleased at how kind the old man had been in return. I bade him farewell and told him to go back to his people.

"Speak well of dragons," I told him. "Perhaps all will not remember us with fear."

I stayed in Great Sire's cavern, falling into a deep depression. Had my addiction fostered a hatred among the humans that led them to kill us all? It seemed my fears had been true. And what was I to do now, but spend my waning years with the knowledge that I alone had wiped us from the world?

I would have stayed in that cavern until I died, but it wasn't long—a few weeks or months, perhaps—that a human came calling.

I didn't do much but eat and sleep those days, so when I heard a crunch of rocks at the cavern's entrance, I lifted my head and squinted into the light. There stood a tall, bulky human dressed in something silver and shiny, the clothing clinking as he walked. Even his head was encased in this silvery clothing; I could not see his face. He carried a shield that had been blackened by fire, a sword tinged with blood, and what I later would learn was a crossbow.

"Are you the last of the dragons?" he asked, and I was surprised. I never thought I would hear another creature speak Dragontongue but me.

"Who are you?" I asked.

"I am Morgan of the Mountain People," he said.

I lowered my head, sighing. I had grown as fat as Great Sire, so even this much movement was an effort. "Hello, Morgan," I said. "I am Larka, and I suppose I am the last. I hope you aren't disappointed."

He raised his crossbow. At the time, I didn't know what it was, so I didn't realize the danger.

"No," he said. "I am not disappointed at all. In fact, I am pleased I will be able to say I killed the last one."

"Killed the—" I began, but I didn't get to finish. The crossbow fired a sharpened stick faster than anything I had seen move before. There was a swish of air for the briefest of seconds and then I felt a sharp pain in my side.

I screamed. The arrow had penetrated the narrow gap between my scales and buried deep in my flesh. Blue blood was oozing from the wound."You hurt me!" I cried.

He had already reloaded his crossbow. "And I shall do so again," he said.

I never thought I would hurt another human, but my survival instinct took over. I blew fire his way, expecting that would be the end of it. Much to my surprise, when the smoke cleared, he was crouched behind his shield.

I opened my mouth to try again, and he fired his arrow right into my mouth. It went straight through my tongue.

I tasted the bitterness of my own blood. I may have been fat, but I knew now that this little human could possibly be the end of me, so a surge of energy bolted me to my feet.

I charged straight at him. I snapped at him with my jaws, but he darted to the side. Rather than stay and fight, I continued forward, and launched myself into the air. I hadn't gotten far when I felt another arrow stick into my side.

A vile rage swept through me. I thought about killing as many of the humans as I could, but I knew where that would lead. Back into temptation. So instead I flew north, returning to the icy home where I had spent so many years.

Dragons are slow to heal, and the long flight had sapped me of strength. I stayed in my cave, listening to the moaning of the winds, and wondering what reason I had to go on living. Because I didn't bother to eat, I grew even weaker, withering, my body feeding on itself. Months passed like this, and when I heard footsteps on the snow at the mouth of the cave, I barely had the strength to stand.

I was not surprised when I glanced up and saw that it was the same human as before, dressed in the same silvery clothes, the snow flurries swirling behind him. Somehow I had been expecting him.

"Persistent, aren't you?" I said in Dragontongue.

He crept closer, all the while keeping the crossbow trained on my head. The disadvantage of the cold was that it made it difficult to summon the fire. It was just as well. I doubt I would have been able to stop him, and it would only have prolonged my misery

A few steps away, he stopped and raised the mask that had been hiding his face. He was old and wrinkled, and there was a sadness in his eyes I didn't expect to see.

"Well?" I said. "Are you going to finish me?"

He sighed and shook his head.

"No?" I said. "But you've come so far."

He sat, placing the crossbow and shield on the ground next to him. He looked less a mighty warrior than a worn out old man. "Killing dragons has been the bane of my existence," he said. "I could think of nothing else when I was younger. If I went a few days without killing one, I would go crazy. I wanted to stop. I wanted to be a simple farmer like the rest of my family, but there was always this need. When there were no more dragons, I was able to have a normal life. Then I heard of you, and the need was back. Just like that, I walked away from everything I love."

He bit down on his lip, and looked at me with glistening eyes.

"If I kill you," he said, "I will never know if I had the strength to beat it on my own."

He was sitting so close. His weapons were out of his grasp. One snap of my jaws and I could have him in my mouth.

"I know exactly what you mean," I said.

And so the dragonslayer cared for my wounds and nursed me back to health. He brought us fish, and I cooked it with what little fire I could manage. There was little to do but talk, and so we talked often—of cravings and weaknesses and the desire to be the masters of our own fates.

Sharing our story was a way of healing.

Sharing our story was a way to remain alive.

A Witness to All That Was

It was just another dead planet, as useless and wasted as their marriage. That was what Marco thought when he saw the brown smudge of a world for the first time—and of course he felt an immediate pang of guilt for thinking it.

"Any signs of life?" he said.

He didn't look at Kelsie when he said this. He was afraid to look at her. He was afraid that if she saw his eyes, she'd know what he'd been thinking. She'd always been so good at that—reading him, knowing exactly what was on his mind. After ten years together, most of it spent almost exclusively in each other's company as they scoured the universe looking for treasures in the aftermath of a war that desolated ninety-eight percent of the colonized universe, you'd think he would have gotten good at reading her too. But he hadn't. He'd never been. And it had only gotten worse since they'd lost Trevor. More and more, he didn't think he knew her at all.

"No," she said.

She sounded mildly irritated, and he thought maybe she was

on to him, but of course she usually sounded mildly irritated. Sometimes not so mildly. Sometimes she sounded like she outright hated him. And who could blame her?

He stole a glance at her. In the cramped cockpit of the *Buggywhip,* wires dangling everywhere as he kept patching their poor ship to keep it running, and half the control panel circuitry exposed, Kelsie was almost invisible. Gray uniform, gray skin, gray hollowed out eyes—even her hair looked more gray than blonde these days. All that gray blending into the circuit boards and the panel doors and the bulkheads. God, she wasn't even forty yet and she looked like a cadaver.

"Any energy signatures?" he asked. The planet really did look awful—like a sweaty fingerprint on the thick glass of their cockpit window.

"No."

"Well," he said, "I guess we'll start on that southern continent. That's likely where there was the most life, near the equator."

She didn't say anything. She didn't even bow her head—just went on staring ahead like some kind of zombie. Or a ghost. That's what she'd become to him, really—a living, breathing ghost. Suddenly he hated her for not looking at him. He'd looked at her, hadn't he? He'd been able to do that much.

"Okay," he said tersely, "I'll set the coordinates—"

"Wait," she said.

"What?"

"There is something," she said, finally a little bit of life in her voice. "It's very faint—but yes, there's something down there. Something running on artificial power."

SHE WOKE IN THE FOREST. The first thing she noticed were the smells—the crispness of the morning air, the moldy wet leaves, the eye-watering scent of the flowering koona trees. These were all smells that were familiar to her, but when she opened her eyes and saw the man staring down at her, she didn't know him.

"Who are you?" she said.

He was tall and gangly, all knobby elbows and blocky knees in his sweat-stained shirt and blue running shorts. He was breathing heavy, hands on those ugly knees, a beard of sweat trickling down his long brown sideburns. She saw a hint of gray in the sideburns, but he could have been anywhere from thirty to fifty—he had that kind of face. He wore some type of video visor, the tinted lenses flipped up; on the visor's tiny twin screens a woman in a finned dress was pointing at a chart.

He removed a black receiver from his ear and said, "I think the better question is, who are *you?*"

She opened her mouth to tell him, but when she grasped for it, the information wasn't there. It felt like it was just out of reach, like a horga bug fluttering just beyond her fingertips. She'd had it just a moment ago, but now it was gone. Of course, she knew what a horga bug was. She obviously hadn't forgotten everything.

"I—I don't know," she said.

"Really?" he said. "This isn't some kind of joke, is it?"

"No." And it wasn't. She was also starting to get afraid. It was as if someone had just turned out the light on part of her brain, and the darkness pressed in from all sides.

"Hey, hey now," he said, extending a hand to her. "Don't be worried. It's probably something to do with that nasty bruise on your head. It'll come back to you in a second."

Since she was already taking his hand with her right—him pulling her up, having to huff a little to do it—she touched her forehead with her left. At the same time she felt the puffy mound over her left eye, she also felt a throbbing pain.

"Ow," she said.

"Ow is right. You could get that thing declared the second largest mountain in New Hyron. You do know you're in New

Hyron, don't you?"

She didn't, and he must have seen that right away by her eyes, because his jocular expression quickly shifted to concern. Or was it pity? She checked herself over; her loose-fitting gray clothes were disheveled and speckled with leaves and dirt. Had she been raped? She didn't feel like she'd been raped. The clothes were a kind of uniform, but crudely made. She saw a matching bonnet half-buried in leaves and she snatched it up. It looked like cloth but it had the hardness of a stone bowl.

"Hmm," the man said. He took a couple paces away and picked up a thick branch about the length of his arm. He brought it to her and pointed at a place where the bark had been chipped to the paler wood beneath. There was a tiny spot of blood. "I'm at heart a scientist," he said, "and I'm going to venture a hypothesis that this is *your* blood."

"Maybe it fell from the tree and hit me," she said.

He looked up at the trees, then grimaced. She followed his gaze and saw what he saw—no tree limbs anywhere close to above where she'd been lying.

"I think it *did* hit you," he said, "but it wasn't because it fell."

THEY FOUND the energy signature in the eastern hemisphere, in the shadows of a jagged mountain range that resembled bloodied teeth. It was a gray basin with no trees, no bushes, no water of any kind—just chalky, black-and-crimson rock. When they drifted down through the smog in the lander and Marco saw what awaited below, he thought it was the most desolate place he had ever seen. If there was a hell, then it would look like this. If it *was* hell, then this is where he would go when he died.

"Are you sure about that reading?" he said.

She was leaning close to the monitor, and when she looked up at him, her face glowed green. She gave him a cold look. "Do you want to check it yourself?"

He swallowed and focused on the landing controls, firing the rotationals, banking to the left as he brought them down in the smoothest area he could see. That look from Kelsie—it was worse than hate. It was murderous. It was the way she'd looked at him several weeks after the accident, when he'd dared to touch her shoulder in bed, thinking maybe she'd have him again, maybe they could strive for something between them even though it would never be the same—and the naked rage she'd flashed him had pierced his heart like a blade. He'd known at that moment she'd never have him again, never touch him again. And he'd been right.

Setting the ship down, feeling the gangplanks shudder beneath his boots, he wondered how many more of these trips they had in them. Five? Two? She'd never asked to stop, never asked for a divorce, never asked for anything, really, which was the problem, but the end had to be coming. It'd been nearly a year. He figured they'd just kept on, not because either of them wanted it, but out of habit. Maybe she wouldn't ask for a divorce. Maybe one of these days, when his back was turned, she'd just leave him, marooned on a world like this. Who would ever know? She could make up whatever story she wanted.

Like usual, she had her suit on first, and like usual, she made no attempt to help him. It was the little things like that he missed the most—how she used to help him with his suit, how she used to put the coffee out for him when he was in the hydro, how she used to touch the back of his neck when she entered the cockpit. When he joined her at the hatch, she was standing there with her gloved white hand on the panel, the glare of the overhead light on her helmet obscuring her face.

"Ready?" she said, her voice crackling over his helmet's speakers.

His suit smelled like old sweat and musty leather—smells he

used to love because they kindled his sense of adventure, but he now despised because they made him remember better times. "Sure," he said. But what he wanted to say was, *He was tethered, Kelsie! I swear to God he was tethered!*

Of course he didn't say that. He'd never once said it, even the day it happened. It was something she obviously knew. Why should he have say it?

The last thing he did was make sure the laser pistol holstered on his hip was fully charged. It probably wasn't necessary, but it was always better to be safe. As soon as the hatch clanked open, pale orange dust swirled into the compartment. It fogged the air, made it impossible to see. Out of instinct, he reached for her hand, but she was already clomping down the gangplank with her handheld in front of her. He followed, her nothing but a blurry shape. Out of the ship's antigrav, he felt the planet tugging him, giving him weight.

The red and black ground was as hard as metal; it made him think of a crusty scab. There were boulders everywhere, and the spires loomed through the haze like wraiths. He couldn't see her any more. Panicking, he started to run and immediately bumped into her bulky air supply. She'd stopped in a ring of boulders, the large misshapen one directly in front of her about half her height.

"Here it is," she said

He studied at the boulder, leaning in to squint at it through the dust. "It's a rock," he said.

"I'm telling you this is it."

"It's a rock."

"Marco, I'm *telling* you—"

"All the places we could look for treasure and you brought us to a rock."

She thrust the handheld at him, blue lights flickering through the protective sheath. "You look at it!"

Disgusted, he pushed her arm away and reached for the

boulder. The swirling dust chose that moment to calm, the air partially clearing. As he leaned, he saw that the boulder did have a very unusual shape, with strange bumps and odd ridges. Still, it was a rock, nothing but a damn rock, so when his hand was nearly touching it and the rock grabbed his wrist, he was so surprised that he let out a startled cry.

HIS NAME was Jahn Klonburr. He'd introduced himself on the way back to his pod, where he quickly flew her to the top of a towering glass building on the edge of a glistening emerald lake that bordered the forest. When they landed, an older fellow with white hair escorted her to the infirmary, where a sleek robot nurse tended to her wounds, its spindly arms humming softly when they moved. The way everyone talked to Jahn, she realized two things: one, he was definitely in charge, and two, he was very powerful man.

While the bandage was being affixed to her forehead, Jahn disappeared for ten minutes. When he returned, he took her hands in his. She expected soft hands, the kind of hands of a man who'd spent most of his life earning his keep with his brains and not his brawn, and was surprised when they were rough and calloused. He was still dressed in his running clothes, though he no longer wore the visor. He must have also put on some kind of deodorant, because she could smell it—a powerful scent, like the ocean before the storm.

"I've got good news and bad news," he said.

She sat up straighter on the wall-mounted cot. "Tell me the good news first. It'll help cushion the blow."

He smiled kindly. He wasn't really all that handsome, but she loved his smile. It was not only warm, but slightly bashful as well. "The good news is that your genetic scan was in the system. Your name is Derra Verne. Ring any bells?"

"No."

"Ah," he said, sounding mildly disappointed. "Well, maybe the bad news will. Unfortunately, it looks like you were a member of The Family of Jorf." He raised his rather thick eyebrows.

"Sorry," she said. "Still nothing. Who are they?"

"A very conservative religious cult—anti-science, anti-technology. Anti-sanity, if you ask me. Their city, Jorf, is a long way from here—half a continent, practically. They are very strict when it comes to their dogma, and if one of their members if found in violation they are summarily expelled. And usually abandoned far from Jorf—which appears to be the case with you."

"Oh, so I'm a rebel, then?"

"Actually, you might have been hysterical at being left behind. From what I've read, they only strike the ones who keep trying to return."

"Oh," she said.

"You sound disappointed?"

"I guess I am. I don't feel like some sort of blind follower."

He squeezed her hands. "You don't have to be. You can be whoever you want to be."

She laughed—a nervous laugh, too high and strained. "What you mean is, I can be whoever I want to be because I don't remember who I am?"

"No," he said, "it's true *especially* if you remember who you are."

He smiled that warm, bashful smile again, and she knew at that moment she was falling in love with him.

It wasn't until the rock stood, still gripping his hand as tightly, that he realized that the misshapen thing was not actually a rock at all.

It was a robot.

The dust swirled and undulated around them, the thicker orange vapors rippling like silk scarves. The dust was so thick and clumpy on the robot's body that it was easy to mistake it for a boulder, especially with visibility so poor. Plus, the way it had been sitting, with its knees drawn to its concaved chest, arms wrapped around the legs, and head bowed to its knees, had made it nearly impossible to recognize it for what it was until it moved.

"Hey!" Marco cried, pulling at the metallic fingers clamping onto his wrist. "Let me go!"

Slowly, as if it required immense effort, the robot lifted its head. For the first time they saw its true color—white, but dull and faded like old wax. Since its face had been shielded, the metal there was smooth and clear, and the ring of dust along its scalp looked like a bad haircut. It had dainty features, its face narrowing to a point, like a downward-pointing triangle. The big hinged jaw, the lack of a nose, and the recessed eye sockets made him think of a skull. The ridged fingers were as small as a child's, but they were damn strong.

"Come on!" Marco said.

It went on holding fast, staring up at him with shadowed eyes. He thought about going for his laser pistol, but it was on the same side as his clamped arm—and really, he didn't want to shoot it unless it was absolutely necessary. Then Kelsie did something unexpected. She laughed. His blood was already flowing, his heart pounding, and he couldn't help his reaction—he wanted to kill her. He might have killed her, if the blasted thing didn't have a death grip on him.

"You're not helping!" he shouted at her.

This only made her laugh harder, her giggles and squeals ringing inside his helmet. She doubled over and he thought, this is it, it really is finished.

"Verna-saff, rik rik?" the robot said.

It broke the spell of Marco's rage, and seemed to take the air out of Kelsie's fits too. He looked down at it.

"What?" he said.

"Verna-saff, rik rik?" the robot again.

"We don't speak your language!"

"Speak language," the robot said, with amazingly clear enunciation even though it had only heard the words once.

"That's right!" Marco said, irritated it was parroting him. "We don't! *Now let go of my hand!*"

The robot let go of his hand. In fact, it had happened so promptly that Marco stumbled, backpedaling, finally coming down hard on his rear. He narrowly missed sitting on a boulder, but his flailing left elbow wasn't so lucky—it flung into the rock, striking a nerve that brought tears to his eyes. The first thing he heard was Kelsie's laughter. Her response was worse than the falling, and he hated her more in that moment than he'd ever hated anyone or anything in his entire life.

It wasn't just the laughter. It was the *contempt* in the laughter.

"Kelsie!" he screamed.

"Speak language," the robot said again. "That's right. Now speak language."

When he glared at it, he saw that the robot was rising. Its legs were as thin as stilts, and when the billowing dust thickened around it, sometimes it looked like it wasn't standing on anything larger than a pair of taut strings. Despite its child-sized features, it was about Kelsie's height.

"I told you—" Marco started to tell it. "Wait," Kelsie said, not laughing now, quickly sobering. "I think it's asking *us* to speak. It's trying to learn our language."

"That's crazy," Marco said, painfully getting off the hard ground, his tailbone smarting. He was lucky had hadn't punctured a hole in the suit. "It can't possibly already—"

"Learn, learn," the robot said. "You speak language. I learn it. Now, speak."

Then Marco was a believer. He realized that every word the robot had spoken so far had been one they had already spoken to it—and not only that, but the robot seemed to comprehend the meaning behind those words instantly. Whether by context or some powerful analysis of structure and sound, he didn't know, but it was certainly beyond any technology he'd seen before.

"I'm Kelsie," Kelsie said, touching her chest. "This is Marco. He's my—husband." It might have been his imagination, but he was sure there was a pause between the words "my" and "husband," one that struck a nerve even deeper than her laughter. "We're treasure hunters," she continued. "Or war scavengers— that's the not-so-polite way of putting it. We travel around the universe in a ship visiting worlds ravaged by the Dulnari, looking for rare artifacts and other finds. To sell them. It's not noble work or anything. It's just, you know, a way to make a living."

With the dust wrapping around its legs like a cape, its upper body momentarily in the clear, the robot listened attentively. Kelsie hesitated, and Marco kept waiting for her to add a few more lines of biography: *We had a son named Trevor. He was two years old. One time, on a dead planet very much like this one, we stopped to make some repairs. I was sick as a dog with some Povian virus we'd picked up at our last stop, so Marco brought Trevor outside with him. There were deep canyons everywhere, but Trevor was on a short tether attached to the ship. Marco says Trevor must have undone it. He only turned his back on him for a second. That's what Marco says happened, anyway.*

But to Marco's great relief, she simply shrugged her shoulders and said, "That's really all I can think to tell you."

"Where is ship?" the robot asked.

Kelsie pointed. "Well, it's right over—"

Before she finished, the robot abruptly started walking in the direction of the ship.

* * * * *

THEY'D BEEN TOGETHER less than three weeks when Jahn proposed. Derra was shocked, of course, but not so shocked that she didn't immediately say yes. It might have taken him three weeks, but deep down she'd known in less than three *hours* that she was going to marry him eventually. It had only been a question of when.

Her memory of her time pre-Jahn—which was how she'd almost immediately begun to classify the events off her life, as pre-Jahn and post-Jahn—never did return. He brought in dozens of specialists, but there was nothing they could do. The great, gaping hole in her past bothered her tremendously in the beginning, but over time the love she felt for Jahn made the memory loss more bearable. In fact, she began to feel *grateful* for her amnesia. If what Jahn said was true, she might have been a completely different person with her full memories intact, a cult-like lamb whose only desire would be to try to get back to the Family. She didn't want to be that person any more. She liked who she was when she was with Jahn.

They had the best of marriages—lovers, friends, the closest of confidants. His company—a technology firm which developed everything from artificial organs to hologaming consoles—took him all over the world, and he always took her with him. They dined in fine restaurants with powerful people. She was no wilting wallflower either; he insisted she learn all aspects off his business, and it wasn't long before she was attending the management meetings. It wasn't long after that when her voice carried just as much weight as his.

He wasn't all about making money, either. It was a trying time for the planet, beset by the dangers of a rapidly expanding population, determined to exhaust all of its natural resources despite the cost. It wasn't long before he was dedicating the majority of his time to trying to solving the world's problems. And where was she? At his side of course.

More than eighty years they spent like this, Derra treasuring every minute of it, until even the best biological enhancements and improvements in medicine could not extend the vitality of their bodies. They retired to the very same forest where they had met so many years before—Jahn had built a castle for her in the center of the forest, where a bevy of robot servants would see to their every need and desire.

Then Jahn got sick—withering away, his body hardly more than a patchwork of bones. She sat by his beside, holding his hand while he was wracked with terrible coughs. Finally, when one of these fits passed, he slumped into the bed and told all the doctors and robots to leave them.

Even in his shrunken state, he looked up at her with the same warm eyes, smiled up at her with the same kind smile. "I'm dying, Derra," he said.

"No, no," she said. "You just need rest."

"We both know it's my time."

"Jahn—"

"No, listen. I've waited too long as it is. I have something to tell you. It's important that you know before I die."

DESPITE CONSTANT entreaties, the robot did not stop as it marched to their ship through the pluming dust. By the time they caught up to it, the robot was already ascending the ramp.

"Hold on, there!" Marco cried.

But the robot didn't heed his warning. Marco grabbed its shoulder, but the robot pulled him right into the air lock, his boots skidding over the ramp's ridges. When they were all inside, Kelsie closed the air lock door.

"What're you doing?" Marco said to her. "I don't want—*hey!*"

Before the outside door was even closed, the robot was already working the controls to the inner hatch. As soon as the outside door beeped that it was closed, the inner hatch whirred and spun open. The robot plunged into their inner sanctum. Marco pursued, working at the latches of his helmet. He was already thinking about his laser pistol. He certainly didn't want to fire it inside the lander, but he would if it came to that.

Out of the dust, it was their first good look at the robot. Its head, which really wasn't all that large, looked enormous on top of its skeletal body; it made him think of the sort of stick figure a child might draw, with a big head and pencil-thin body. The orange stains looked like a funky sunburn—the metal white in some areas, stained in others.

Marco dropped his helmet with a clank on the metal floor, and behind him he heard Kelsie do the same. The lander was much smaller than the *Buggywhip*, so the robot didn't have far to go before it reached the cockpit. There was barely room for the three of them inside, poorly lit by a strip of amber lighting, made darker still because their bodies cast shadows everywhere. The robot quickly surveyed the room, then opened an access panel and yanked out a yellow wire.

"Stop that!" Marco said.

Then the robot did something even more outlandish—it put the exposed wire inside its mouth. Marco, expecting some type of sabotage, lunged for the wire, but the robot held him at bay with a hand squarely in the middle his chest.

"I won't—let you—" Marco cried.

"Marco, stop," Kelsie pleaded.

Struggling against the robot, finding it futile because of its superior strength, he couldn't understand why Kelsie was being so calm. Of course— she probably really did want to be marooned on this hellhole. But not him. He didn't know it until this moment, but he still wanted to live.

Giving up on using his brute strength, he sprang away from the robot and yanked his laser pistol out of its holster. It was huge and heavy in his gloved hand. He aimed it directly at the robot's head.

"Marco!" Kelsie screamed.

"I'm going to count to three," Marco warned.

"Marco, no!"

"If you don't put down that wire, I'll blast your head off. One …"

"Marco! It's not trying to hurt us—"

"Two …"

She grabbed his arm. He couldn't believe it. They struggled briefly, and then he pushed her and she toppled against the bulkhead, thudding to the gangplank. He was so surprised at what he'd done that he briefly forgot the robot; by the time he looked at it again the robot was lowering the wire from its mouth. It cocked its head slightly to the side, holding up the yellow wire as if it was a candle waiting to be lit.

"The weapon is unnecessary," the robot said, now speaking in perfect Prime. "I have finished interfacing with your ship's computer. I mean you no harm."

Rising to her feet, Kelsie glared at Marco. "I told you!" she said.

"What did you do?" he said to the robot, ignoring her. He aimed the pistol at its head again. "Are you trying to take over my ship?"

"Of course not," the robot said.

"Then what?"

The robot returned the wire to the compartment, fixed it in its original location, then closed the panel. It looked at the weapon in Marco's hand. "Please," it said, "it would be quite unfortunate if you damaged your ship with an errant shot."

Kelsie's hand was on his arm again, lowering it, and this time he let her. He still wasn't sure what was going on, but he still had the gun. He could still use it. "Who are you?" he said to the robot.

It did not answer at first, though it did stiffen. With no cheek muscles to tighten, no lips to part or compress, no eyebrows to raise or lower, it was impossible to get any sort of read on the robot's reaction. But when it spoke, he was quite certain he heard sorrow in its voice.

"I am a witness to all that was," it said.

THERE WERE DOZENS of things Jahn could have said that would have surprised her—after all, she'd chosen not to learn much about her past—but nothing could have shocked her as much as what he actually said. It didn't seem real. It hung in the air between them like just another mote of dust in the light slanting in from the window, the silence stretching out so long that she started to wonder if he'd said it at all. So she finally had to say it herself, just to test the reality of the word on her own lips.

"A robot?" she said.

"That's right," he said.

He started coughing again, his body wracked with convulsions so severe he looked like he was having a seizure. She stared at him, trying to comprehend.

"I'm a robot?" she said.

He cleared his throat into his fist. When he'd finally gotten some air in his lungs, he said, "But more, too. Obviously a lot more."

"I don't feel like a robot," she said.

"No, of course you wouldn't. That's the way I made you—so that you would think you were alive."

"Jahn," she said sternly, "if this is some sort of joke—"

"No, Derra. You need to know the truth. Once I'm gone, you

were bound to find out anyway."

She wiped away a tear from her eye, and she wondered if she was really crying or if it was just an automated response to a certain external stimuli. "So my whole life is a lie?"

"Not a lie," he said. "A necessary myth."

"So all that about the Family of Jorg, finding me in the forest—"

"All part of the illusion."

"But why?"

He started to answer, but on the first word his throat seized up on him. The anguish on his face—it was terrible, made him seem so sickly and old. He turned toward the window.

"I wanted a witness," he said quietly.

"A what?"

He didn't look at her. "It wasn't for me. At least not at first. I just—well, you've been there with me, Derra. You know how fragile life is on this planet. If we don't destroy ourselves, and there's still a good chance of that happening, then something else might—an asteroid with our name on it, a series of volcanic eruptions that black out the sun, something else. Someday we'll all be gone. It's inevitable. The odds aren't on our side."

"Jahn—"

"I wanted there to be a witness," he said. "Someone made to last. Someone who would survive, who would be able to tell others about who we were, what we lived for, what we were like."

"But there are robots everywhere," she said. "Any of them might—"

"No!" he said fiercely, turning to look at her. "You're different! You lived as one of us. You *are* one of us. I have given you everything that we have—pain, emotion, even the illusion of age and disease. Though you won't die. And you will shed this outward form soon enough. What's inside was built to last forever."

It was an absurdity, all of it, but she knew instantly that it was true. She wondered bitterly if it was because he had programmed her to accept the truth when he finally told her. "So what we had between us," she said, "that was a myth too?"

"No! I didn't expect to love you, Derra, but I do. You mean everything to me. You are my witness too. And now, as I lay here at the end of my life, I wonder if that's all I ever wanted. Maybe my motive was never pure. What are we if we have no witness, no one to be there with us through all of life's travails? Everything that we are fades to nothing—except the memories that other people have of us. Your memories, Derra. You will carry them inside you, forever."

He squeezed her hand. They had held hands the entire time. Even in her confusion, even in her anger, she had not let his hand go.

WHEN THE ROBOT was finished with its story, Kelsie was crying. Marco stood mute. The wind whistled against the cockpit window, and the jagged mountains appeared and disappeared in the sheaths of crimson fog billowing past the cockpit window.

"How long have you been out there?" Marco said.

"A long time," the robot said.

"Did the Dulnari—"

"Oh no. We had destroyed ourselves long before they arrived. It has been a least a thousand winters since I last spoke to another living being. The Dulnari did not even stop. There was nothing for them here."

"A thousand …" Kelsie said. She wiped her cheeks on her suit's sleeve. "You've been alone for a thousand years?"

Instead of answering, the robot motioned to the control panel. "Everything that I am, all of my memories, and all of the collected knowledge and wisdom of my people—it has been downloaded into your ship's computer. I ask that you make sure that it is distributed to any and all who would appreciate it."

"Wait," Kelsie said. "You're not going with us?"

"No," the robot said. "I must return to where you found me."

The robot stepped past them, heading to the air lock. Kelsie followed. Marco holstered his gun, trailing both of them.

"But there's nothing out there," Kelsie pleaded.

"On the contrary," the robot replied, *"everything* is out there."

"It's a wasteland!"

At the hatch, its hand on the handle, the robot faced them. It may have just been the angle of the light, but Marco finally got a good look at the robot's eyes—and he was startled to see that they did not look like robot eyes. They were a rich, expressive blue, oval in shape, with widening dark pupils. They were deeply recessed, nearly hidden behind tiny gears and tightly-packed wires, and may have still been artificial, but to him they seemed every bit as alive as his own.

"That wasteland," the robot said, "was once a lush forest. Where you found me was once my home. You may see nothing but dead rock, but I see a world alive with memories—my memories, everything that ever mattered to me."

It turned to go, but Kelsie grabbed its narrow arm. "We can't just leave you alone out there!" she said.

The robot placed its metallic hand over Kelsie's glove, and it spoke to her as a mother might speak to a troubled child. "I will not be alone," it said.

Then it opened the hatch. Marco reached for Kelsie, thinking he might have to hold her back, but Kelsie did not resist when the robot pulled away. The robot stepped through, then turned to face them.

"Wait," Kelsie said. "I'll get my helmet—"

"No," the robot said, peering at them through the crack. Marco stood slightly behind his wife, looking at the robot over her shoulder. It stood that way for quite a while, frozen like a photographer trying to capture the perfect shot. Another moment. Another memory. "Remember," it said, "no matter what happens, it is good to have a witness. It is good to *be* a witness."

With that, it clanged the door shut. Kelsie let out a little whimper and continued to stand there. They heard the air whooshing into the compartment on the other side. Marco felt numb—not so much by the robot's story, but by what Kelsie had just said. *I'll get my helmet.* Had she been she offering to accompany the robot to where they'd found it, to say goodbye to it there—or had that been her way of saying goodbye to him?

It was then that Marco realized he didn't want Kelsie to say goodbye. He wanted her to forgive him. He didn't know if it was possible, but he wanted to try. What had happened with Trevor, it was an awful thing, but it was something they shared. They were a witness to it, just like they were a witness to each other's lives. If they went their separate ways, it might be easier to forget the pain, but it would be easier to forget everything else, too.

They heard the robot clanging down the gangplank. Kelsie's shoulders slumped. He was looking at the back of her blonde head for a time, but then he found his gaze drawn to her right hand, still gloved, hanging limply at her side. If he reached with his left, he could take it. He could not turn and go back to that cockpit and leave this planet until he reached for that hand. She might spurn him, she might reject him, and if she did, it would probably be for the last time.

But he had to reach.

He had to try.

FROM HER WINDOW, gazing out at the lush forest that surrounded her home, Derra watched the tiny ship lift into the sky. The sun was bright and warm on her face. She shielded her eyes, watching the ship go, rising into the blue heavens over their precious planet, the ship now as small as a bird, now a black dot vanishing into the white clouds. She watched until she could no longer hear the thunder of the ship's engines, until she once again heard the chirping of the birds and the whisper of the breeze.

"They're good people," she said. "There's pain there—I could see it. But there's hope for them too. There's hope for all of us."

Standing behind her, his breath warm on her neck, her beloved husband said, "I think so too."

Lincoln and the Dragon

He walked alone on a country road two miles from Springfield, only his labored breathing and the crunch of his boots on the snow breaking the stillness. The bright cloak of stars would ordinarily have given him some solace, but he could find no comfort in them this night.

"Abe! Abe, for God's sake, man, slow down!"

The voice came from far behind him, and he recognized it immediately—Joshua Speed. It was too late to duck into the woods encroaching on the road to his right, his first instinct, so he turned and waited, breath fogging in the starlight, hands clasped behind him as if he was arguing a case in the courtroom. He only wished that were true; when he was in the courtroom, there was no problem that seemed insurmountable.

It took a full minute for Joshua to emerge from the darkness with lantern in hand. His flush face was the only visible skin; the rest of him was bundled in overcoat, scarf, wool gloves and hat. He was a short man, but not slight, his arms and shoulders broad

207

from years of working in his store. When he held up the lantern, his breath formed white clouds in the sphere of yellow light.

"Dear God, man, you going to walk all the way to Chicago?" Joshua said.

"You should go home, my friend," Abe said.

"Not without you. This is hardly the way to celebrate the new year. You might catch your death out here." Then he paused, reading his friend's face. When he spoke again, it was with less levity. "What is it? What's happened?"

There was no one else in the world Abe trusted more than Joshua. When Abe first came to Springfield, practically penniless, the man had been kind enough to offer him free room and board. For the past five years, there had been little about their most intimate feelings they had not discussed. But he found it difficult to summon the words.

"I broke off the engagement," he said, and it was all he could manage before something dark and fierce got a choke hold on him."Why?" Joshua said.

Abe, feeling the muscles in his face tighten, could only shake his head.

"It's not because of me, is it?"

"No, no," Abe said. Although Joshua's decision to return to Kentucky, to manage the plantation of his recently deceased father, had rocked Abe more than he would care to admit. "Mary Todd—she's a fine woman. It's just … not to be."

"But I thought you loved her?"

Before Abe could answer this question, they heard something crashing through the woods—the breaking of branches, the crunch of snow. Abe expected a spooked deer, but he watched as the shape of a man materialized from the darkness. He was lean and wiry, and as he drew nearer the lamp, Abe saw carrot-colored hair. The man's clothes were certainly odd: blue pants, a brightly colored shirt patterned with flowers that left his arms bare, and white shoes.

The last thing Abe saw was the Colt pistol clasped in the man's right hand, dangling at his side like an afterthought.

Abe felt the hairs on the back of his neck rise. "Hold there, sir," he said. "What's your business?"

The man took a few more unsteady steps, then drew to an abrupt halt. He had a pale face and long sideburns, and his forehead and cheeks were spotted with sweat.

"So here we are," the man said, his accent so thick Abe could barely understand him. It was vaguely southern.

"Do we know you?" Joshua said.

The man rocked a little on his feet. "I thought he'd be alone," he mumbled.

"Who?" Joshua said.

There was an uncomfortable silence, and Abe cleared his throat. "We'd all feel a might bit more comfortable, traveler, if you'd give up your pistol."

The man looked at his gun as if he had just realized it was there. "I'm not a killer," he said. "I'll have you know that."

"That's a fine thing," Abe said, advancing a step. "Why don't you—"

He stopped short when the man raised his weapon.

"I'm sorry," the man said. The pistol trembled at the end of his outstretched arm.

Lincoln swallowed. "I don't have but a few small coins—"

"No, no, no. I want you to come with me. There." He tipped his head toward the forest.

"Why?"

"No more questions!"

The man cocked the Colt and pointed it at Abe's face. Despite the poor light, Abe could clearly see the end of the barrel, and it seemed enormous. He raised his hands in a gesture of surrender.

"Of course, friend. Just don't shoot."

"Now wait," Joshua said quickly, "perhaps we can discuss this like civilized—"

The man swung his gun toward Joshua. It was in that moment that Abe acted. Because he tended to lope from place to place, people usually underestimated his speed, but he knew himself well: he grabbed the man's arm and pointed it skyward just before his startled adversary managed to squeeze off a shot. The blast echoed off the trees, reverberating in the stillness, but Abe did not relinquish his grip.

The small man was surprisingly strong and the two of them grappled with each other, the smaller man cursing, spittle flying from his mouth.

Then Abe tore the Colt free, the stranger tumbling to the ground. He was back up in a hurry, but the fight had gone out of his eyes. He looked at Abe, at the gun, and then he sprinted back toward the forest, kicking up snow behind him.

Abe hesitated for only a second, then pursued.

"Abe, no!" Joshua called after him.

The small man was fast, and he stretched out an early lead, but Abe's long legs allowed him to close the distance. He wanted to get to him before he reached the cover of the trees. He was almost upon him when the stranger glanced over his shoulder, feverish eyes widening, and then he was fumbling for something inside his pants pocket. Dear God, Abe thought, he has another pistol, and he threw himself on the smaller man.

Again they wrestled in the cold snow, Abe clutching at the wrist of the man's right hand. Abe caught only a glimpse of the object, and it was white, no bigger than a hen's egg. He tried to pry it out of the man's fingers, convinced it was some kind of weapon, but the stranger warded him off with his free arm and managed to push something on the device with his thumb.

There was a click, and then a low buzzing like a hummingbird's wings—

* * * * *

*Bodies. He had never seen so many bodies—the twisted car-
casses crowding the barren field, young men all, garbed in blood-
stained uniforms, vacant eyes. Was this what his pride had
wrought? The air was still hazy and smelled of gunshot. He heard
a cry somewhere up on the rise, a piercing shriek, and he thought
for a moment it might be a survivor. He felt a lump in this throat.
Then he saw the crow, shrieking, rise up from behind one of the
bodies. Then another crow, and another, rising to form a swarm,
all of them crying out with what seemed to him the voices of young
men ... With each new crow, another piece of his heart was rendered away ...*

—and then they were suspended darkness. His breath froze
in his lungs. His stomach lurched as if he were falling, but he
felt no rush of wind. Then it passed, and his shoulder thudded
against hard rock.

Dusk. Sky the color of blood. The scent of sulfur. The
stranger took advantage of Abe's disorientation to knee him in
the groin. Abe groaned and doubled-over, the man springing to
his feet, laughing gleefully.

"Yes, yes!" he cried. "I've done it! I've done ... done ...
aaaieeeee!"

Abe looked up through tears of pain just in time to see the
stranger waving his arms. It looked comical, as if the man was
an ungainly, brightly-colored bird doing its best to fly, but then
Abe realized that the man had unknowingly back-stepped off a
precipice.

Body twisting, hand still clutching the small white device,
the man plummeted out of sight. Abe could not see how far the

drop-off was, but it was only a second before he heard a thud—then, a few seconds after that, a more distant crash of something breaking against the rocks; moaning.

Abe blinked away the sweat in his eyes. They had appeared on a mountain of some sort, the ground beneath him hard, black rock. A forested valley, hazy in the purple light, stretched out far below them—and beyond, an ocean that melted into the hazy horizon.

Gathering himself, he crawled to the edge of the precipice. The man had been fortunate: the drop had only been about ten feet, to a small outcropping. He lay on his back, hugging his stomach, his eyes closed. His device, however, had not been so lucky. It had fallen another twenty feet to a gently-sloping rocky hillside where it had smashed into dozens of pieces.

The man groaned and rolled onto his side. Abe brought himself up to his knees. He felt queer, and it wasn't the pain; his head felt thick, like it was filled with lead. There were still lingering images in his mind that he couldn't explain—a field littered with the dead, a sky full of crows.

What was this place? He looked behind him and saw that they were about halfway up the small mountain, the top half which seemed to be made of nothing but rock. There, just below the rounded peak, was the opening to a cave. He felt cold looking at this cave, a cold that started in his spine and spread outward along his extremities. The longer he looked at the cave, the colder he felt, until it was so unbearable he had to look away.

"No!" the man below wailed. "No, no, no!"

Abe glanced over the precipice. The stranger was on his stomach, looking down at the remains of his device. He rolled onto his back, hands pressed against the sides of his face, eyes pressed tightly closed. When he opened his eyes, he was looking directly at Abe, and his cheeks flushed red and his eyes flared wide.

"Look what you've done!" he cried. "Now we're *both* trapped here!"

"Where is here?" Abe said.

But the man just closed his eyes and wept. Abe was going to ask again, but then there was a roar so loud it shook the ground. The sound seemed to come from all around him, but when he looked up at the cave, he saw something emerging from the darkness, a glowing white oval. It was only when it blinked, with a thin, filmy lid, that Abe realized it was an eye. The glow from the eye shed its pale light on leathery, ash-colored skin. Abe could just make out a pair of nostrils and the hint of jagged teeth.

A monster?

Where *was* he?

Whatever that thing was, it did not appear friendly, and he would be easy pickings out in the middle of the barren mountainside. He scrambled over the precipice, lowering himself with his long arms, then dropping the remaining few feet. His companion had already scrambled halfway down to the more gently sloping part of the mountain.

"Where are you going?" Abe shouted.

"Away from that!" the man said.

"What is it?"

The stranger leaped a good six feet to the ground beneath him, landed awkwardly, but got up and continued limping down the slope. Bits of rock and dirt spilled after him. Abe did not want to let the stranger get away. Before he started down, however, that strange pressure in his head increased, as if a man with huge hands had suddenly grabbed hold of his skull and was trying to crush it. He fell back against the rock wall, cradling his head in his hands.

... letters piling high on his desk, more every day ... young men charging, gunfire and clouds of white smoke, and bodies cut down like blades of grass under the sweep of a scythe ... the sky the color

of an anvil, filled with cannonballs on the way to their targets ... the letters, so many letters, he would answer every one, he would write until his fingers bled ...

Another roar broke his reverie, this one even louder. He heard a whooshing and then a snap, the sound repeating, like bursts of wind filling a sail, slackening, then filling it again. The stench of sulfur burned in his nose. He looked out between his fingers just as a shadow passed over him. Then he saw the creature: black and magnificent, as big as a frigate, its huge, vaporous wings trailing a sooty cloud. The yellow talons, curled back like a hawk's, each big enough to scoop up a cow with room to spare. As the thing soared away, the scaled neck bent back, revealing the wolfish head and the single eye.

Just for a moment, Abe thought it was looking at him, but then the creature looked forward. In moments, it disappeared over the horizon.

SOMEONE BEAT a drum inside his head. His vision blurred, tears streaking his cheeks and salting his lips. He cradled his head, pressing his fingers hard against his skull, but it gave him no relief. He was up and walking, but he hardly felt his feet. He floated through a world of shadows and slants of light. He lost all feeling in his arms. There was only the throbbing, the overwhelming pain. Dear God, he would give anything to make it go away.

... bodies piled on bodies piled on bodies ...

The fog in his brain made time meaningless. He was vaguely aware of scaling a few rocks, of trotting down a rocky hillside, falling, tasting dirt, getting back up, passing into the cool embrace of the forest, wet air on his face. Smelling moss and bark and ferns. Cold water seeping into his boots. Falling again in mud. Back up, still walking, his head on fire. The hoot of an owl, high above.

... the sky was filled with crows ...

Stumbling through a thicket of bushes. Falling onto a dirt road. Rolling into the rut left by a wagon wheel. The pain, the pain, it had to end ... He heard the clop of horse hooves. A man's shout.

Then his vision narrowed to a point, a tiny white dot. The dot shrank, and with it went the pain, until the dot itself was gone and he was swallowed by the cold comfort of darkness.

HE MIGHT HAVE SLEPT for a thousand years or a day, and he did not dream. He woke to the sound of rain and to the whisper of a woman's voice.

"Mary?" he said, his voice groggy.

"No," the woman said.

"Who—?"

"Be still."

It was not Mary. This voice was much softer than Mary's, musical almost. The room was dark, but not completely so; there was a pale flickering light from what must have been a candle. He could only make out the vaguest shape of a person, her face cast in shadow, the fringes of her hair a vibrant red. He was aware of a pillow beneath his head, heavy blankets up to his chin, the softness of a mattress beneath his back. The air was musty and smelled of lilacs.

She started whispering again, some sort of chant. She dabbed his forehead with a moist cloth. When she leaned close, he caught a glimpse of her face in profile, shrouded in shadow. It was a lovely face, with gentle curves and a small nose, no hard angles.

When she leaned back, he saw why she held her head just so: for a moment the candlelight illuminated the fringes of the right side of her face, and he saw a startling patchwork of disfigured skin. She wore her hair long on that side.

She caught him looking, and she turned quickly, moving her whole body so that she was sitting on the edge of the bed. In silhouette, he saw a small woman with a pleasing shape, her lavender dress fitting tightly against her curves above her waist and flowing more gently below.

"I'm learned in the ways of healing," she said softly. "I've spent the better part of two days singing the *Baliko*, the blood song. It has given you strength, I trust?"

"Two days?" he said. "Have I slept that long?"

"That and some, tall one. It took Harmon nearly all night of riding to bring you here, and you have slept since."

"Harmon?"

"My brother," she replied. She rose and walked through the dark room, her dress rustling against the floor. She walked in a wide berth around the bed, and he couldn't help but guess that it was so the shadows kept her face hidden. "I trust you are thirsty. I will have the chambermaid bring you water. She can also light the lamps, if you desire."

He heard the creak of a door.

"Wait," he said.

"Rest," she said.

"Who are you?"

He heard the rattle of the door closing.

IT WAS NOT LONG before the chambermaid bustled into the room, extinguishing the candle and tossing the curtains open. The pale gray light of late afternoon flooded the room; weak as it was, it still stung his eyes. Squinting, he saw the shape of a stout woman standing before him. He heard the metallic clank of something being put down on the cabinet next to the bed.

"A little daylight's all's you need," she said. "Sit up, now."

He started to rise, and he felt a hand against his back, helping him. Cold metal touched his lips, and then water soothed his parched throat. When the chambermaid pulled it away, he found he could see again. The old woman before him was short and round, with bright silver hair tied up in a bun. She wore a simple, moss-green gown with russet accents. The dress made Abe think of a costume a Shakespearean actor would wear. The rest of the room was no less anachronistic: stone brick walls and floors, decorated with the occasional tapestry or rug.

She put the tin cup on the chest next to the bed. "There now," she said, smiling. Feeling better?"

"A little," he said, and he did. The throbbing in his skull was gone. "Where am I?"

"In the castle of good King Talsey, sir."

"And the country?"

She chuckled. "What a silly thing. The land of Howander, of course."

"Is that somewhere in South America?"

They woman gave him a puzzled look. He was going to ask her another question, but then he heard approaching footsteps in the hall. The door swung open and two men entered, one older, perhaps in his fifties, and another that must have still been in his twenties.

"Ah, so you are awake," said the older man.

As they approached his bed, the chambermaid curtsied and retreated. The older man was short and broad-shouldered, dressed in finely woven silk and wool. A purple velvet cape flowed down his back to the middle of his knee, and a gold sash was tied around his waist. The young man, with much the same build, only slightly taller and thinner, was dressed more simply in a brown tunic and crimson vest. Where the young man's shoulder-length hair was a light brown, the older man's was a mixture of dark brown and silver. They had the same ruddy complexion and bold green eyes.

"I am King Talsey," the old man said. "This is my son, Prince Harmon. Could you tell us who you are and why you were found wandering around the Mountain of Ashes?"

Abe realized that the disfigured woman, then, must have been the King's daughter. "My name is Abraham Lincoln," he said. "I do not know this place you name, but if that is where that mountain creature—"

"So you did see it!" Harmon exclaimed. "You were mumbling about a monster when I found you, but I didn't know what to make of it. Few have ever spied the Black Dragon and lived."

Dragon. It seemed so silly to use such a word, and yet that's exactly what the creature appeared to be. "If it was you who saved me," Abe said, "then I offer my thanks."

"I only brought you here," Harmon said. "Which, as big as you are, was no easy task. But the person who truly deserves your thanks is Lady Madora. Tell me about the Black Dragon. Did you feel the effects of the cave? How did—"

The King held up his hand for silence. "Let the man tell his story." He looked at Abe intently. "You are obviously not from here. Your clothes, your manner of speaking … We find you wandering, half-mad, near the Mountain of Ashes, where no sane man in our land would dare go. I have brought under my protection, and offered you the talents of my daughter to save you. I want to know who you are, and I want the truth."

He spoke like a man who was used to having his requests obeyed. Abe did not know what they would make of his story, but he always found the truth to be his best ally. So, his voice still hoarse, he told them how he came to find himself on the mountain. He told them about Springfield, Illinois, and the United States. The more he said, the more their eyes grew wide. There was something other than just astonishment on the King's face—a dimming of the eyes, a slight frown. Disappointment? It confused Abe.

"And then I find myself here," Abe said, "in your care. I thank you, humbly, sir, for taking me in."

The King nodded thoughtfully. "It is a fantastic tale. I have not decided whether to believe you."

"It is the truth as well as I know it," Abe said.

"There *were* other tracks in the vicinity," Harmon said. "It is possible they belonged to the man he speaks of. The man had no horse and his load was light."

"Perhaps he will turn up," the King said, "and we will learn more of why you are here. In the meantime, Abraham—"

"Call me Abe," Abe said. "All my friends do."

The King smiled. "Abe, then. In the meantime, rest and eat. When you are fully recovered, we will talk." He started toward the door, his son trailing him, and then turned back. "Oh, one other matter," he said, speaking more softly. "When you see my daughter again, if you would be so kind as to refrain from staring at her … *wound*, I would be most appreciative." His expression was pained, his eyes downcast. "She bears the burden well, but we do what we can to lighten it."

Abe swallowed away the lump in his throat. "I will do my best, sir. I am in her debt. May I ask, how did it happen?"

The King looked at him sharply, and Abe thought perhaps he had been too impudent. There was a long moment in which the King stared at him, as if he was trying to decide something, but then finally his eyes softened. He sighed.

"It is the dragon that is to blame," he said, and left without another word.

For several days, Abe did not see the Lady Madora again, or anyone else except the chambermaid. He hated to spend his time so prone and useless, but had no choice; those first few days, he hardly had the strength to make his way to the chamber pot. But finally, after much rest, warm soup, and the motherly attentions of the chambermaid, he finally felt strong enough to walk for more than a few steps. The trouble regarding Mary no longer haunted him quite so much; the whole business truly seemed to be something that happened in another lifetime, in another world.

In fact, despite his illness, and his uneasiness about this strange place, he'd never been in better spirits. The chambermaid had been given instructions to fetch the King or the Prince when Abe was well enough, and so Prince Harmon came for him. Abe had just finished putting on his clothes, which had been washed. They had also put out clothes more fitting, which the chambermaid had suggested quite strongly that he wear, instead of his "foolish rags," but Abe wanted to wear his button-up white shirt, black pants, and boots.

"I've been dying to talk to you," Harmon said, "but father insisted you get your rest."

Abe already liked Harmon. He had an easy manner and a quick smile.

"To be honest, I could have used the company," Abe said. He held onto the wall for support. While he was certainly better, his legs still felt weak.

"Yes, I can imagine. Would you like to go watch the knights train? They are in the courtyard."

He led the way through dark castle halls lit by oil-burning lamps. It was cooler and draftier than in his room. Abe walked slowly, each step measured, but the pace did not seem to bother the Prince, who peppered him with questions about his homeland Abe answered as best he could. They passed through a wooden door, stepping out onto a stone balcony, a cool breeze hitting in full in the face.

The sunlight brought water to his eyes. The sounds of combat—shouting, the clomp of boots of dirt, the clank of swords against shields—greeted his ears. He saw that there was someone already there, standing at the stone wall and looking down into the courtyard. The person wore a green cloak with the hood up, and when she turned slightly, he saw that it was Madora.

She stood on the right, so it was mostly the better half of her face she revealed. Her thick locks of red hair and the hood mostly hid her scarred face, but he still caught a glimpse. It was hard not to be taken aback by the discolored, badly wrinkled flesh, so out of place on a woman so beautiful.

"Oh, hello," Harmon said. "I did not know you would be here, sister."

"Good morning, Harmon," she said. "Hello to you as well, Abraham."

He did not tell her to call him Abe. He liked the way she said his full name. "It is good to be upright, miss," he said. "If I was in bed any longer, I'm afraid I would sprout roots."

"I thought he might like to watch the knights," Harmon said. "Would it be all right if we join you?"

"Why wouldn't it be all right?" Madora said.

"Oh, I just thought, you know, your privacy …"

"Yes, of course. My *privacy*." She sighed. "Shouldn't you be training down there as well?"

"Oh. All right." He smiled at Abe. "I really do need the training. You don't mind, do you?"

"By all means," Abe said.

He bowed and left. Madora turned back to the balcony. Abe joined her on her left, her better side, holding onto the wall for support. The stone felt cold and rough and gritty. Dozens of knights trained down in the square courtyard. Some rode on horseback, others walked on foot. Some were dressed in suits of armor, while others wore heavy leather and chain mail. Many were engaged in hand to hand combat, working at half-speed as they practiced their moves, while a few practiced on an archery range.

"Do you truly feel better?" Madora asked.

"Much improved," Abe said. "Still weak in the knees, but I'm sure that will change in short order."

"I have herbs that could help restore your strength. I could have them added to your lunch."

"I'd be most obliged. Have you always been a practitioner in the art of healing?"

"Ever since I was a little girl," she said.

He sensed there was more she wanted to say, but if so, she kept it to herself. Abe saw Harmon appear from one of the tunnels, dressed now in light armor, sword in hand. The young man threw himself into the exercises with total abandon.

"Do they always train like this?" he asked.

"Most days."

"Are you at war?"

She said nothing for a time, but he noticed, on the part of her face he could see, that a dark cloud passed over her features; her eyes dimmed, her lips curled in a slight frown. He wondered if he'd crossed some line of impropriety.

"The reason they train," she said, her voice as soft as the breeze, "is the same reason I have the face I do. The same reason I have studied the healing ways since I was a child. The same reason my father was so eager to talk to you, in hopes you might possess information that could help us. The reason is the dragon. Around here, it is always about the dragon."

She spat out the last word as if it was acid on her tongue. He waited to see if she would say more, and when she didn't, offered tentatively, "The same one I saw?"

"There is only one. *The Kalendune,* in the old language. The Beast of the Mountain of Ashes. Dweller in the Cave of Lost Souls. Most just call it The Black Dragon."

"He must be a terrible foe."

Her lips formed a thin line, the color bleaching to white. "Ask, then."

"Ask what?"

"Don't be foolish!"

"I'm afraid I don't—"

"You're the only one in the whole kingdom who doesn't know, and I imagine you'll hardly rest until you know the answer. How did the dragon give me this face? Isn't that what you want to know?"

She whirled toward him abruptly, giving him the first full look at her face. He was going to offer a retort, but his words died stillborn. Once, when he was a small boy in Indiana, living with his family in a muddy dugout when life was at its worst, he'd had the misfortune to be one of the first on the scene after a log cabin burned during the night. Most of the bodies had been hidden in the charred rubble, but he had gotten a good look at what must have once been the face of a child. The withered, sinewy face, with its patchwork of black and crimson, gave him nightmares for weeks.

Madora's face—the scarred part, at least—brought back that memory.

The skin on that side had the same sinewy look, shiny in places, full of ridges and grooves. It was as if the cheek had been glued together from various plates of hardened skin, some pink, some crimson, some a deep shade of brown. It seemed impossible that she could have lived after such a wound.

But there was the other part of her face, too, and it was the first time he'd truly gotten a good look at it, either. It was the kind of face that inspired poets and painters. It was a face that belonged to the kind of woman Abe knew was forever beyond his reach. It wasn't just the physical nature of her beauty; it was her *presence*, that thing that reached out from her startling green eyes and took hold of his soul.

"Well?" she said. "What do you think now?"

He bowed his head. "I don't want you to speak of anything that gives you pain."

"Liar," she said. "You want to know. How could you not? It is the Curse of Kalendune. The Black Dragon's Bargain."

"My Lady," Abe said, "you don't have to—"

"Quiet! You might as well hear it from me."

So SHE TOLD him the tale. Looking him in the face, never once turning away, she told him how many generations ago, the Black Dragon had come to Howander, using its fiery breath to turn what was once a beautiful mountain into the scorched place that was now known as the Mountain of Ashes.

It burrowed into its lair at the top of the mountain, creating what eventually became known as the Cave of Lost Souls, and there it slept for seven months, undisturbed. After that, it began to emerge from its cave and feed, but only two or three times a year, and usually only taking livestock that was aged or sickly.

Though its passing shadow filled anyone who saw it with dread, the dragon did not attack humans. No one knew where it had come from or why it had come to Howander; dragons were ancient and mysterious creatures who followed their own internal sense of purpose. Still, it went on this way for over a decade, and soon the dragon became just another nuisance, like drought and disease, everyone learned to simply endure.

It may have stayed that way, too, if not for Madora's grandfather's grandfather, the young King Ilian. When his Ilian's father died early, Ilian had the kingdom thrust upon him when he should have been still enjoying what remained of his carefree youth. But despite the early burden, his kingdom prospered, and the people loved him. He took a young bride from one of the old families, and she soon bore him a daughter. He had hoped for a son, an heir to his throne, but it took only one glance at his infant daughter for her to steal his heart.

But during her fifth winter, the girl became quite ill. She lay for days in bed with a fever, and it soon became obvious that no herb or root would turn the tide. The royal couple were beside themselves with despair.

Despite the Queen's protests, the King traveled to the Mountain of Ashes on horseback, his daughter's frail body wrapped in a bundle of blankets upon his lap. When his horse would go no further, he carried her up the mountainside, both the smell of sulfur and the terrible feelings of pain and sorrow emanating from the Cave of Lost Souls getting stronger.

Because it was by then widely known: the closer you got to the Cave of Lost Souls, the more it drew out the darkest, most sorrowful parts of your heart. The worst things you'd seen, the worst things you'd felt, all those awful memories you kept locked inside you—they would all come rushing out as you neared the cave. Not only that, but the cave was not bound by the hands of time: all the sorrow and despair that awaited you in the years ahead might be shown to you, too.

When the King could bear to go no farther, he knelt and placed daughter's mummy-like body on the rock before him.

He cried out that he wished to make a bargain.

For a long time, there was nothing but the hiss of the wind, and the King thought he had come all that way for nothing. Then, finally, there was a rumbling from the cave, and then the head of the great one-eyed beast appeared in the opening. It fixed its eye upon him, slender pupil narrowing. Puffs of smoke rose from its nostrils, and a forked tongue licked its cracked lips. Despite his trembling legs, the King held his ground.

"Come closer."

The dragon's mouth did not move. The deep voice seemed to come from all around, rolling down the mountain like thunder.

"Come closer, little man. Come closer, and let me see the child."

The King picked up his daughter and carried her up the mountain. Each step closer to the cave made his heart heavier. The man he was disappeared in the overwhelming despair, but such was the love for his daughter that still he pressed on. His vision blurred with his tears, his heart pounded fiercely, but he made it all the way to the dragon—close enough he could not only smell the dragon's rancid breath, but feel the warmth of it on his face.

The great eye studied him. By itself, the eye was as tall as a man, and the King saw his own desperate face reflected in the widening pupil. Wild thoughts buffeted the King's mind like currents in a storm. He wanted to impale himself on his blade or throw himself from the mountain, and it was all he could do to keep himself in place.

"I am impressed," the dragon said. "I never thought a man would be strong enough to stand this close to my lair." His eye narrowed, focusing on the bundle in the King's arms. "Your child has death about her. Your bargain is for her life, I take it?"

"Yes," said the King.

"What price are you willing to pay?"

"Any … any price."

"Well, then. What can you offer?"

Speaking was a near-impossibility, but somehow the King managed. "We have … gold. Livestock. Wine. I'll—I'll bring it by the wagonload. All that I have …"

"Trifles. Anything else?"

"I—I don't know."

"Then go away," the dragon said. "You show courage, so I shall let you live, but you have nothing for me." He started to retreat into the cave.

"Then kill me," the King said.

"What?"

The King bowed his head. "I can't bear to live without my daughter. Kill me. Kill us both, and then bother our suffering will end"

The dragon studied him for a long time, puffs of smoke rising from his snout. "All right, then, I am intrigued. Here is your bargain. I can save your daughter's life, but all the first daughters of all the future kings of your land will belong to me. I shall mark them when they are a child, so all will know this, and then I will come for them when each is twenty years old. She will spend a fortnight with me in my lair entertaining me, and then I will eat her. Are you willing to trade all of those lives who have not been born for the life of your daughter? Are you willing to pay that price?"

"... AND IT IS SAID that the King hesitated," Madora continued. Her fingers, gripping tightly to the stone balcony, had turned white. "It is said he thought a long time before agreeing, but who is to say? He was the only one who knew the truth, and he may have altered the story to ease his own conscience. But agree he did. The dragon blew his smoke on the King's daughter, and she was healed. She lived a long life and died of old age. But two daughters before me have suffered the fate the dragon promised. The dragon comes for us when we are just old enough to walk, and, with a single lick from his hot tongue, scars us forever. On our twentieth birthdays, he finds us and takes us to his lair."

"You could flee, or hide—" Abe began.

"No. My great-grandfather tried this, going so far as to spirit his daughter away to another land. The dragon still found her to mark her, and found her again when she was twenty, despite his efforts to hide her again. And my grandfather tried attacking the dragon in his lair with his whole army before the dragon came to mark his daughter, but only a handful could get within a few steps of the cave without succumbing to madness. No one has ever been able to get inside. The visions are too terrible."

"But surely, something can be done," Abe insisted. "Isn't there—"

"No!" Madora cried. "It is my lot in life, Abraham! Some things are just the way they are and there's nothing that can be done." He could see that she was trying to stay in control, but a single tear on the scarred part of her face betrayed her. It followed the path of the ridges and grooves, and she did not bother to wipe it away. "So now you know," she said. "Now you know why I am this way. And no matter how much I learned about the art of healing, I could not change it."

Before he could say anything, she turned and fled, leaving him alone on the balcony.

WHEN ABE ATE DINNER that night with the King and his son, at their insistence, Madora did not attend, and no one spoke of her absence. Instead they asked many questions about life on Earth. Because he did not want to seem ungrateful for the help, he did his best to answer every one as frankly as he could, even those the son had already asked. And though the food and wine was plentiful and good, the roasted lamb being the finest Abe had ever tasted, he sensed a dark pall over the proceedings.

The King began to tell Abe of their plight with the dragon, and when Abe said Madora had already told him, the King seemed surprised. He said he hoped Abe would help. Since no magic on their world had managed to stop the dragon, perhaps some magic from *his* world would. Abe did not have the heart to tell them he knew no magic, nor did he believe that on his world there was such a thing.

He just told them he was grateful for their hospitality, and he would of course help them in any way he could. He also learned that Madora's twentieth birthday was only a month away, which he assumed was why the mood in the room was so somber.

It was later that night, when he was alone in his chambers, that he saw her again. He was in bed, with the lamp extinguished, but he was not sleeping. He was trying to make sense of this world in which he found himself. For the first time since he was but a young boy, he had no plans, nor did he feel any desire to make them. Starting his law practice, getting elected to the legislature, finding an upstanding woman who wouldn't think it was beneath her to marry him—those goals had motivated him the last ten years, but now they seemed rather empty and pointless.

He heard the creak of the door, and he sat up in bed. A beam of light lanced across the floor.

"Who is it?" he said.

"Don't be alarmed," Madora said.

He felt a cool draft of air. She carried a lantern into the room, closing the door. She wore the same green cloak with the hood, but this time she wore it over a white sleeping dress that swished across the stone floor. She placed the lantern on the table by the window, then sat in the high-backed chair next to it. Her face was full of shadows, but he had no trouble seeing her eyes. They stared at him fixedly.

"I came to apologize," she said.

"There's no need," Abe said. "What you've been through—"

"It doesn't excuse anything. You must feel terribly lonely here, away from your friends and family. It's selfish of me to add to your burden."

He nodded thoughtfully. "My burden has nothing to do with you. And to be honest, I'm not entirely sure there's much of a place for me back on my world. I reckon it would be quite happy to do without me."

"Why do you say this?"

"Just a feeling."

"But there must be a reason. What of this woman you named when you woke? Mary? Is she part of your troubles?"

His mood soured. He'd forgotten that he'd said Mary's name to her. "Let's just say I feel more at home here, after a few days, then I did in a lifetime back on my world. I doubt I'll ever amount to much back there, despite my best intentions." He did, however, wonder why that strange traveler had found it so important to bring him here. It didn't make any sense.

She looked down at her hands. He hoped she wasn't considering leaving.

"Did you love your mother?" she asked.

The question surprised him. "Very much," he said. "She died when I was nine years old. Though I was fortunate my father married again, and I think of her as my mother, too. She is a good woman."

She was silent for a time. "We have something in common, then. I lost my mother when I was only seven. But my father never married again."

"I'm sorry."

"I still think of her sometimes. She was so kind to me, so tender. I think Harmon is more fortunate than I, because he doesn't remember her."

"Oh, I don't know," Abe said. "It still hurts a little when I think of my real mother, but that doesn't mean I'm not glad I remember her. Even a sad memory can be a good one, I think. Just because a penny is tarnished doesn't mean it isn't worth saving. They're all pennies in our pocket in the end."

She laughed softly. "You certainly have a colorful way of talking, Abraham."

"Well, when you have a face like mine, you have to rely on more than your looks to make friends."

It was an old joke, one he often used to disarm people, but he realized right after he said it how insensitive it might seem. And indeed, she looked away. His first instinct was to apologize, but he thought that would only make matters worse. In fact, he was pretty sure another apology was the *last* thing she needed.

"Forgive me if this is bold," he said, "but at heart I am a simple country boy, so I just can't help myself. I reckon you should stop wearing that hood."

She looked up, startled. "Excuse me?"

"Be proud of your face and stop hiding it."

"I'm not ... I can't believe you would ..."

"You don't see me hiding my face, do you? And I look like the south end of a mule. A person is about as happy as they make up their minds to be. No matter how bad things are, we don't have to give in to despair."

"Abraham! I can't believe you would make light of what happened to me, after what I told you—"

"I'm not making light of it. I'm saying if you don't want people to treat you like you're a broken chandelier, then stop treating yourself like one."

He could see the tears welling up in her eyes. "But the way they stare ..."

"Then paint it."

"What?"

"Paint your face. If they're going to stare, show them you're not ashamed. Make it something folks would pay good money to see."

That got a laugh out of her, and he was glad, because he was worried he'd gone too far. "Seems foolish," she said.

"So be foolish, then. A little foolishness never hurt anyone. I myself am foolish at least four times a day, and three of those are by accident."

She laughed again. It was the restrained laughter of someone not used to laughing, and he decided right then that as long as he was able, he would make it his goal to make her laugh as much as possible.

"You are a strange man, Abraham," she said.

"I have often heard it spoken so."

"Are all the men from your world as strange as you?"

"A few. It takes practice, you see."

She nodded. "I would like to see your world. It's too bad …" she trailed off into silence.

"Perhaps you will," he said.

She said nothing for a long time, her head slightly bowed. Finally, she rose and gave him a weak smile. "Good night, strange man," she said, and left.

LIFE THE NEXT few days fell into a comfortable routine. Abe watched the knights in the mornings. Later, he went for long walks with Madora over the rugged countryside surrounding the castle. He dined with King Talsey and his son in the evenings, and occasionally with Madora, when she chose to attend. Each day he felt more himself, stronger of mind and body.

His old life back in Springfield became foggier by the day. All the angst and worry he'd felt back then seemed silly now, far removed from his present circumstances. He still felt a tinge of homesickness for a few things from his old life—the solitary walks through the Springfield countryside, exchanging wry jokes with sharp-witted lawyers and judges—but even that, too, was fading. He also hadn't suffered through one of his black moods since he'd been there, not even a brief one, which was a pretty good stretch for him.

More than that, he knew his feelings for Madora were deepening. It wasn't just concern for her safety. It was something stronger, something that made him feel a bit like he was betraying Mary. He may have broken off the engagement, but he couldn't deny that he still cared for Miss Todd.

In fact, she may have been the *only* reason he had to go home.

But would he? Would he go home now, if the opportunity presented itself? He wasn't sure, and it was that very question he was wrestling with the morning Harmon burst into his bedchamber, his hair disheveled, his tunic and pants wrinkled and untucked.

"Come quick!" he said breathlessly. "We've—we've captured a man who speaks of you."

Abe dressed hastily and followed Harmon into the bowels of the castle, down several flights of stairs, until they reached a dungeon. Only a scattering of lanterns staved-off the darkness. The stone floor was coated with something that squished beneath his boots like wet leaves.

Finally, they came to a place where a group of soldiers and King Talsey were gathered. It wasn't until Abe reached them that he was able to see the man in the cell, cowering behind a bed of hay. It was the same man who had abducted Abe, yet he had undergone such a radical transformation in the previous week—his body rail-thin, his eyes bugged out like a toad's, his skin splotchy and pale—that Abe scarcely recognized him. His clothes had been reduced to muddy rags.

"Some peasants caught him trying to steal one of their chickens," the King said. "Is it the same—"

"Lincoln!" the man cried. "Abraham Lincoln! I knew you'd be here!"

"Hello, friend," Abe said.

"Friend?" the stranger said. "No friend of yours! My ancestors would be kings if not for you! Butcher! Killer of thousands! I'm a savior! I changed the course of history!"

Abe thought of the visions he'd had of bloody battlefields and felt a chill run up his spine. "What are you talking about?

The stranger began to pace, and when he spoke, it was more

to himself than to Abe. "They thought they could stop me. But I was smarter. The risks—the risks were great. But I did it. You'll never make your war on my world. Never!"

Abe moved closer to the bars. "Is that why you brought me here?"

The man looked at him and jumped back a little, as if he had just realized Abe was there. "Butcher! Slayer of the innocent! You won't get answers out of me! Torture me and I won't talk! I won't!"

"Are you from the future?" Abe asked.

The stranger scampered to the corner, sunk to his knees, and plugged his fingers in his ears. Then he began to repeat a *na-na-na* sound as a small child would.

"Answer, or I'll drive my sword through your heart!" the King threatened.

When the stranger still didn't respond, the King growled and took a step toward the cell. Abe blocked him with his arm.

"Please, sir," he said. "No good can come from inflicting more pain on this man. Give him time, and perhaps he'll tell us more."

The King did not seem happy about this request, but he relented, and they left the stranger to his own ravings. To Abe, this seemed the best course of action, because although he was desperate to know more about why the stranger had brought him to this place, it seemed that even a little more prodding would push the man into complete insanity

Unfortunately, no more answers were to be had. The next morning they found him dangling from one of the top bars of his cell door, having used what remained of his pants as a makeshift noose.

* * * * *

THE STRANGER'S DEATH had an oddly quieting effect on Abe. Rather than falling into despair that he might never learn why the stranger had thought it so important to abduct him, Abe instead saw it as a sign that he should fully embrace his new life. There seemed no way to get home, so why worry about it? Besides, if what the stranger said was true, perhaps he was better off *not* returning home. He did not know what odd contortions in history would have to take place to put him in a position to cause the deaths of thousands, but was it not possible?

His political ambitions had always been grandiose, despite his humble beginnings. Might he rise to a national office in the future, such as Secretary of War, where his choices might lead to the tragedy he'd seen in his visions? He wouldn't dare say the thought aloud, for fear it would smack of hubris, but his ego told him it could be true.

The best course of action seemed to be to focus on repaying those who had helped him. With his strength fully recovered, and with the King's blessing, he started to train with the knights. Madora's birthday was only two weeks away, and Abe decided that he, too, would do what he could to protect her, meager as his abilities might be.

And yet, he surprised himself. Though he lacked formal training in swordsmanship, he more than made up for his raw skills with his long reach and his quick reflexes, testing even the best knights. His archery, too, was better than he thought it would be; though he'd never wielded a bow, it seemed that his fair marksmanship with a rifle helped him. It wasn't long before the "tall foreigner," as people had started to call him, was the talk of the castle.

Madora, however, was singularly nonplussed.

"I don't see what good can come from you placing yourself in harm's way because of me," she told him one night.

Outside his room, the rain pounded the countryside, and an

occasional bust of lighting illuminated his purple curtain, followed by a rumbling of thunder. Lincoln was nursing what remained of his mug of ale, his muscles aching from a long day of training. Madora sat across from him at the small table, a book of ancient poetic myths open in front of her. Abe had been amused at how similar the myths were to the biblical tales he knew so well.

"You think I should sit by and do nothing?" he asked.

She sighed, looking at him. He'd long gotten used to her scarred face, and no longer reacted when he got a good look at it. It seemed that around him she had forgotten about it as well, which he counted a small blessing.

"I don't want anyone getting hurt because of me," she said. "What's going to happen is going to happen, and there's nothing anyone can do about it."

"I don't believe in that sort of fatalism."

"When it concerns the Black Dragon, it's not fatalism. It's destiny."

"I see. You have no hope at all, then?"

"Hope is for fools and small children," she scoffed.

Abe was silent a moment. "I don't think you believe that."

"Oh? What do I believe then?"

"I think you have taught yourself to forsake hope, because living with hope also means living with the possibility of disappointment. But without hope, Madora, we have nothing at all."

He could see that he'd gotten to her; her eyes misted, and her head bowed slightly. "It is so hard for me," she said softly.

She did not need to elaborate. He knew what she said encompassed all that was difficult about her life: her scarred face, the fateful curse, the burden that came from a whole kingdom striving to protect her. He reached across the table and placed his hand over hers.

"I will not rest until the dragon is destroyed," he said.

"Why would you do this for me?"

The easy answer was because it gave purpose to his life, and he was a man who needed purpose, but he knew this was not the whole truth. His throat had grown tight, but he forced himself to speak. "Isn't it obvious?"

He sat close enough that he saw her pupils widen. His heart pounded, and he heard the blood rushing in his ears. Abe had never gotten over his awkwardness around women, but he thought there would never be a more opportune time for a kiss. Slowly, he leaned forward, closing the gap between them. She did not move until his lips were mere inches from hers, but then she turned away.

"I don't want your pity," she said.

He leaned back, an aching hollowness eating him up from the inside. "If it was only pity I was offering, then I would not feel so stung by your rejection."

"I didn't reject you. I spared you."

"Nonsense."

She looked at him, and now there was fierceness he saw instead of sadness. "You have another life to return to! Another woman who cares for you! And despite what you may believe, in a matter of days I will be gone. You've suffered so much as it is, I don't see any reason to make your suffering greater."

"Madora—" he protested.

"Do you think I have no feelings for you?" she said, rising. "Of course I do! Your coming here, soon before I leave, has been the best and the worst thing that ever happened to me. You made me want something I can never have—a life that can never be. You speak of hope, but it does not change what will be. I'm sorry, Abraham. I wish I could believe."

She hurried from the room. He called after her, but she did not answer, and the heavy door swung shut. He sat there silently for a time, listening to the sounds of the storm. In the past, he would have succumbed to a black mood that would have threatened to overwhelm him, but he refused to give in to those feelings. Not this time. Not now.

"I have enough hope for both of us," he said to the empty room.

THE NEXT DAY, Madora caused her own stir in the castle. She showed up at breakfast not only without a hood, but with the scarred part of her face painted a bright rainbow of colors. Not only that, but her mood was bright and cheerful, and she showed no lingering effects from their conversation the previous night. He did not know whether to feel happy or discouraged by this; it made him wonder, since it seemed so easy for her to recover, whether her feelings for him were very deep.

His doubts only grew when she did not come to visit him the next few nights, nor did she accompany him on any of his walks. He was stubborn enough, and prideful enough, that he didn't want to ask her about the change, but it finally became too much. He pulled her aside by the elbow one morning after breakfast, two days before her birthday.

"Are we to be strangers now?" he said to her.

The King and the Prince had already gone ahead. A few of the nobles passing them in the grand hall eyed them curiously. Madora waited for them to pass, offering them a polite smile. Her scarred face has been painted over with red and yellow roses. Up close, it could not hide the texture of the scars, the folds and ridges, but she had painted the flowers with such skill that the imperfections caused by her deformity seemed almost intentional.

"I thought we would both be happier this way," she said.

"Why would *not* seeing you make me happy?"

She shook her head. "You must let me handle things in my own way." Before he could offer a retort, she pulled away from him and hurried to join a group of noble women chatting as they walked the hall.

During his training the rest of that day, he fought with such fierceness that no man could best him. He was also invited to join the King and the knights in their planning; it seemed they were determined to make a pre-emptive strike against the Black Dragon the next day. Despite his ancestors' failures with such an approach, the King wanted to take matters into his own hands.

Abe was glad to focus on something other than his wounded pride, and when he lay down that night—another night without a visit from Madora—he could hardly sleep, his anticipation was so great. The plan would work. The dragon would be killed. And a new life would enfold for them with all the current awkwardness between them a distant memory.

But the next morning, the princess was already gone.

THE NOTE SHE had left behind gave them little doubt her disappearance was intentional: *"To all my friends—Do not search for me. I could not bear it if any of you were hurt because of me."*

The King had fortified his guards the last few days, but he did not doubt that she had departed the castle. There were secret passageways known only to royalty, passageways intended to let them escape in an attack, but it had never crossed his mind that his daughter would use them to slip out undetected. There were reports from peasants in one of the villages of a lady in a gray cloak who had been seen traveling through the forest, but the most skilled woodsman could find no tracks. It seemed that the Princess was good at more than just the art of healing.

Every knight who could ride a horse was sent to scour the countryside. Abe went, too, despite his unfamiliarity with the land, and the king even granted his request for a horse. Abe looked not in the villages, but in the thick wooded areas where she had last been seen. Many of the other knights did the same, and as he rode and called out to her, the forest was filled with echoes of her name.

He had no luck, and as the hazy purple light of dusk settled over the forest, things got even worse. Riding along, he suddenly felt light-headed. Then it was as if he passed through a current of warm air, and he was sick to his stomach. He dismounted and slumped against a tree, vomiting. A pain was growing in his skull, a pain he had felt before, and he collapsed to the ground.

The cold, mossy ground pressed against his forehead. He stayed hunched over, breathing slowly, steadying himself.

"Megawatts, baby," a man said behind him. "I'm not only good, I'm lucky."

Abe spun around. Sweat blurred his eyes, and he blinked it away, looking up at the man standing before him—a young black man in a russet-colored tunic. The man's head was completely shaved bald, but he had a tuft of bright orange hair on the end of his chin. He had a cocksure smile. The horse shuffled its feet and snorted.

"Pardon me?" Abe said.

"The calculations have to be just perfect," the man said. "You get one shot otherwise you have to recalibrate for months earlier or months later. The wavefront gets too rumpled." He studied Abe's face. "Hmm. You look cooked."

"Cooked?"

"Beat up. Tired. Run through the meat grinder. I bet when you first got here, you were a wreck for days."

"How did you know?"

The man shrugged. "A side effect of the dimensional shift. If you don't take the proper meds, it can really wipe you out. And if you're close when somebody else makes a shift, like you were when I just appeared, you can feel the effects, too." He smiled. "So ... ready to go home?"

It was then that Abe noticed the small white device in the man's right hand, the same device the stranger had possessed. He felt both a surge of excitement and a sinking feeling in the pit of his stomach. He rose unsteadily to his feet, holding onto the trunk of the oak for support.

"Home?" he said.

"Yep," the man said. "One shot in a million that I can slip you in at the exact moment of your departure, which is what we need for zero distortions, but I'm good enough to pull it off. I'm Rashawn, by the way. Big fan. Lots of happy family potlucks because of you." He went on smiling.

"Who was the man who brought me here?" Abe said. "Why did he do it?"

Rashawn looked uncomfortable. "Ah ... Not really supposed to answer questions, even if you won't remember any of this. Against the code."

"Wait," Abe said. The lingering effects of the vision were making it hard to think clearly. "Wait, what do you mean, I won't remember?"

"Once you're home, yeah. Your mind just isn't made to accommodate memories from multiple planes of reality, not without a surgical implant. Anywho, we really should be going." He opened up his device and hit a few buttons. There were some whistles and beeps that reminded Abe of the calls of small birds.

"I'm not going with you," Abe said.

Rashawn stared. "Huh?"

"I'm staying here."

The man's smile quickly vanished. "But-but-but ... you *can't!*"

"Why not?" Abe said. "I've never felt more at home than here in the Kingdom of Howander. And if what your companion told me is true, my return can only cause misfortune and misery to thousands. I think I've been offered a glimpse of such misery in those visions. I have no desire to make them true."

Rashawn gaped at him. His mouth opened and closed a few times, a few sputterings of words came out, but in the end all he could manage was a strangled, "No!"

"Well, that's certainly forthright," Abe said. "But it doesn't change my mind. Now, if you'll excuse me, there's a young woman I'm trying to find." He headed for his horse.

"It's because of her, isn't it?" Rashawn said. "You want to stay because of her."

Abe took his horse's reins and lead her onto the narrow trail. "Not the only reason, but a good enough one."

"I could force you. I could force you to come with me."

Abe glowered at the man. "I'd like to see you try, friend."

"I wouldn't need to win a fight. Just touch you when we slip into the wave."

"As I said, I'd like to see you try."

"This is ridiculous! Do you know what's at stake?" Rashawn began to pace back and forth. "No, no, of course you don't—the code won't let me tell you. Worthless code! I'll have to zipvid the committee, really let them know how I feel about ... hey, wait, don't go!"

Abe had one foot in the stirrup when he felt the man grab onto his other leg. With one swift kick, Abe sent the smaller man sprawling. Rashawn let out a startled *"Ooomph!"* and fell hard on his backside.

"I told you that wasn't a good idea," Abe said.

"Please ..." Rashawn begged, getting slowly to his feet. He rubbed his back with both hands. "Don't go. Everything—everything depends on you."

"What are you talking about?"

Rashawn shook his head. "I shouldn't do this. They're going to kill me. But, well, you probably won't remember ... All right, look. It's like this. You're going to become President. Not for a couple decades, but it's going to happen. There will be a Civil War in the United States, and it will have to do with slavery. North versus South. It'll be a long and bloody war, but your side will win, and that will be it for slavery. The guy who brought you here, Gaston Schmidt, one of his ancestors was Jefferson Davis, who was President of the South during the war. And Gaston—who was suffering from severe dimensional sickness—got in his head that removing you from the time continuum would restore the power to his ancestors that was lost after the war."

Abe's head was spinning. President? Only in his wildest fantasies did he think he'd ever have a shot at the highest office. He took his foot out of the stirrup and faced the man. "How do I know you're telling the truth? Maybe the other fellow is right and me staying here is best for everyone."

"Right … and they'd send a black man to try to fool you."

"Hmm."

"Hey, maybe I'm not black at all. I'm just wearing lots of makeup. That's me, blackface Rashawn." He chuckled.

"I gather your point." Abe scratched his chin. The other fellow's state of mind certainly seemed in question, and Rashawn, despite his boastfulness, seemed level-headed.

Ever since Abe had witnessed a slave auction as a young man, while delivering a floatboat of farm produce to New Orleans, he had known that the barbaric practice was not only immoral, but that it would eventually rip the country apart. Anyone who thought slavery was justified should try on the role of slave himself was what he always said. A civil war was certainly not out of the question.

He looked at Rashawn. "President, you say?"

Rashawn grinned. "Hard to turn that down, huh?"

"One term or two?"

"Oh, well, can't give it all away, now can I? I'm already in enough hot water with the Committee as it is."

But Abe had seen a dimming in the man's eyes that clued him in that it wasn't really about this nebulous Committee at all. "You're not telling me something important."

"Huh?"

"What happens to me?"

"What happens? You're a hero! They erect monuments in your name—"

"Monuments! They do that for the dead. Do I die? Do I die on the battlefield, is that what happens?"

"Er ..."

"Something worse, then? An assassination?"

Rashawn held up his device and stared fixedly at it. "I don't know what good will come from all this."

"That's it, then," Abe said. "I'm assassinated. I can see why you didn't want to tell me. You're afraid that if I learned too much, I wouldn't want to go back with you."

Rashawn stared at his device a while longer, then sighed and slipped it back in his pocket. "Maybe what you say is true. All right, it is true. But we still need you. The country needs you."

"Are you telling me slavery won't end unless I go back with you?"

"No, it ends. But much later. And there's a much worse war—with weapons far more powerful. Not much left of the planet after that."

"I see," Abe said. "This Gaston must have known someone like you would come to stop him."

"I hate to say it, but I got lucky. Our devices protect us from the time distortions—we ride in our own pockets of time, really— so it's true we *could* stop him. But the crafty devil also modified his Shifter—that's the lay term for the dimensional transporter— and it was nearly impossible to trace him without wreaking havoc everywhere. Of course, he didn't count on someone brilliant like me. Kind of ironic, isn't it? A black guy being the one to beat him." He smiled, and then his smiled faded a little. "I *have* beaten him, haven't I? You are going to go back?"

Abe was silent. Becoming President, and playing such a lofty role in the preservation of his country, certainly appealed to his ego. More than that, any man with a conscience should do whatever he could to end an abomination like slavery. And yet ... he had no desire to be a martyr, to have statues erected in his name. He wanted love and family. He wanted to be with Madora. The thought of being assassinated filled him with dread.

There was still Mary Todd, of course. He did love her, but it was not the same kind of love. It was a love he would have to choose, rather than a love that chose him.

"Will I be happy?" he asked.

"I think so," Rashawn said.

"Speak the truth."

"The truth? I don't know, man. You get married. You have children. But I can't say you're always happy. That's not the way you're described."

"And I suppose I continue to suffer my black moods?"

Rashawn looked away. So that was it, then. Abe could go back to his old life of perpetual melancholy, supposedly playing a big part down the road in saving his country and ending slavery before he met his end by assassination, or he could stay and choose this life, and the love of a woman who loved him back. But could he really have that? Madora was doomed to die by the Black Dragon, and even if he saved her, he didn't know for certain that she would want to be his wife.

Still, what Rashawn said may have seemed logical, but it also seemed like a lot of conjecture, too.

"Well?" Rashawn said hopefully. "What's it going to be?"

"I reckon I don't know," Abe said. "But I'm going to stay for now."

"What?"

"I can't leave Madora. At least not until she's rescued."

"Are you out of your mind? If you die here, that's curtains for us, man. I won't be able to jump back to try to save you. The wavefront will be too rumpled."

"I realize what's at stake," Abe said. "I'll make my decision then, and it won't be made lightly, I assure you. You'll just have to trust me."

Rashawn sighed. "And once again it comes down to a black dude having to trust a white dude. Figures."

"No," Abe said, "it comes down to *you* having to trust *me*."

"Sure, fine, whatever. What's the difference?"

Abe clapped Rashawn on the shoulder. "My friend, it's all the difference in the world."

As NIGHT FELL, the knights returned to the castle. No one had found even the smallest trace of the Princess. The King and his subjects were suspicious of the dark-skinned man Abe brought back with him. Seeing no reason to lie, Abe told them Rashawn offered Abe a way to return home, but that Abe wouldn't leave until the Princess was rescued. This seemed to give everyone a little extra cheer, and the King gave him a few sidelong knowing glances over a truly somber dinner. Did he know of the nights Madora spent talking with Abe? Did he know how Abe felt about his daughter? Abe supposed he did. It was just as well.

"And you can offer no special means to help us?" the King asked Rashawn. "Perhaps some magic or tool from your world that would give us an advantage?"

"Sorry, no," Rashawn said, his mouth full of steak. "Even if it was allowed, I wouldn't be able to leave and then come back. It doesn't work that way."

"A pity," the King said.

He did not let them eat long. His face grave and haggard in

the candlelight, he asked for silence.

"My friends," he said, when the sound of tinkling silverware and plates ceased, "I know you are tired, but I see no reason to wait at the castle until tomorrow. There is little doubt in my mind the *Kalandune* will succeed where we have failed, and that the Black Dragon will find Madora tomorrow. We have the half-moon's light, which is more than enough. We will ride hard, hoping to make it to the mountain by dawn."

They had already prepared for this possibility, so the provisions were ready, the blades sharpened, the bows freshly strung. Only a few men were left behind to guard the castle; nearly a thousand men headed out for the Mountain of Ashes. Several hundred, including Abe and Rashawn, rode on horseback, while the rest followed more slowly on foot. Under normal circumstances, no sane king would have dared leave his home so lightly guarded, but Abe knew what King Talsey was thinking: if the King failed to save his daughter, it would not be because he did not use *all* the resources available to him.

The men rode in near-silence, the dark forest filled with the thumping of hooves on soft dirt and the labored breathing of their beasts. The air felt cool and moist on Abe's face. Shafts of moonlight pierced the canopy of trees, giving the woods a celestial atmosphere. The silence did feel holy to Abe, and more than once he caught the murmuring of some nearby rider offering up a prayer.

They reached the mountain just as the first gray light brightened the eastern horizon. Free of the protective cover of the forest, and the scorched mountain looming above, the horses began to whinny and pull on the reins. The small army rode as high as the horses would go, then the King had them dismount and spread out around the cave, two hundred strong. Arrows were readied, swords unsheathed, shields put into position. There was no point in trying to hide.

Tendrils of mist curled past the cave. Abe was much farther away now than when he first appeared next to the cave, but he could still feel that same coldness in his spine. The King's simple command was passed along by whisper: "When the Black Dragon shows itself, hold nothing back."

Abe knew there was no guarantee the dragon was in the cave at all; and even if it was inside, Abe knew how easily the creature could evade them. But what else could they do? They waited for a good hour, the gray light turning pink, the pink light turning crimson. Another hour passed, and some of men on foot began to trickle in around them. The fog melted. Soon the sun was high overhead, and all the King's soldiers had reached the mountain.

Then, just when the men began to shift on their feet and mutter, there was a rumble. The horses had been tied down with stakes, but they pulled violently, a few breaking free and galloping for the trees. The great eye emerged from the darkness of the cave. The charred snout, skin dusky and uneven, sniffed at the air. The lips parted, pulling tight against teeth longer and sharper than their swords, forming a demented smile.

For a long time, the dragon emerged no further. Then there was another odd rumble, this one much different than the first, and it took Abe a moment to realize it was laughter—a horrible, thunderous laughter. Without warning, the dragon launched himself into the air and flew straight toward them.

In seconds, the sky was full of arrows. The dragon sent a plume of fire cascading in front of him, enveloping the arrows in his path. He continued plummeting toward the army, and it was only at the last moment that he pulled up, streaking over the trees at blinding speed. The wave of air from his passing knocked Abe back a few steps, and half the men around him fell on their backs.

When they managed to gather themselves, the dragon was long gone.

The men began to stir, and Abe could sense the despondency

settling over them, but they didn't have long to wait. Only a few minutes later the dragon returned, faster than anything Abe had ever seen move before, so fast it was just a blur of gray and black.

The wall of air buffeted their backs. By the time Abe noticed the dragon, it was already to its cave, but it did not go inside. Instead, it slowed, banking around, virtually crawling through the sky. When it was close enough, Abe saw, clasped in one of its gnarled, black claws, the Lady Madora.

Her black robe fluttered in the wind. For a brief moment, he saw her face, and she looked terrified. The dragon seemed to be mocking them with its slow pass. No one dared fire an arrow so long as it held the princess.

The dragon made three complete loops, then turned, finally, to the cave entrance. Then it was gone.

THE KING GATHERED with his most trusted Knights; Lincoln, along with Rashawn, were also asked to attend. They crowded into a tent his men had hastily constructed. A warm breeze swirled about them, carrying the scent of sulfur.

"You are my daughter's last hope," the King said. "One of you *must* be strong enough to enter the cave."

The Knights all began to chime in their encouragement, but it sounded like false bravado to Abe. Options were discussed, plans debated. They were settling on everyone charging the cave as one, hoping that their sheer numbers might weaken the cave's magic. When there was a lull in the conversation, Abe finally spoke.

"Let me go alone," he said.

Everyone gaped at him.

"Nonsense," the King said.

"Hear me out," Abe said. "The dragon's weakness, as far as I can tell, is his arrogance. He does not believe it's possible that any man can enter his cave. That will be our only chance—to surprise him. If we all charge up there as one, he'll hear us coming."

They were silent. The King glared at him.

"One arrow right in the eye ought to kill him," one of the knights said finally. "Or a sword straight up into his neck."

"It's suicide!" the King bellowed.

"Your highness—" Abe began.

"No, no, I won't hear any more of it. You wouldn't stand a chance, and I can't ask it of you anyway. We will charge as one."

The entire army was given the instructions to charge on the King's command. Any man who could endure the cave magic was to press on inside and dispatch the dragon. Abe thought the King was being foolish, but there was nothing to be done. The King's hoarse voice pierced the air, and the small army charged—save Rashawn, who said he didn't sign on for the rescue operation.

There would be no element of surprise now; they made enough noise to wake the dead. Wanting to save his strength, Abe stayed to the back, watching the first line draw nearer the cave. Just as he expected, as they got close, they slowed, clutching their skulls as if they were suffering a great pain.

One by one the men turned aside until there were just a few—Harmon and the King among them—who were almost to the cave, their progress unbearably slow. But even these last few eventually could go no further.

Each successive wave of men suffered the same fate, until at last Abe was nearing the cave. His hand dampened the hilt of his sword with sweat. He felt the same coldness he felt the day he first came to Howander, a coldness that started in his stomach and spread outward along his extremities, getting colder the farther up the hill he went. He also felt a steady pressure at the back of his skull, something burrowing into his brain.

His mood darkened. It was the worst despair he'd ever felt, worse than any black mood he'd ever suffered. His mind was filled with images that brought bile to his throat: an old woman's rotting face, filled with maggots, a child's severed hand floating in a pool of blood, a skeletal man, so thin his skin was like a tattoo on his bones …

A voice screamed inside his head: *Turn back! Turn back! Turn back!*

But he did not turn back. He was accustomed to living with darkness, and though this was worse, he knew he could endure it. All but a few men turned away, some openly wailing, but Abe continued. He came at last to the King and the Prince, both of whom sat on a rock, gasping for breath. The King looked up at Abe with bleary, bloodshot eyes.

"I tried," he said.

"If I make it," Abe said, "do one thing for me, sir."

"Yes?"

"Wait twenty minutes, then have all of your men retreat."

"Retreat?"

"Yes. Head for the castle."

"But if you need help—"

"Please, just do it. No time to explain."

The King nodded. Abe pressed onward. The rocky peak, stark black against the vanilla sky, was only a few dozen steps away, but each step was like stepping on a bed of nails. Still, he climbed, alone now, and the plague in his mind became even worse.

He heard women screaming, dozens of them. He smelled blood and rotting flesh and excrement. Now the peak disappeared, and instead he saw a blood-soaked battlefield filled with slaughtered men, the air smelling of gunshot. Now they weren't young men. They were all Madora, every single one, and they rose on bloody stumps and reached for him with hands charred from fire.

"*Abraham …*" they whispered, "*look at what your pride has wrought ..."*

He focused on the ground. The bony fingers of the many Madoras brushed against his tunic, but he did not stop. Was it pride that made him press on? Perhaps it was. If he was strong enough to save a nation, as Rashawn had said, then he would be strong enough for this. Suddenly something dark loomed before him like a shade, and he looked up to see that he had reached the mouth of the cave.

He leaned against the jagged rock, steadying himself. The opening had seemed small from far away, but the roof was at least three times his height. Cobwebs hung sparsely across the rocks. The path led quickly into darkness. He was so cold, his teeth chattered, and his fingers and toes felt numb. He heard nothing from within the cave, and there was no wind, but something pulsed from the depths of the darkness all the same. His thoughts were terrible; his hand wanted to plunge his sword into his own heart, and it took all his strength not to do so.

Each step happened with frustrating slowness, the movements broken down into their tiniest components. Bend ankle, push, lift foot, lean, down now ... Each step, the light behind him receded, and the terrible shackles on his mind tightened. He felt something hot burning his cheeks, and touching his skin was surprised to find that he was crying.

Something brushed his clothes, and he saw that it was an arm protruding from the rock, the hand bearing only three bloodied fingers. The arm wore the tattered sleeve of a blue army uniform. Hundreds of arms lined the cave all the way around like teeth, and gritty fingers grasped at his clothes. The light vanished and he walked in complete darkness, but not for long. A flickering glow appeared ahead.

He had no idea how much time had passed, but he knew he didn't have long until the King retreated. Approaching the light, he moved along the wall. His path jutted out along a precipice that overlooked a giant chamber. Getting down on his hands and knees, he peered over the edge, and immediately saw the hunched back of the dragon. A massive fire burned off to the right, filling the chamber with flicking orange light.

… *blood gore gun fire mud smoke sword strike kill kill kill* …

Abe felt dizzy, his vision blacking in and out, but he forced himself awake. It took all of his will power to keep from sobbing.

"I won't do it!" he heard the Princess cry.

"Temper, temper," the dragon replied, the voice booming in the cave. "You still have two weeks with me, but I could get bored. Now, dance."

"No!"

"Dance!"

The dragon's shout brought dust raining down on them. The Princess sobbed, and then Abe heard the clinking of metal, the soft padding of footsteps on the stone. The dragon shifted a little to the right and finally Abe saw her: she was nearly naked, only a few tatters remaining of her clothes, and her skin was spotted with soot. She had black iron shackles fastened to her feet, which were in turn attached to chains. The chains were tied around a stalagmite as thick around as a sequoia's trunk and taller than the dragon. She was trying to do a little dance, but the chains made it difficult; it amounted to little more than an awkward shuffle.

"Faster," the dragon said.

"I'm trying," she sniffed.

"Faster!"

Side to side she went, turning around, sobbing, until she finally lost her balance and fell. The dragon laughed.

"Good, my pretty!" he said. "Again, again!"

She struggled to her feet. The distance was too great for an arrow, and the only thing worth aiming for was the dragon's eye.

Abe had to stick to his original plan … He moved away from the opening, looking for a place to hide. Ah, there was an opening in the wall, down near the ground. If he could get down on his stomach, he might be able to roll himself inside and out of sight. Trying it, he found it a tight fit, but he managed.

It was just in time. The sounds of the army retreating—the thumping of hundreds of footsteps, the clopping of horse hooves, the shouts of men—rolled down the tunnel. Abe tensed, waiting.

"Ah," he heard the dragon say. "Hear that, my pretty? They're leaving you."

"I don't care," Madora said weakly. "I want them to leave."

"Oh, surely you do," the dragon said. "You are a strong one, maybe the strongest I've had yet. But I must check for certain. They may just be trying to trick me, poor fools."

Abe felt the thunderous vibrations through the rock. He held his breath, his heart pounding in his ears. The tunnel darkened, and through the crevice, Abe saw black scaly flesh pass just inches from his face. He felt a waft of air. Then the dragon passed, the cave brightening again with the faint glow of firelight, and Lincoln slowly let out his breath.

But there was no time to delay. When he no longer felt the vibrations, he rolled out the crevice and scrambled down into the chamber. The burning logs, as big as trees, crackled and hissed, and the heat from them was like a wall.

"Abraham!" Madora cried.

There were tears pouring down her face, heading down the alleys and crevices on the scarred side, streaking the soot on the other. He tried the chains, and, as he feared, it would take more than his sword to break them. "I'm going to hide right behind you," he said, "behind this rock column. When he comes back, you have to distract him."

"How?"

"Dance for him! But get him to look away if you can."

"But—"

"No time! I think I hear him coming."

He dashed behind the stalagmite, and sure enough, he felt more tremors. As quickly as he could manage, he pulled out his bow and cocked an arrow. He knew he would most likely have only one chance to hit the dragon's eye.

The ground shook so badly he was nearly knocked off his feet. He pressed his back against the jagged rock, sucking in his stomach. He heard the chains clink, saw them slide off to his right. There was a rush of foul, sulfur-stinking air, and soot swirled around him. The dragon's immense shadow appeared on the far wall.

"The cowards have abandoned you," the dragon said. "What do you think of that, little one?"

"It's for the best," Madora said. There was clinking of metal.

"Liar. What are you doing?"

"Dancing," Madora said. "I thought that's what you wanted."

"Hmm. I'm surprised to find your mood so changed."

"In truth, I want something from you. I thought if I dance, you might grant my wish."

"Ah, I see. What is it, then?"

"I was wondering if you might … heal my face."

"Heal your face!"

"Yes. I know you have the power to heal. I just thought, if I could live my last few days without the scar, if I could touch my face without feeling the wrinkled flesh …"

The dragon laughed. "Foolish, girl. Why would I want to grant any wish of yours?"

The chains stopped clinking.

"I don't know," Madora said. "I just thought it might be more pleasing for you, looking at me without the scar. But it's all right if you can't do it."

"Can't! Well, of course I *can*. I simply don't wish to do so."

Madora muttered something.

"What was that?" the dragon said.

"Nothing. I just said, well, we'll never know."

"Insolence!"

"There's no need to get angry just because you can't undo something you did."

The dragon cried out—a horrible sound that made Abe think of the shrieking of dozens of horses at once—and stomped his foot. "You know what I will do, girl? I *am* going to heal your face, just to show you I can—and then I'll give you a scar on *both* sides, too! Come here." Abe watched the shadow of the dragon's head bend down to Madora's shadow.

The chains rattled, then strained against the rock column. "No!" Madora cried. "Please, don't!"

"Foolish girl," the dragon said. Abe heard him take a breath, then exhale. There was a pause before the dragon spoke again. "Touch your face. Touch it! Feel that smooth skin? I have more power than you can possibly imagine. Now, as to your punishment …"

Pulling the bow string taut, Abe stepped out from behind the column. The dragon was turned away, bent over Madora, but his eye's slender pupil pivoted in Abe's direction just as Abe let loose the arrow.

The great black beast started to jerk back, but he was too late: the arrow found its mark, burrowing deep into the eye socket.

The dragon roared, jerking his head skyward. Black blood streamed from the protruding arrow, darkening the dragon's teeth. Abe had hoped the first arrow would kill the dragon, but he wasn't so fortune. He cocked another arrow and fired it at the eye. This one, however, missed its mark and merely bounced off the dragon's tough scales.

The blast of fire came so fast from the dragon's mouth that Abe just barely managed to dodge behind the column. Flames danced on both sides of him, searing the air. He dropped his bow and unsheathed his sword.

"Come out, little man!" the dragon cried, coughing. "Come out and face mee*eaaargh!*"

Abe didn't know what caused the beast to cry, but he took it as his cue to act. He bolted from his hiding place and rushed directly toward the blinded dragon. As he ran, he saw Madora with her arm outstretched, and a black rock falling to the cave floor. With the dragon distracted, Abe wove from side to side, hoping that an indirect path might fool the dragon.

He was right. The dragon must have heard his approach, because he sent out a long blast of fire that scorched the ground to Abe's right—but far enough away that it didn't slow Abe.

Now he was directly under the dragon. It was fortunate he was tall, because it took every inch of his reach to plunge his sword into the dragon's belly.

Blood fell upon him like black rain, stinging Abe's eyes. The dragon jerked back onto his hind legs, sword still stuck in his belly, his head crashing against the chamber's ceiling.

Rocks and dust fell upon them. The dragon's hind legs crunched out the fire, reducing the light in the room to an ember glow. Abe scrambled back, not knowing what to do now that he had no weapon, but expecting that the dragon would attack.

Madora screamed.

Looking up, he saw why: the dragon wasn't attacking, it was falling, its body suddenly going limp, its mouth going slack. It was a great tree falling directly toward him, as deadly to him as the dragon's fire.

Abe ran to the side, leaping at the last moment to try to escape the crushing blow. He thought he'd just made it, but then he felt a terrible pain in his back, and the world went dark.

HE TUMBLED in a cold, soundless void, and when he woke, it was again to the sound of a woman's singing. This time he recognized the voice. The bright lamplight brought tears to his eyes, blurring his vision. He could just make out the vague shapes of people.

"Lucky bastard's got more lives than a cat," he heard Rashawn say. "He's even grinning about it."

"Shh," Madora said. "Your prattle will disturb my magic."

Finally, the people gathered around him came into focus. He was on a cot in a tent, covered with blankets. The flaps of the tent fluttered in the cool breeze. There was Rashawn off to his left. King Halsey stood behind him, his face a mask of worry. Prince Harmon stood at the foot of the bed. Madora was on the other side, sitting on a chair and leaning over him.

The most amazing thing was looking at her face: the scar was gone, both sides equally beautiful. What made her even more beautiful was her smile.

"That's the second time I've healed you, Abraham," she said.

"You're a vision," he said, his voice hoarse. He was struck by a coughing fit, and when he finished, said, "I thought you were an angel at first."

It was enough to make her blush.

"My sister will have every man in the kingdom courting her," Harmon said, beaming.

"She could have had any man before," Abe said. "She just didn't believe it."

She looked at Abe intently. "There's only one I'm interested in."

Abe felt a warmth spread to his own face. Among the others, there were lots of uncomfortable glances and shifting on their feet, but Madora continued to look at him. He tried a smile, but she must have seen the hesitation in his eyes.

"What is it?" she asked, taking his hand.

Her skin felt warm and soft on the back of his hand. It was a wonderful feeling, and he wished the moment could just go on forever. He could clearly see the two roads his life could take from his point, and the road with Madora was far more appealing of the two. Perhaps there was greatness waiting for him on the other path, greatness and immortal fame, but there also a violent end and no guarantee of much happiness along the way.

He didn't need to see the future to know it. He could feel it in his bones.

The choice was between his own happiness and the future of his beloved country, and he could not live with himself if he chose the former.

"You're going home," she said, seeing the truth of it in his eyes.

His throat clenched, but he managed to nod.

A STORM was blowing in from the north, the evening sky filled with heavy, dark-violet clouds. Rather than prolong his departure, Abe decided it was better to leave that night. If he dallied, he knew he might change his mind. The King's army was preparing to return to the castle, and Abe said his goodbyes, shaking hands with as many of the knights as possible. King Talsey and Harmon wished him well, and said he would always be a knight of Howander in their eyes.

When finally he was ready, he went to the edge of the forest where he had agreed to meet Rashawn, and there he found the black man standing next to Madora.

"I'll give you two a moment to take care of all that mushy stuff," Rashawn said, heading into the trees.

Madora smiled, but he could see the moisture at the edges of her eyes.

"I'm sorry I have to do this," he said.

"I know you are," Madora said. "But it's *because* you are going that makes me love you all the more."

"Madora—"

She placed a finger over his lips. "Shh. There's no sense pretending otherwise. You wouldn't be able to live with yourself if you knew your home country fell into ruins in your absence, and I wouldn't be able to live with myself if you left without knowing my true feelings. I do love you Abraham Lincoln, and I always will."

She kissed him. It was a long and tender kiss, then she patted his cheek and walked away. Watching her go, he wondered if he would ever find happiness without her—if such a thing was possible, after seeing what true happiness was.

He didn't think he'd spoken aloud, but he must have, because Madora turned. "Just remember, Abraham, a person is as happy as they make up their minds to be. No matter how bad things are, we don't have to give in to despair."

"Hmm," he said. "What fool told you that?"

"A wise man," she said.

Then she walked away. His heart heavy, he followed Rashawn into the trees. What little light there had been from the shrouded moon was gone, and he stepped into a place that was as dark as any place he'd ever tread. There were no shadows or hues to guide him, just an impenetrable blackness, and he couldn't help but think it was a fitting place for his journey on this world to come to an end. The darkness matched his mood.

"Rashawn?" he said.

"I'm here," the man said, not far away. He pressed something small into Abe's palm. "Chew this up and swallow. It'll prevent you from getting cooked."

Abe chewed up the pill and swallowed it. It tasted like cherries, with a slightly bitter aftertaste.

"Ready, then?" Rashawn asked.

The wind was cold, and Abraham tucked his arms around his body. Were those the faces of young soldiers he saw staring at him from the darkness? Was that the sound of cannon fire he heard deep in the forest? A man could go mad if he stayed too long in a place without any light at all.

"You say I won't remember her?" he said.

"Doubtful," Rashawn said.

Abe nodded. "It's a good thing." But he didn't believe it. He would have liked to remember her, painful as it was.

Rashawn offered no further comment. Abe heard a few bird-like chirps, then a rising, high-pitched whine. He looked back the way he had come, hoping to catch one more glimpse of Madora, but it was too late. The darkness embraced him.

ABE WAS ON TOP, both of the man's arms pinned, and he was prying the thing loose, almost had it—

—and then a chill swept across his body. His vision went dark, and just for a moment, he felt as though he were floating in a cold, soundless void. When he blinked, he was back in the forest on his hands and knees. The stranger was gone. Abe's hands and knees pressed against the snow.

"Abe!" he heard Joshua cry somewhere behind him.

Dizzy, Abe managed to struggle to his feet. Where was the stranger? He looked around him, but saw only the lonely trees standing in dark shadows.

Joshua burst through a bush off to his right. "Abe! What happened?"

"I don't know. He was just … gone."

Joshua bent over, hands on his knees, struggling to regain his breath. "We'll—we'll report it to the sheriff. He's got to be out there somewhere." He looked up, squinting at Abe. "What is it? You look like you've seen a ghost."

Abe held up his hand for silence. He thought he heard something amidst the rustling of the leaves, a woman singing in a whisper, a sound that seemed familiar to him for a reason he could not explain.

"Do you hear that?" he said.

"Hear what?"

Abe shook his head. Strangeness abounded. Even stranger, his black mood was gone. Completely vanished. *Something* had definitely made him feel better. He wished he could explain what it was. But all he could think was that it had something to do with that woman's whisper in the trees. There was something more, something tantalizingly close, something of profound importance, but he could not grasp it. Just as he thought this, he found himself speaking.

"Most people are as happy as they make up their minds to be," he said.

Joshua looked perplexed. "Did I miss something?"

"No, but I think I did."

"Abe, you are strange man, indeed."

Abe peered into the trees, watching them sway in the night. If he strained, he thought he could still hear her. The longer he looked into the darkness, the more he thought he saw something there in the shifting shadows: a woman's face, turned to the side, obscured by a veil. He stared for a long time, wondering if he was going mad.

Finally, he shook off the feeling, clapping his friend on the shoulder.

"Many have said so," Abe said. "Come on, let's go home."

Afterword and Acknowledgments

Even though the majority of my writing time these days has been devoted to novels, I still love writing short stories. I cut my teeth as a storyteller on short stories, writing well over a hundred of them before I even attempted a novel, and it's a path I recommend to a lot of aspiring writers.

Although the skill set required to write a successful short story isn't identical to what's required for the novel, it's similar enough that there's nothing wasted in devoting some early years to short fiction, even if you see yourself primarily as a novelist. And there's *lots* to be gained. If you have any hope of getting a reader to laugh or cry in the span of a few thousand words (or sometimes in the span of a single page!), you learn how to get to the good stuff quickly.

Of course, if you're going to write short stories, you've got to read them too—and even better if you love them. My tastes as both a reader and a writer have always been pretty broad, and reading short stories was a great way to sample lots of kinds of writing with a much shorter time investment. Ray Bradbury, Harlan Ellison, Ernest Hemmingway, Raymond Carver, Edgar Alan Poe, Arthur Conan Doyle, Stephen King—the list goes on and on, writers who produced stories as diverse in content and style as the lives they led (or still lead). All the writers I just mentioned were key inspirations for me, and I'm pretty sure there's echoes of all of them in my own work.

And that's how it is, isn't it? Writing short stories is like being part of a great conversation, one that continues from generation to generation, one writer inspiring another. It's the Great Literature Cocktail Party, the guests coming and going, lots of little side conversations happening in this corner or that one, but the overall party continuing unabated, the lights always on, the music playing in an endless loop. You want to join? The cover charge is the written word, the ink formed from the blood, sweat, and tears of many lonely hours. But the door is always open to another guest. You can count on it.

What you can't count on is whether any of your own stories withstand the test of time. All you can do is be part of the conversation, which is what I've tried to do. If readers laugh or cry in a few spots, then so much the better. It's all I can hope for, really.

My general rule of thumb with short stories—well, with all my fiction—is to let the tales stand on their own. No matter how hard I try to write as truthfully as possible about a story's origins, it still seems to have a whiff of make-believe about it—an indulgence here, a bit of fanciful recreation there, and before you know it, even the writer isn't sure what's true. And honestly, if I'm going to write fiction, I might as well do the real thing.

But I've always enjoyed it when other writers offer a "behind-the-scenes" glimpse into their work. I assumed this was just the writer in me, but I've been told by a number of readers that they enjoy them too, so I offer a few words here for those of us in this camp, for what it's worth.

The title story, "The Man Who Made No Mistakes," is actually a good example of being part of the Great Literature Cocktail Party I mentioned. I originally made a run at this story—a man who has the ability to rewind time, commits a terrible act just to see how it feels, and then finds he can't undo it without destroying the world—about ten years ago, calling it "The Switchbacker's Song." It didn't quite work, so I shelved it and worked on other things. Then a few years ago I read Stephen King's story, "Mute," in his collection *Just After Sunset.* I don't need to spoil the story itself, but what inspired me was its structure. It's a frame story told to a priest, starting off with a line like "Well, I'm not sure I sinned," or something very similar. For whatever reason, that line made me see the switchbacker story in a new light.

Now a frame story—a story within a story—is tough to pull off, largely because you're starting out fairly passively, one character talking to another, and a man talking to a priest is probably one of the most passive openings of all. So there is a bit of an extra challenge, but I love those extra challenges. It's one of the games I play with myself to get my mind out of a critical space. And while I enjoyed "Mute," there was one aspect that I didn't find quite satisfying. Frame stories work best when both tales— the frame and the story within the frame—work as stories, both the teller and the told affected by the events in some way. The priest in King's tale was really just a prop. I made sure my Father Holder had his own back story, his struggle with his faith, and tried to make his own journey compelling.

My intrepid interstellar investigator, Dexter Duff, who appears in "The Bear Who Sang Opera" and "The Android Who Became a Human Who Became an Android," was just my attempt to take the hardboiled detective and put him in space. They both appeared in Analog. I've got more Dexter Duff stories to tell, maybe even a novel, so hopefully you haven't seen the last of Duff.

"The Time of His Life" is one of the most personal stories I've ever written. At its heart, it's a story of addiction (one of two stories of addiction in this collection; "The Human Addict" being the other), but it's also about the guilt I've often felt as a writer trying to carve out time away from my family to work on my craft. If only I had a room where time didn't pass, I mused, I could get so much more done ... I set it in my own first house, a little cottage where my wife and I lived before we had children, and it had a cramped office above the garage with a closet much like the one described in the story. With a day job and a young family, I'm often asked how I find the time to write. Well, now you know my secret.

I owe a special thanks to my father for, "A Witness to All That Was." A number of years ago, he said something like, "What a lot of people want is a witness to their lives, someone who can say yes, this person's life mattered." The comment inspired the title, which I came back to a few years later. In a sense, this was another frame story, though I think it was a little more hidden this time. What better witness than one who witnesses not only the life of a spouse, but that of an entire civilization?

I've always had a special fondness for our sixteenth President, an interest I know is shared by lots of people. I've read three or four biographies, and each one seems to deepen my appreciation for him—not just as a man, and the admirable qualities that allowed him to rise to the occasion during one of the most trying times in the history of the United States, but also as a character, how complex and intriguing he was, how troubled and conflicted. The idea for "Lincoln and the Dragon" started when I came across the little nugget of information about how Lincoln briefly broke off his engagement with Mary Todd on New Year's Day in 1841, and how he deemed it "the fateful first of January." What happened to him that day, I wondered? And what made him get back together with her? It's a bit dangerous taking one of the most revered figures in my nation's history and using him as a character in a fantasy adventure, but I hope my sincere admiration for him comes across.

That said, I'll let the rest of the stories stand on their own. I *do* want to briefly thank a number of people who helped make this book possible:

To the editors who published many of these short stories originally, my sincere thanks: Stanley Schmit, Shawna McCarthy, George Scithers, Tim Deal, and Mark Rudolph. Since short story collections don't often make much money—you and I may love short stories, dear reader, but we are a tiny subset of the reading population—publication in magazines or anthologies, and more importantly, the *money* a writer earns for those original publications, encourages writers like me to keep writing them.

To Lyn Worthen, thank you for your astute proofreading on not just this book but on the many others I've sent your way—I appreciate all your hard work.

To Billy Norrby, whose cover art for this book is a remarkable piece of work, my deepest appreciation. Originally appearing as an illustration for the title story, "The Man Who Made No Mistakes," in the magazine *Realms of Fantasy* where the story was first published, I knew when I saw it that I wanted it to grace the cover of my next collection.

To Kristine Kathryn Rusch and Dean Wesley Smith, superb writers, great teachers, fine friends—it's hard to believe it's been twenty years since I walked into that writing workshop in Eugene, Oregon. But I wouldn't be the writer I am today without your generous spirits. Since I can never truly pay you back for all you've done for me, all I can do is pay it forward to the next generation of writers. I'll try to faithfully do so whenever I can.

And last but never least, all my deepest gratitude and love to my wife, who has served as my first reader and most trusted editor long before I published anything. Since it would be a cliché to say I couldn't have done it without you, dear, let me say instead that I'm very glad I never had to try.

About the Author

SCOTT WILLIAM CARTER's first novel, *The Last Great Getaway of the Water Balloon Boys*, was hailed by Publishers Weekly as a "touching and impressive debut" and won the prestigious Oregon Book Award. His short stories have appeared in dozens of popular magazines and anthologies, including *Analog, Ellery Queen, Realms of Fantasy,* and *Weird Tales*. His fantasy, *Wooden Bones*, chronicling the untold story of Pinocchio, is due out from Simon and Schuster in summer 2012. He lives in Oregon with his wife, two children, and thousands of imaginary friends. Visit him online at *www.scottwilliamcarter.com*.

www.ingramcontent.com/pod-product-compliance
Lightning Source LLC
Chambersburg PA
CBHW032023240626
47154CB00003B/763